D0104242

THE LEAST OF THESE MY BROTHERS

Classic Fiction by Harold Bell Wright
Retold for today's reader by Michael Phillips

A Higher Call
The Least of These My Brothers
The Shepherd of the Hills

THE LEAST OF THESE MY BROTHERS

HAROLD BELL WRIGHT

MICHAEL R. PHILLIPS, EDITOR

BETHANY HOUSE PUBLISHERS
MINNEAPOLIS, MINNESOTA 55438

Copyrite 1902, Harold Bell Wright. Originally published as *That Printer of Udell's* in 1902 by Book Supply Company, Publishers and A. L. Burt, Co., Publishers.

Copyright © 1989
Michael Phillips
All Rights Reserved

Published by Bethany House Publishers
A Division of Bethany Fellowship, Inc.
6820 Auto Club Road, Minneapolis, Minnesota 55438

Printed in the United States of America

Library of Congress Cataloging-in-Publication Data

Wright, Harold Bell, 1872–1944.
    The least of these my brothers.

    I. Phillips, Michael R., 1946–   . II. Title.
PS3545.R45L4   1989   813'.4   89–6713
ISBN 1–55661–056–4

HAROLD BELL WRIGHT (1872–1944), the American novelist, was born to the farming life in upstate New York, working in the fields at an early age. As he grew he sought an education, which eventually led him into the ministry. Traveling to the Ozarks in the 1890s to recuperate from pneumonia, Wright began the work of a fill-in preacher in a little mountain log schoolhouse, remained there, and eventually was offered a regular pastorate. Over the next ten years he pastored churches in Missouri, Kansas, and California until declining health forced him once more back to his beloved Ozarks for a time of rest and seeking God.

After publishing his best-known book, *Shepherd of the Hills*, Harold Bell Wright went on to become one of America's top-selling inspirational authors. His nineteen books achieved estimated sales in excess of ten million copies.

CONTENTS

And the King shall answer and say unto them, Verily I say unto you, Inasmuch as ye have done it unto one of the least of these my brethren, ye have done it unto me.

INTRODUCTION

Harold Bell Wright (1872–1944), American novelist, originally studied for the pastorate and planned to preach, which he did for some eight to ten years. When he began to write, however, his books became such unexpected bestsellers that he eventually gave up the pulpit so he could write full time. A more comprehensive outline of his life can be found in the introduction to the Bethany House edition of his book *The Shepherd of the Hills*.

Wright's second pastorate started in 1898, in his 27th year, just a year before he was married. He was called to the bustling mining town of Pittsburg, located in the southeastern corner of Kansas, just across the state line from Missouri. He eagerly accepted the challenge of the new parish, which was very near the Ozark region he dearly loved and in which several of his books are set.

He came as a green, young pastor, full of ideas and hoping to make a difference for the cause of Christ. The response of the congregation to their new minister was very enthusiastic (although from what follows we may assume not *everyone* thought highly of his preaching). The church grew, attendance and finances mounted. But still Wright remained unsatisfied. Something was missing. Somehow he did not feel he was making an impact in the community—in the daily lives of the people. He was deeply concerned that the church be more than a mere social club for its members while those on the outside and those in the town's business community felt no impact of the Gospel.

Pittsburg was a rough mining town, with saloons and brothels doing a rampant turn-of-the-century business. Only a few short years earlier, this had been the wild west of the American prairie. Kansas City lay just to the north. Wichita and Dodge City were not far over the plains to the west. The Oklahoma Territory, which was only twenty-five miles south, was not even a state yet. The remnants of wild western life remained strongly evident. Men still wore guns, the saloon was the center of the town's night life, and arguments were settled with fists and bullets.

In this environment, Wright's heart yearned to make a lasting, moral impact, to demonstrate the teachings of Jesus in a dynamic way. With the hope, therefore, of arousing the people of his congregation to action, and of clarifying their priorities with respect to Jesus' words, he began writing what eventually became his first book, intending to read it by installments in the weekly evening services.

Wright wanted to capture his congregation's attention. So he began his tale as a story—complete with intrigue, mystery, romance, murder, and betrayal. But he was trying to accomplish a purpose as well. Thus, woven throughout the drama and characterization, were unmistakable themes he did not want his people to miss. It turns out, as we read his words ninety years later, his message is as timeless as is the scripture around which Wright based the events of his narrative.

When it was completed, Wright called his story *That Printer of Udell's*. It was the story of a church and its people, the sort of place Wright envisioned his church at Pittsburg should and could be. No doubt he drew many of the characters of the fictional Boyd City from the real life Pittsburg. And one wonders whether Wright himself occasionally stepped into the shoes of young Cameron and spoke through Cameron's voice.

Wright had the book copyrighted, and through the efforts of one of his churchmen, it was published in 1902. From this inauspicious beginning, the writing career of Wright, who was destined to become one of America's best-selling writers of the early twentieth century, was launched. The book became, if not an overnight success, certainly a moderate one. Wright's reputation grew, and his courage in combating the evils of the little mining town, both from his pulpit and pen, brought him great admiration from friends and enemies alike, and earned him an expanding reputation in the Midwest. After his next book, *The Shepherd of the Hills* (1906), became a runaway bestseller, *That Printer of Udell's* began to sell on a national scale as well, and ultimately became a bestseller in its own right, eventually selling several hundred thousand copies.

One of the reasons I like the books of Harold Bell Wright so much is that he is a good storyteller. He is able to paint lifelike characters, and then weave through their lives complexities of mystery and plot that keep the stories interesting and fast-paced. Yet, at the same time, he writes on a deeper level; and it is the emotional and spiritual themes he explores that really set his books apart.

I found myself compelled by this present work. The further into it I progressed, the deeper Wright's message of Christlike behavior took hold of me. I found myself thinking about everything I did and said from a new light, contemplating my business from fresh perspectives, viewing relationships with new meaning. I began praying anew for God to show me exactly what He wanted me to do and how He wanted me to do things. I found myself praying about a vacant piece of property adjoining our bookstore, asking, "Lord, do you have some purpose of ministry in mind for that place which my eyes cannot yet see?"

In a host of ways I have found myself looking at the world through different eyes.

Years ago I read *In His Steps*, in which the striking question "What would Jesus do?" is made a daily way of life. I think Wright takes that question a step further in this book, asking what Jesus would have of us after we move beyond that necessary starting point. Once the foundation of Christlikeness has been laid in our personal interactions with one another, then what are the consequences in wider spheres—in our churches . . . *between* our churches . . . in our towns, cities . . . even in our nation?

I find my mind simply reeling from the implications of the impact we would have if Wright's message were understood and lived out in churches across America. If pastors and city leaders and business men and women, teachers, professionals, congressmen, bankers, and most importantly the lay members in the congregations of every church . . . if such individuals were to read this book, and then—by the hundreds and thousands—began asking one vital question, I think we would be astonished by the results. That question is simply this: "Lord, what would you have *me* do—right now, here, where I live and function—to make this scripture of Matthew alive and life changing? Show me, Lord . . . and I will do as you say."

Can you imagine the staggering impact if thousands, perhaps even millions of Christians began, in deepest prayerful sincerity, praying that prayer and then looking for God's answer? The result would be an astounding move on the part of the unbelieving world toward Jesus Christ.

The reason the world of today is not listening to the message of the church is not because the message is not vital and alive and meaningful. Rather, it is because we do not back up that message with our lives. Our steeples are raised high, but our doors are closed. Our sermons every Sunday morning and our Bible studies through the week are preached and conducted for the benefit of ourselves, scrutinizing Scripture rather than living it, seeking to increase our *knowledge* rather than change our behavior. Our ceaseless activities more resemble those of widespread social clubs than an effort to live out the revolutionary, fateful, and sobering thirteen verses at the end of Matthew 25.

Surely I am not suggesting we attempt to adopt Wright's exact social agenda, or to copy his methods, proposals, and solutions. This book, after all, is almost ninety years old. Times change. The world of today is vastly different than Wright's world of 1902. New specifics will have to be found to live out these unchanging priorities. In every town, in every church, in every human heart, the need will be different, as will be God's leading. But though the details have changed, the principles involved have not. Nor have Jesus' compelling and portentous words.

Lord, what would you have me do . . . ?

When we begin asking this question, the Lord will begin to work mighty miracles in our generation.

Lord, how would you have me put my time and resources and money and energy to work to obey your command?

When we are asking these questions, churches will begin getting together in ministry rather than remaining locked in their *own* little independent spheres. When we are asking these questions, ministers and pastors and clergymen will begin breaking down the walls of theology between them to minister *together* to the heartbroken and downtrodden of their communities.

. . . how would you have me minister to the least of these, my brothers and sisters?

These are questions the Lord longs to hear from us. As long as our hearts are willing to follow them with the words that turn the whole process into dynamic life which no one can stop:

Show me, Lord . . . and I will obey.

But at all levels, from the laity to the clergy, as long as we place our *own* independence and the preservation of our *own* doctrinal positions (which we prefer to think of as the illusory mirage we call "doctrinal purity," as if the finite and sinful mind could ever approach such a thing) above the humble and openly prayerful asking of these simple questions, the Spirit of God will be vastly limited in what He is able to do in this generation.

We pray for our churches, our cities, our nation, and all the problems they contain. But until we lay down our own self-interests and our own doctrines and our own prejudices and our church-club mentality and really begin to put ourselves on the line, willing to obey in practical ways those very clear words of Jesus, we are only fooling ourselves by thinking God will be able to answer our prayers. We might as well not even pray them if we are thinking God is going to take care of the world's ills by some divine magic.

He cannot answer them until we are willing to do our part.

Ah, if we could but pray these prayers—earnestly, with willing hands and hearts and feet and pocketbooks!—what God could do among us! What changes there would be in our churches and families and cities! What powerful ministry of the Gospel would go forth into the world!

The vision of Harold Bell Wright has infected me. This is an exciting message! I believe it is a prophetic message. It's a message God gave to one of his servants ninety years ago—and it is still His message for us today.

It is impossible for me to remain "detached" when editing a book such as this. I take every piece of writing I do very seriously and personally. I find myself seeking to "know the mind and heart" of an author if I am re-doing one of his works, realizing that my ability to faithfully represent his original is largely dependent on my awareness of his thought processes, his motives in writing a certain book, his authorial perspectives and priorities, as well as the prevailing social and spiritual conditions in his life and time that formed the backdrop for his words.

Even more than the research I do into an author's life and the time and places where he lived, however, the whole response becomes highly personal as I find my own inner being drawn into the process. I find my perspectives changing. I discover myself almost "taking on" the very attitudes and priorities and values of the original author himself, to the point where I feel myself driven to communicate his original intent from the "inside." It's very different than an analytically detached exercise in "editing," in which certain rote rules are followed that are supposed to lead to a predictable end. There are no formulas. Part of me must, in a sense, "become" that author for a time so that I can exist as a channel through which his original purposes are able to flow.

People often ask me *how* I edit. I am always stumped for an answer. They are looking, I think, for a list of things I *do*—the procedures, the patterns, the recipe that anyone could apply to a piece of writing in a similar way.

But there is no such list. I don't *do* the same thing over and over. Every job I tackle is altogether new. Certainly I bring the writing and editorial principles I have learned to bear on every sentence I re-work. I try hard to be exacting and precise to find just the right words and phrases. But on another level, I'm no "expert" editor, so to speak. I've had no professional training and probably know very few of the "rules" of what an editor is supposed to do.

What I do, which for me is most important of all, is attempt to feel the pulse of the original writer. So after I apply all the specific principles I know, I then try to plug into the emotional and spiritual heartbeat of a book, and let it carry me along.

My hope is to get inside the author's mind and heart, and then try to write as I sense *he* would write a certain section. In a way, my editing is not a *doing* at all, but rather a *feeling*. I apply no hard and fast formulas, but rather just relax and let myself enter into the author's being, letting his perspectives, thoughts, vision, concerns, and ideas flow out through me.

A man's spirit lives on through his books. Therefore, I truly feel there is something of the man himself that can be touched through the words he labored over long before. My object as an editor is to touch that something, that deep soul of the man, and then allow it to come out onto my printed page with even greater clarity of focus. My prayer is that when you read something I have done, you will encounter—perhaps in some cases even more vividly than you could have in a hundred-year-old original—the spirit and person of the author, while my editorial scalpel, as well as the scars it leaves behind, remain invisible. I am only human, and I know that here and there evidences of my incisions will probably not heal over perfectly. Yet such remains my hope.

With every piece of work, the author's personality and spiritual being is either more or less visible. Sometimes the author is right there on the surface, easy to see. At other times he is obscurely removed from the words of his story. In some of George Mac-Donald's stories and fairy tales, I can hardly detect the man. On the other hand, his *Alec Forbes of Howglen* and *Robert Falconer* (retitled *The Maiden's Bequest* and *The Musician's Quest* in the edited series from Bethany House Publishers) simply overflow with the author's presence, and become doubly intriguing for that reason. The first two books by Ralph Connor that I have edited (*Jim Craig's Battle for Black Rock* and *Thomas Skyler, Foothills Preacher*, published through Sunrise Books) are similar expressions of the author—Connor himself is a character who intrudes in and throughout the stories, even though he penned many of his later books from a more distant vantage point.

The same can be said of Harold Bell Wright, who was interestingly sometimes called "the Ralph Connor of Kansas." Wright was an author sometimes obscure and at other times highly visible within the pages of his books. In the case of this present volume, he is very much in evidence, and the vision of his spirit is profoundly present.

It is this cry of Wright's heart that has had such a profound impact on me as I have worked on this book. For I cannot take lightly the fact that God spoke a vision to a man—whether it be nine or ninety or nine hundred years ago—which has implications in my life.

God's word to man is unchanging—the same yesterday, today, and forever. If God spoke this message to Harold Bell Wright in 1902, then perhaps it remains for us today, in the closing years of the same century, to bring that vision of God to fulfillment—a vision of unity among Christians, a vision of common purpose and shared efforts between all of God's people from all denominations and churches, a vision of ministry to those in need.

Yes, Harold Bell Wright is here, in these pages. But more significantly, *God's Spirit* is speaking here, calling to *us*—to you . . . and to me.

That is why I cannot escape the imperative of this book's message. Because I believe through it God has spoken to me.

In this new edition of *That Printer of Udell's*, here retitled *The Least of These My Brothers*, for the Bethany House series, it is my sincere prayer that you enjoy the story and learn from the various characters. And especially that you, as I have, touch God's Spirit as you read, perhaps gaining a message from His heart to yours.

Fruitful reading to you all! I hope you enjoy some of the other books by my favorite old authors as much as I enjoy finding them and making them available to you.

I would be delighted to hear your responses. God bless you!

Michael Phillips
One Way Book Shop
1707 E St.
Eureka, CA 95501

PROLOGUE

In a rude, one-room cabin, standing beneath the high sort of hill midwesterners sometimes call a mountain, with what breath was left in her, an aging woman lay praying.

"God, take care o' Dickie!" she pleaded in a soft voice. "He'll have a tough time when I'm gone—an' I reckon I'm goin' mighty fast. I know I ain't done much t' brag on, Lord. I always tried t' do better . . . but it's kept me scratchin' jist fer me an' Dickie t' keep us from starvin' . . . An' somehow I ain't had 'nough time fer ye like I oughta."

Outside, the dull gray of approaching dawn was barely visible. Inside the room, however, all was black. Even the fading fire could not keep the chill away. For the cabin was filled with a deeper cold than could be explained by the late October storm that had passed in the night. The boy who was the object of the woman's prayers felt the unfriendly nip of approaching change, and shivered where he sat—though he knew not the reason for the involuntary quiver that his mother's fading voice sent through him.

"An' my man," she continued, though the words were barely audible, "he's o' no account an' trifflin', Lord . . . 'specially when he liquors up—an' then ye know how he be t' me an' Dickie. But Dickie, he ain't no ways t' blame fer what his dad an' mammy is—an' I ask ye t' be fair, O Lord, an' take care o' Dickie—fer Jesus' sake . . . Amen."

She paused, then called out a little louder, "Dickie! . . . Dickie . . . where are ye, my boy?"

A hollow-cheeked wisp of a lad arose from the dark corner where he had been crouching like a frightened animal, and with cautious steps drew near the bed. Timidly he touched the wasted hand that lay upon the dirty cover.

"What ye want, Ma?"

The woman hushed in her moaning and turned her face, upon which the shadow was already fallen, toward the boy. "I'm goin'—mighty fast—Dickie," she said in a voice that was scarcely audible. "Where's yer pa?"

Bending closer to the face on the pillow, the boy pointed with trembling finger toward the other end of the cabin. His eyes grew big with fear and he whispered, "Shhh. He's full again. He's been down t' the stillhouse all evenin'. Don't stir him, Ma, or we'll git licked some more. Tell me what ye want."

But his only answer was that broken prayer as the suffering woman turned to the wall again. "O Lord, take care o'—"

A stick of wood in the fireplace burned in two and fell with a soft thud on the ashes. A lean hound crept stealthily to the boy's side and thrust a cold muzzle against his ragged jacket. In the cupboard a mouse rustled over the few simple dishes and among the scanty handful of provisions.

Cursing foully in his sleep, the drunkard stirred uneasily and the dog slunk under the bed, while the boy stood shaking with fear until all was still again. Reaching out, he touched once more that clammy hand upon the dirty coverlet. No movement answered to his touch. Reaching farther, he cautiously laid his fingers upon the ashy-colored temple, awkwardly brushing back a thin lock of the tangled hair. The face, like the hand, was cold.

With a look of awe and horror in his eyes, the child caught his mother by the shoulder and shook the lifeless form, while he tried again and again to make her hear his words.

"Ma! Ma! Wake up!" he whispered in despair. "It'll be day

purty soon an' we can go an' git some greens, an' I'll catch some fish fer ye. Ma! Oh, Ma, the meal's almost gone. I only made a little pone last night; there's some left fer ye. Shall I fix ye some afore Dad wakes up?"

But there was no answer to his pleading.

Ceasing his efforts, the lad sank on his knees by the ramshackle old bed, not daring even to give open expression to his grief lest he arouse the drunken sleeper by the fireplace. For a long time he knelt there, clasping the cold hand of his lifeless mother. Again the lean hound crept to his side, and thrusting that cold muzzle against his cheek, licked the salty tears that fell so hot.

At last, as the first flush of day stained the eastern sky, and the light tipped the old pine tree on the hill with glory, the boy rose to his feet. Placing his hand on the head of his only comforter, he whispered, "Come on, Smoke, we gotta go now."

And together the boy and dog crept softly across the room and stole out of the cabin door—out of that cabin where lay only darkness, into the beautiful light of the new day. The drunken brute still slept on the floor by the open fireplace, but the fire was dead upon the hearth.

"He can't hurt Ma no more, Smoke," said the lad when the two were a safe distance away. "No, he sure can't lick her again, an' me an' you can rustle fer ourselves, I reckon."

CHAPTER ONE

NEW ARRIVAL IN THE CITY

In the early gray of morning, a young man crawled from beneath a stack of straw. He had spent the night on the outskirts of Boyd City, a busy, bustling mining town of some fifteen thousand people at the turn of the twentieth century, located in one of the middle western states, many miles from the one-room cabin that stood beneath the hill. The young man, who wore the aspect of a common tramp, appeared to be about twenty-six.

The night before, he had approached the town from the east along the road that leads past Mount Olive. Hungry, cold, and weary, he had sought this friendly shelter, much preferring a bed of straw and the companionship of cattle to any lodging place he might find in the city, less clean and among a ruder company. Economics might also have been a factor in his decision.

It was early March and the smoke from a nearby block of smelters was lost in a chilling mist, while a raw wind caused the young man to shiver as he stood picking the bits of straw from his clothing. When he had brushed his garments as best he could and had stretched his numb and stiffened limbs, he looked long and thoughtfully at the city lying half hidden in its shroud of gray.

"I wonder . . ." he began, talking to himself and thinking

grimly of the fifteen cents in his right-hand pants pocket . . . "I wonder if—"

"Mornin', pardner," said a voice at his elbow. "Rather late when ye got in las' night, warn't it?"

The young man jumped, and turning, found himself facing a genuine specimen of the genus hobo. "Did you sleep in this straw-stack too?" he asked in surprise, while taking in the ragged fellow's measure with a practiced eye.

"Sure. This here's the hotel whar I put up—slept in the room jist acrost the hall from your'n," the hobo answered, then asked with a hungry look, "Whar ye goin' t' eat?"

"Don't know. Did you have any supper last night?"

"Nope."

"Same here."

"I didn't have nothin' fer midday dinner neither," continued the hobo, "an' I'm gittin' powerful weak."

The other thought of his fifteen cents. "Where are you going?" he asked.

The ragged man jerked his thumb toward the city. "Hear'd as how thar's a right smart o' work yonder an' I'm on the hunt fer a job."

"What do you do?"

"Tendin' mason's my stronghold. I've done most ever'thin' though. Used t' work on a farm, and puttered 'round a sawmill some in Arkansas. Aim t' strike a job at somethin' an' then go back thar where I know folks. Nobody won't give a feller nothin' in this here godfersaken country. No one hain't asked me t' sit down with 'em fer a month. Back home they're always glad t' have a man eat with 'em."

The fellow's voice dropped to the pitiful, pleading of the professional tramp.

The young man looked at him. Good-for-nothing was written in every line of the shiftless, shambling figure, and pictured in every rag of the fluttering raiment. And yet, the fellow really was hungry—and again came the thought of the fifteen cents.

The young man himself was hungry. He had been hungry

many times in the past. And downright gnawing, helpless hunger is a great leveler of mankind. In fact, it is one of the few real bonds of fellowship between men.

"Come on," he said at last, "I've got fifteen cents. I reckon we can find something to eat." And with that the two set out toward the city together.

Passing a deserted mining shaft and crossing the railroad, they entered the southern portion of the town, and continued west until they reached the main street, where they stopped at a little grocery store on the corner. The young man carrying the wealth of fifteen cents invested two-thirds of his capital in crackers and cheese, his companion reminding the grocer meanwhile that he might throw in a little extra, "seein' as how they were the first customers that mornin'." The merchant good-naturedly did so, and then turned to answer the other's question about work.

"What can you do?"

"I'm a printer by trade, but will do anything."

"How does it happen you are out of work?"

"I was thrown out by the Kansas City strike and have been unable to find a place since."

"Is he looking for work too?" the grocer asked, with a glance and a nod toward the fellow from Arkansas, who sat on a box near the stove rapidly making away with more than his half of the breakfast.

The young man shrugged his shoulders. "We woke up in the same strawstack this morning and he was hungry, that's all."

"Well," returned the storekeeper as he dropped the lid of the cracker box with a bang, "you'll not be bothered with him long if you are really hunting a job."

"You put me on the track of a job and I'll show you whether I mean business or not," said the young man.

"There's lots of work in Boyd City and lots of men to do it," the grocer replied as he returned to his task of dusting the shelves.

The young man turned and left the store, but had only walked a little way down the street when he heard the voice of the tramp behind him. "I'm obliged t' ye fer the feed, pardner. Reckon I'll shove along."

The younger traveler stopped, and the other continued as he came up alongside him. "Don't much like the looks of this place nohow. Reckon I'll shove along t' Jonesville, forty miles below. Might be work there. Ain't got the price of a drink, have ye? Can't set 'em up jist fer old times' sake, ye know?" As he spoke a cunning gleam crept into the bloodshot eyes of the vagabond.

"What do you know about the old times?" the young man shot back, staring keenly at the bloated features of the man before him.

The tramp shuffled uneasily, then replied with a knowing leer, "Ain't ye Dickie Falkner, what used t' live cross the river from Simpson's stillhouse?"

"What of it?"

"Nuthin' much; only I'm Jake Tompkins that used t' work fer Simpson at the still. Me an' yer daddy were pards. I used t' set 'em up fer him a heap o' times."

"Ah, yes," replied Dick with a note of bitterness in his voice. "I know you now. You gave my father whiskey and then laughed when he went home drunk and drove my mother from the cabin to spend the night in the brush. You know it killed her."

"Yer ma always was weakly-like," faltered Tompkins. "She'd no call t' hitch up with Bill Falkner nohow. She oughta took a man with book learnin' like her daddy, old Judge White. It always made yer pa mad 'cause she knowed more'n him. But Bill 'lowed he'd tame her, an' he shor' tried hit on her. Too bad she went an' died, but she oughta knowed a man o' Bill's spirit would a took his liquor when he wanted it. I recollect ye used t' take a right smart lot yerself fer a kid."

The bitterness in the young man's voice gave way to a note of hopeless despair. "Yes," he said, "you and Dad made me drink the stuff before I was old enough to know what it would do to me. Sometimes I wonder why I fight it," he continued, half to himself.

"That's the talk!" exclaimed the other with a swagger. "That's how yer pa used t' put it. Yer ma wasn't much good nohow, with her finicky notions 'bout eddication an' such. A little pone an' baken with plenty o' good ol' red eye's good 'nough fer us. Yer ma she—"

He never finished. Dick made a threatening move toward him and grabbed him by the shirt. The tramp shrank back cowering.

"If you dare take my mother's name in your foul mouth again," cried the young man, "I'll make you live to regret it!"

"Lemme go, Dickie. I didn't mean no harm. Me'n yer daddy were pards. Lemme go. Yer pa won't bother ye no more, Dickie. He can't. He's dead."

"Dead!" Dick released his grasp and the other sprang back to a safe distance. "Dead!" he repeated, staring forward with blank expression.

The tramp nodded sullenly. "Yep, dead," he said hoarscly. "Me an' him were bummin' a freight out o' St. Louie, an' he slipped. I know he was killed 'cause I seen 'em pick him up. Six cars went over him an' they kept me in hock fer two months."

Dick sat down on the curb and buried his face in his hands. "Dead," he softly repeated to himself. "My dad is dead—dead."

With a slowly gathering rush, all his past life came back upon him: the cabin home across the river from the distillery, the still-house with the rough men who gathered there, the neighboring shanties with their sickly, sad-faced women and dirty, quarreling children, the store and blacksmith shop at the crossroads in the pinery seven miles away. In his mind's eye he saw again the river flowing sluggishly at times between banks of drooping willows and tall marsh grass as though smitten with the fatal spirit of the place, then breaking into hurried movement over pebbly shoals as if trying to escape to some healthier climate. There was the hill where stood the old pine tree, the cave beneath the great rock by the spring, and the persimmon grove in the bottom. Then once more he suffered with his mother from his drunken father's rage, and every detail of that awful night in the brush, with the long days and nights of sickness that followed before her death . . . It all came back so vividly that he wept again with his face in his hands as he had cried by the rude bedside in the cabin sixteen years ago.

Then came the years when he had wandered from his early home and had learned to know life in the great cities. What a life he had found it! He shuddered as his recollection quickened: the many times when inspired by the memory of his mother, he had tried to break away from the evil, degrading things that were in and about him, and yet the many times he had been dragged back by the training and memory of his father—the gambling, the fighting, the drinking, the periods of hard work, the struggle to master his trade, and the reckless wasting of wages in times of wild despair.

And now suddenly . . . his father was dead. Dead—he shuddered. All at once there was nothing to bind him to the past. Could he perhaps finally be free?

"Can't ye give me that drink, Dickie? Jist one little horn. It'll do us both good, an' then I'll shove along. Jist fer old times' sake, ye know."

The voice of the tramp broke in upon his thoughts.

For another long moment he sat on the curb, then started to his feet, a new light in his eye, a new ring in his voice.

"No, Jake," he said slowly, "I wouldn't if I could now. I'm done with the old times. Done—forever."

He threw up his head and stood proudly erect while the tramp gazed in awe at something in the man's face he had never seen before.

"I have only five cents in the world," continued Dick. "Here, take it. You'll be hungry again soon. Goodbye, Jake—"

He turned and walked swiftly away, while the other stood staring in astonishment, first at the coin in his hand, then at the retreating figure. Finally, with an exclamation, the ragged fellow wheeled and started in the opposite direction toward the railroad yards, to catch a south-bound freight.

CHAPTER TWO

HARD FIRST DAY

As young Dick Falkner walked along the block after leaving his father's friend, a lean hound came trotting across the street.

"Dear old Smoke," he said to himself, his mind going back to the companion of his boyhood—"dear old Smoke." Then as the half-starved creature came timidly to his side and looked up at him with pleading eyes, Dick remembered his share of the breakfast, still untouched, in his pocket.

"You look like an old friend of mine," he continued as he stopped to pat the bony head; "a friend who's never hungry now—but you're hungry, aren't you?"

A low whine answered him. "Yes, you're hungry all right." And the next moment a wagging tail was eloquently giving thanks for the rest of the crackers and cheese.

The factories and mills of the city gave forth their early greeting, while the sun tried in vain to drive away the chilly mist. Men with lunch buckets in their hands went hurrying along at the call of the whistles, shopkeepers were sweeping, dusting, and arranging their goods, a streetcar full of miners passed with clanging gong, and the fire department horses out for their morning exercise clattered down the street. Amid the busy scene walked Dick—without work, without money, without friends, but with a new purpose in his heart that was more than meat or drink. A new feeling of freedom and power made him lift his head and move with a firm and steady step. It could not be said he was *glad* to hear his father was dead. He was too much a man for that. But mingled with the sadness, which must come with earthly loss, was a feeling he could not explain . . . a freedom at last to stand on his own and for the first time *be* the man he had all the time been struggling to be, a release from the bondage of the past which had kept him down.

All that morning he sought a job, asking at the stores and shops, but receiving little or no encouragement. Toward noon, while waiting for an opportunity to interview with the proprietor of a store, he picked up a daily paper lying on the counter. He turned to the "help wanted" column, read an advertisement for a man to do general work about a barn and yard, and when he had received the usual answer to his request for work, left the shop and went at once to the address given in the paper.

"Is Mr. Goodrich in?" he asked of the young man who came forward with a look of inquiry on his face.

"What do you want?" was his curt reply.

"I would like to see Mr. Goodrich," came the answer, and the young man conducted him to the open door of an office.

Dick stood still until a portly middle-aged gentleman had finished dictating a letter to the young lady seated at the typewriter. "Well," he said, as he looked up and saw Dick before him, "what do *you* want?"

"I came in answer to your ad in this morning's *Whistler*," answered Dick.

"Humph—Where did you work last?"

"At Kansas City."

"Doing what?"

"I'm a printer by trade, but willing to do anything until I get a start."

"Why aren't you working at your trade then?"

"I was thrown out by the strike and have been unable to find anything since."

A look of scorn swept over the merchant's face. "So, you're one of that lot, are you? Why don't you fellows learn to take what you can get? Look here—"

He pointed to a pile of pamphlets lying on the table.

"—Just came in today. They cost me fifty percent more than I ever paid before only because you cattle can't be satisfied. And now you want me to give you a place! If I had my way, I'd give such like you work on the rock pile." He wheeled his chair toward his desk.

"But I'm hungry," said Dick. "I must do something—I'm not a beggar—I'll earn every cent you pay me."

"No, I tell you!" shouted the other. "I won't have men about the place who think they're above their position." He picked up his pen.

"But, sir," said Dick again, "what am I to do?"

"I don't care what you do," returned the other. "There is a stone yard here for such as you."

"Sir," answered Dick, standing very straight, his face pale, "you will someday learn that it does matter very much what such fellows as I do. As a man, I am every bit your equal, and I will live to prove it."

With the words, he spun around and marched out of the office like a soldier, leaving the young lady at the typewriter motionless in amazement, and her employer dumb with rage.

What induced him to utter such words Dick could not imagine. He only knew they were true, and they seemed somehow to have been forced from him. He found himself laughing at the ridiculousness of the situation before he was barely away from the building.

The factory whistles blew for dinner, but there was no dinner for Dick.

They blew again for work at one o'clock, but still there was nothing for Dick to do. All that afternoon he continued his search with the same result: "We don't need you." Some were kind in their answers. One old gentleman, a real estate man, seemed about to help him, but was called away on business, and poor Dick went on his weary search again.

At six o'clock the whistles blew again, and the workmen, their faces stained with the marks of toil, hurried along the streets toward home. Through hungry eyes, Dick watched the throng, wondering what each worked at during the day and what they would have for supper.

The sun went behind a bank of dull, lead-colored clouds, and the wind sprang up again, so sharp and cold that the people who were still out turned up the collars of their coats and drew their wraps more tightly about them. Dick sought shelter in an open hallway.

Suddenly a policeman appeared before him.

"What are you doing here?" he asked.

"Nothing," answered Dick.

"Well, you'd better be doing something. I've had my eye on you all afternoon. I'll run you in if I catch you hanging around anymore. Get a move on now." And Dick stepped out on the sidewalk once more to face the bitter wind.

Walking as rapidly as possible, he made his way north on Broadway, past the big hotel all aglow with light and warmth, past vacant lots and factories, until he reached the ruins of an old smelter just beyond a network of railway tracks. He had noticed the place earlier in the day as he passed it on his way to the brickyard. Groping about over the fallen walls of the furnace, stumbling over scraps of iron and broken timbers in the dusk, he searched for a corner that would in some measure protect him from the wind.

It grew dark very fast, and soon he tripped and fell against an old boiler lying upturned in the ruin. Throwing out his hand to catch himself, by chance he struck the door of the firebox, and in a moment more was inside, crouching in the accumulated dirt, iron, rust, and ashes. At least the wind could not get at him here.

Leaning his back against the iron wall of his strange bedroom, tired and hungry, he fell asleep.

CHAPTER THREE

MOVE ON!

The next morning, stiff and sore, Dick crawled from his rude lodging place and started again on his search for employment. It was nearly noon when he met a man who in answer to his inquiry said, "I'm out of a job myself, stranger, but I've got a little money left. You look hungry."

Dick admitted that he had had no breakfast.

"Tell you what I'll do," said the other. "I ain't got much, but we can go to a joint I know of where they set up a big free lunch. I'll pay for the beer and you can have something to eat."

Poor Dick, weak from hunger, chilled with the March winds, tired and discouraged, forgot his resolve of the day before and followed his would-be benefactor. It was not far and they soon stood in a well-warmed saloon. The grateful heat, the polished furniture, the rows of bottles and glasses, the clean-looking, white-jacketed and aproned bartender, and the merry air of those he served were all wonderfully attractive to the poor shivering wanderer from out in the cold. And then there was the long table well loaded with strong hot food. The starving fellow started toward it eagerly. "Two beers here," cried his companion.

Suddenly Dick remembered his resolve of the previous day. He withdrew his hand, his pale face grew even more haggard, and he thought to himself, *What am I to do? I must eat.*

He saw the bartender take two large glasses from the shelf. His whole physical being pled with him, demanding food and drink. Now one of the glasses was in the hand of the man, filling with the amber liquid. A moment more and—"Stop!" he cried. "Stop! It's a mistake. I don't drink."

The man paused and looked around with an evil leer, one glass still unfilled in his hand. Then with a brutal oath, he growled, "What are ye in here for then?"

"I—I—was cold and hungry—" Dick trembled, glancing involuntarily at the food on the table. "And—and—the gentleman asked me to come. He's not to blame; he thought I wanted a drink."

His new-found friend looked at him with a puzzled expression. "Oh, take a glass, stranger," he said. "You need it. And then help yourself to the lunch."

Dick shook his head, but no words would come.

"Look here!" broke in the bartender with another string of vile language as he quickly filled the empty glass and set it on the counter in front of Dick, "You drink this or get out. That there lunch is for our customers, and we ain't got no room for temperance cranks or bums. Which'll it be?"

Dick's eyes went from the food to the glass of beer, then to the saloon man's hard face, while a strange hush fell around the rest of the room. Slowly the young man swept the faces of those gazing upon the scene, but he met only curious indifference on every side.

"I won't," he said finally; then to his would-be friend he added, "Thank you for your good intention."

The silence in the tavern was broken by a shout of harsh laughter as the bartender raised the glass of beer he had drawn for Dick and mockingly drank him good luck as Dick stumbled back through the doorway, leaving warmth and food behind.

All he could hear behind him as the door closed was the voice of the bartender, followed by rousing laughter from all sides.

All that day Dick continued his search for work. Night came

on again, and he found himself wandering, half dazed, through the better part of the city. He was too tired to go to the old smelter again. He could hardly think clearly as he stumbled aimlessly along.

The door of a house opened, letting out a flood of light, and then a woman's voice called out, "Dickie, oh, Dickie, come home now . . . supper is waiting."

A lad of about ten, playing in the neighboring yard with his friend, answered with a shout as he bounded across the lawn. Through the windows Dick caught a glimpse of the cozy home: father, mother, two sisters, bright pictures, books, and a table set with snowy linen, shining silver, and sparkling glass.

Later, still wandering, strange voices seemed to call him out of the night, and several times he paused to listen. Then someone in the distance seemed to say, "Move on . . . move on."

The words echoed and reechoed through his exhausted brain. "Move on, move on," the weary, monotonous strain continued as he dragged his heavy feet along the pavement. "Move on . . . move on." The words seemed repeated just ahead. Who was it? What did they want, and why couldn't they let him rest?

He drew near a large building with beautiful stained glass windows, through which the light streamed brilliantly. In the center was a picture of the Christ, holding in His arms a lamb, and beneath was the inscription: "I came to seek and to save that which was lost."

"Move on! Move on!" the words now shrieked in his ears. Looking up he saw a steeple in the form of a giant hand, pointing toward the stormy sky. "Why, of course"—he laughed with mirthless lips—"of course . . . it's a church. I ought to have come here long ago. This is Thursday night and that voice is the bell calling people to prayer meeting.

"I ought to have remembered the church before," he continued to himself as he leaned against a tree near the building. "I've set up and printed their notices many a time. They always say 'Everybody welcome.' Christians surely won't let me starve—they'll help me earn something to eat." He tried hard to straighten his tired frame.

By this time, where Dick stood muttering to himself, well-dressed people were passing and entering the open door of the church. Then the organ began to play, and arousing himself by a supreme effort of his will, Dick followed them into the building.

The organ now filled the air with its solemn tones. The bell with its harsh command to move on was forgotten, and as Dick sank onto a cushioned seat near the door, his heart was filled with restful thoughts. He saw visions of a gracious being who cared for all mankind, and who had been all this time waiting to help him. Had he not heard his mother pray, many years ago in the cabin, "O Lord, take care o' Dickie"? How foolish he had been to forget. He ought to have remembered, but he would never forget again.

The music and the singing stopped. The pastor rose and read the lesson, calling particular attention to the words recorded in the twenty-fifth chapter of Matthew: "Inasmuch as ye have done it unto one of the least of these my brethren, ye have done it unto me." Then after a long prayer and another song, the man of God spoke a few words about the Christian's joy and duty in helping the needy; that the least of these meant those who needed help, no matter what their positions in life; and that whoever gave aid to one in the name of Christ glorified the Master's name and helped to enthrone Him in the hearts of men.

"The least of these . . ." whispered Dick to himself.

And as one after another of the Christians arose and testified to the joy they found in doing Christ's work and told of experiences where they had been blessed by being permitted to help some poor one, his heart warmed within him; and in his own way he thanked God that he had been led to such a place and to such people.

With another song, "Praise God from whom all blessings flow," the congregation was dismissed and began slowly passing from the building, exchanging greetings, with more or less warmth, and remarking what a helpful meeting they had and how much it had been enjoyed.

Hat in hand, Dick stood near the door, patiently waiting. One by one the members passed him; two or three said "Good evening"; one shook him by the hand. But something in their faces as they looked at his clothing checked the words that rose to his lips, and the poor fellow continued to stand silent, his story untold.

At last the minister came down the aisle, greeted Dick, and was about to pass out with the others. In a choked voice, Dick faltered, "Sir . . . may I speak to you a moment?"

"If you'll be brief," replied the preacher, glancing at his watch. "I have an engagement soon."

Dick told his story in a few words. "I'm not begging, sir," he added. "I thought some of the church members might have work I could do, or know where I could find employment."

The minister seemed a little embarrassed, then beckoning to a few who still remained, he began to question them. "Brother Dickson, here's a man who wants work. Do you know of anything?"

"Umm . . . I'm sorry to say, but I don't," promptly replied the good deacon. "What can you do?" he asked, turning to Dick.

He made the usual answer and the officer of the church said again, "Find it rather hard to strike against anything here in Boyd City, I fear; so many tramps, you know. Been out of work long?"

"Yes, sir, and out of food too."

"Too bad, too bad," sympathized the deacon. "Too bad," echoed the preacher with attempted compassion in his voice, while the few other followers of the meek and lowly Jesus nodded and mumbled their condolences. "If we hear of anything we will let you know. Where are you staying?"

"On the street," replied Dick, "when I am not moved on by the police."

"Oh—well—umm . . . we'll leave word here at the church with the janitor if we learn of anything."

"Are you a Christian?" asked one good old mother in Israel.

"No," stammered poor, confused Dick. "That is . . . I guess not."

"Do you drink?"

"No, ma'am."

"Well, don't get discouraged. Look to God. He can help you,

and we'll all pray for you. Come and hear our Brother French preach. I am sure you will find the light. He's the best preacher in the city. Everybody says so. Good night."

The others had already gone. The sexton was turning out the lights, and a moment later Dick found himself once more on the street, looking with a grim smile at the finger of the Christ, wrought in the costly stained glass window. "One of the least of these," he muttered to himself.

Then the figure and the inscription slowly faded as one by one the lights inside the church went out, until at last it vanished, and he seemed to hear his mother's voice, "I ask ye t' be fair, O Lord, an' take care o' Dickie—fer Jesus' sake . . . Amen."

The door shut with a bang. A key grated in the heavy lock that guarded the treasures of the church. Soon the footsteps of the church's humblest servant died away in the distance as Dick turned to move on again.

The city rumbled on with its business and its pleasure, its merriment and its crime, its big meals and its comfortable beds. Guardians of the law protected the citizens by seeing to it that no ill-dressed persons sat too long upon the depot benches, sheltered themselves from the bitter wind in the open hallways and alleys, or looked too hungrily through the bakery windows.

On the avenue the homes grew hushed and still, with now and then a gleam of light from some library or living room, accompanied by the tones of piano or guitar or singing voice—or sound of friends laughing together. And the house of God stood silent, dark, and cold, with the finger of the Christ upon the window, practically invisible now, and the spire, like a giant hand, pointing upward.

CHAPTER FOUR

A Printer Called Udell

"I declare if that ain't the third tramp I've chased away from this house today!" exclaimed Mrs. Wilson, half slamming the kitchen door and returning to her dishwashing. "We'll have to get a dog if this keeps up!"

Her daughter carried on her half of the work without reply.

"The idea of giving good food to them that's able to work," she went on. "Well, I won't do it. Let them do as I do!" As she spoke the good lady plied her dishcloth with such energy that her daughter hastily removed the clean plates and saucers from the table to avoid the necessity of drying them again.

"But this man wanted work, didn't he, Mother?" asked Clara. "And I heard you tell Father at dinner that you wanted someone to fix the cowshed and clean up the backyard."

"There you go again!" snapped the older woman, resting her wet hands on her hips and pausing in her labor, the better to emphasize her words. "Always finding fault—since you took up with that church Young People's Society, there ain't been nothing right. Your mother and father and home ain't good enough for you nowadays." She turned to her dishwashing again with a splash.

"And then what about George Udell?" she went on, after but

a brief pause, in a tone that seemed to indicate she thought the two conversations had some bearing upon each other. "He ain't going to keep hanging around forever, I can tell you. There's too many young women that would jump at his offer of marriage. He won't wait around much longer for you to get through with all this religious foolishness. All of a sudden you'll find him married and settled down with some other girl, and then what will your father and I do when we get too old to work, the Lord only knows. If you had half an ounce of sense, you'd take him up on his offer quick."

Clara made no reply, finished her work in silence, then hung up her apron and left the kitchen.

When a little while later Mrs. Wilson went into the pleasant little sitting room, where the flowers in the window *would* bloom and the canary *would* sing in spite of the habitual crossness of the mistress of the house, she found her daughter dressed for going out.

"Where are you off to now?" she asked. "This is no weather fit to be traipsing around in."

"I have to go to the printing office this afternoon, Mother, to see to the printing of some things for our society meeting tomorrow night."

"Where are you going?" asked the mother.

"Why, to George's, of course," replied Clara.

"Oh, well, get along then. I guess the weather won't hurt you . . . it's clearing off a little anyway. Why don't you bring George home to supper with you?" As the old lady spoke, her voice suddenly grew almost cheerful at the thought, while she watched the sturdy figure of her daughter making her way down the boardwalk and through the front gate.

George Udell was the owner of a thriving print shop in Boyd City, and stood high in the favor of the public generally, and of the Wilson family in particular, as might be gathered from the conversation between Clara and her mother. "I tell you," the older woman had said on more than one occasion, "George Udell is good enough for any gal. He don't put on as much style as some, and ain't much of a churchman. But when it comes to making money, he's all there, and that's the main thing nowadays."

As for Clara, she was not insensible to the good points in Mr. Udell's character, of which money-making was by no means the most important, for she had known him ever since the time, when as a long, lanky, awkward boy, he had brought her picture cards and bits of bright-colored printing. She had been just a small girl then, but somehow her heart told her that her friend was more honest than most boys. And as she grew older, in spite of her religious convictions, she had never been forced to change her mind.

But George Udell, in her mind, was not a Christian. At least he was not a member of any church. Some said he was a heathen, and when he was approached on the subject of his religious beliefs, he always insisted that he did not know exactly what he believed and that he doubted very much if many church members knew any more of their beliefs than he did. Furthermore, he had been heard upon several occasions to make slighting remarks about the church, contrasting its present standing and work with the law of love and helpfulness as laid down by the Master whom they professed to follow.

True, no one had ever heard him say that he did not believe in God. But they hardly took notice of that. Had he not said that he did not care about the church? And was not that enough to mark him as a heathen!

Clara, in spite of her home training to the contrary, was a strong church member, a zealous Christian, and an earnest worker for the cause of Christ. Being a practical girl, she admitted that there were many faults in the church of today, and that Christians did not always live up to their professions. But you could not expect people to be perfect, and the faults that existed in the church were there because all churches were not the same, which to most people—including Clara—meant, "All churches are not of *my* denomination."

And so, in spite of her regard for the printer, she could not bring herself to link her destiny with one whose eternal future was so insecure, and whose life did not chord with that which was to her the one great keynote of the universe, the church. Besides, did not the good book say: "Be ye not unequally yoked with unbelievers"? What could that mean if not, "Do not marry a heathen"?

Meanwhile, as Clara made her way through the mud of Boyd City, Udell, at the printing office, was having a trying day. To begin with, his one printer had gone off on a drinking spree the Saturday before and had not been back to work since. Then several rush jobs had come in all at once. He had tried to get help, but thus far had been unsuccessful, and was trying to get the jobs out with only himself and a young boy helper in the shop. Everything that could possibly have happened to make things worse had happened to George Udell that morning.

Clara walked into the shop just when the confusion was at its height. The room was littered with scraps of paper and ink-stained cloths. The printer's towel was lying on the desk. The stove, whose hearth was piled high with ashes, seemed to be emitting smoke and coal gas in equal portions. And the printer was emptying his vials of frustration upon the public in general because all wanted their printing done at the same instant. His young helper, with a comical look of fear upon his ink-stained face, dodged here and there, attempting as best he could to avoid the threatening disaster.

Clara's coming was like a burst of sunlight. In an instant the storm was past. The boy's face resumed its usual expression of indifference, the fire at once burned freely in the stove, the towel was whisked into its proper corner, and she was greeted with the first smile that had shown on the printer's face that day.

"You're just in time," he said gaily as he seated her in the cleanest corner of the office he could find.

"I should think so," she answered, smiling and glancing curiously about the room. "Looks as though you wanted a woman here."

"I do," replied George. "I've always wanted one particular woman. Haven't I told you that often enough?"

"For shame, George Udell. I came here on business," Clara answered with glowing cheeks.

"Well then, that makes it mighty important business for me."

"What's the matter here, anyway?"

"Oh, my man is off drunk somewhere, and everyone wants their orders at the same time. I worked until two o'clock last night, and I'll have to do the same tonight. I'm—"

Just then the telephone rang.

"—you see, there's another order!" he said as he picked up the phone. "Hello . . . yes, this is Udell's. . . . Yes, we have it set up and will send you the proof as soon as possible . . ."

There was a pause while he listened at the receiver.

" . . . I'm sorry, but we are doing the best we can. . . . Yes . . . all right . . . I'll get at it right away—three o'clock—can't possibly get it ready before—"

He hung up the phone. "I tell you, this is making me thin."

"Why don't you get help?" asked Clara.

"I've tried! I've prayed and threatened and bribed and promised, all to no avail."

The girl noted the worn look on his rugged face. "I wish I could help you, George," she said.

"You know you could," he replied quickly. "You could give me more help than the ghost of Franklin himself. I don't really mind the hard work, and the worry of it all wouldn't amount to anything if only—"

He stopped as Clara shook her head.

"George, you know I have told you again and again—"

"But, Clara," he broke in, "I wouldn't interfere with your church work in any way. I'd even go with you every Sunday, and you could pay the preacher as much as you liked."

"You don't understand, George," she answered, "and I can't make you see it. There's no use talking about it until you change your ideas about the church."

Before he could reply further, the door opened and a weary, hungry, unshaven face looked in. The door opened wider and the uncertain visitor came timidly toward the man and girl.

"Yes, what is it?" said Udell, a little gruffly at the interruption.

"Are you the foreman of this office?" the newcomer asked.

"Yes—and the owner."

"Do you need any help? I'm a printer."

"A printer! You're a printer!" exclaimed Udell. But taking a second look at the disheveled figure before him, he checked his outburst of enthusiasm. "No, I—" he began. Then changing his mind again, he interrupted himself. "I don't care if you're wanted for horse stealing. Can you go to work now?"

The man nodded.

Udell showed him to a case and placed copy before him. "There you are, and the faster you work the better I'll pay you."

Again the other nodded, and without a word caught up a stick and reached for the type.

George turned back to Clara who had risen. "Don't go yet," he implored.

"I must. I have been here too long and you are busy. I only wanted to get that society printing." He found the package and handed it to her.

"Who is he?" she whispered, with a look toward the new-comer.

"Don't know. Some bum I suppose. Doesn't look too good. I only hope I can keep him sober enough to help me over this rush."

"You're wrong there," said the girl, moving toward the door. "He asked for work at our house early this morning. That man is neither a drunkard nor a common tramp."

"How do you know?"

"Same as I know you. By the look," laughed Clara. "Go talk to him and find out. You see, your prayer was answered, even if you did pray like a church member." She turned and left.

The printer returned to his work with a lighter heart. Somehow he felt that things would come out all right someday, and he would do the best he could to be patient. For Clara's sake, while he might not be all she wished, he would make of himself all he could.

For a while he kept himself busy with some work in the back of the office. Then, remembering Clara's strange words about the tramp, he walked over to the case where the new man sat perched upon his high stool. The stranger was working rapidly and doing tolerably good work. George noticed, however, that the hand which held the stick trembled slightly and that sometimes a letter dropped from the nervous fingers.

"What seems to be the problem?" he asked, eying him keenly.

"Nothing," the man muttered, without lifting his head.

"Are you sick?"

A shake of the head was the only answer.

"Been drinking?"

"*No!*"

This time the head was lifted and two keen gray eyes, filled with mingled suffering and anger, looked full in the boss's face. "I've been without work for some time and am hungry, that's all," he said. His head bent again over the case and the trembling fingers reached for the type.

"Hungry! Good night, man!" exclaimed Udell. "Why didn't you say so?"

Turning quickly to the boy he said, handing him a dollar, "Here, run down to the restaurant and bring a big hot lunch. Tell 'em to get a hustle on it too."

The boy fled the shop and George continued talking to himself. "Hungry—and I thought he had been on a spree. I ought to have known better than that. I've been hungry myself—Clara's right, he's no bum printer. Great shade of the immortal Benjamin F! He's plucky, though—and proud—you could see by the look in his eyes when I asked if he'd been drunk. Poor fellow—knows his business too—just the man I've been looking for, I'll bet."

When the boy returned with the basket and gave it to his boss, George called out cheerily, "Here you are, stranger. Come and fill yourself up. Rush or no rush, we'll have no hungry men in this establishment."

He was answered by a clatter as half a stick full of type dropped from the trembling hand of his new printer.

"Thank you," the poor fellow tried to say as he staggered toward the food; and as he fainted, Dick's outstretched fingers just touched the edges of Udell's feet.

CHAPTER FIVE

A FAMILY CONVERSATION

For a town of its size, Boyd City had more than its fair share of active churches. To one of these a young man by the name of Cameron had come as a relatively untried minister in his mid-thirties. He had studied divinity rather late and had only two years before he stepped into his first pastorate.

Thinking himself prepared for the ministry, Cameron's sensitivities were in for a rude shock. The unemployment, the drink, the constant influx of wanderers and vagrants, and the poverty of the neighboring Ozark region worked mightily within the spirit of the new minister. He soon found himself thinking about Christ's words in the Gospel accounts in a far different manner than what he had learned from the commentaries and professors at the seminary. Before his first year in Boyd City was out, the question of how to practically live the gospel amid the anxieties and sufferings of life was one that knocked constantly on his heart's door.

It was not long before this yearning to discover the practicality of Christ's words began finding its way into his sermons, to the occasional discomfort of those more staid members of his congregation, who now began to wonder what they had ever seen in the young man to possess them to invite him to be their pastor.

It was a strange coincidence that the Rev. James Cameron

should have preached his sermon the very next Sunday on what he called "The Church of the Future."

If he had only known, he might have found a splendid illustration of the points he sought to make in the story of Dick Falkner's coming to Boyd City and his search for employment.

But the minister knew nothing of Dick or his trouble. He simply desired to see a more practical working of Christianity. He wished to see Christians doing the things that Jesus Christ did, and using, in matters of the church, the same business sense they brought to bear upon their own affairs. He thought of the poverty, squalor, and wretchedness of some for whom Christ died, and of the costly luxuries of the church into whose hands the care of these unfortunates had been given by the Master. He thought of the doors to places of sin, swinging wide and inviting the young to enter, while the doors of the church—with the exception of but a few hours a week—were often closed against them. He thought of the societies and agencies and clubs and orders doing the work the church was meant to do, and of the honest, moral men who refused to identify themselves with the church because of its lack of practical, daily involvement in the lives of those in need. Some who even professed belief in Jesus Christ, he said, were doing His work outside the confines of the church because they could not tolerate the hypocrisy inside it. Thinking of these things, and more besides, Cameron confessed to his congregation—some of whom nodded their heads in agreement, others whose angry hearts burned within him at his presumption—that he was forced to say that the church must change her methods. "The church of the future must talk less and do more," he said. "She must rest her claims to the love of mankind where Jesus rested His—upon the works that He did."

Cameron went on to say that the church was proving false to God himself, that her service was a service of the lips only, that her worship was form and ceremony—not of the heart, but rather a hollow mockery of the obedience that comprises true worship. He saw that as great and hallowed as was the ancient institution, she was not touching the great problems of life. While men were dying for want of spiritual bread, the church was offering them only the stones of ecclesiastical pride and denominational egotism. He saw all this, and yet—because he was a strong man—he remained full of love for Christ. He told his people that these things were not Christianity, but the lack of it. He placed the blame where it justly belonged: upon the teaching and doctrines of men, not upon the principles of Christ; upon the shepherds who fattened themselves while the starving sheep grew thin and lean, not upon Him who came to seek and save that which was lost.

Adam Goodrich walked out of the church that morning with his aristocratic nose elevated even beyond its usual angle. He was so offended by the plebeian tastes of his pastor that he almost failed to notice Banker Lindsley who passed him in the vestibule.

"Fine discourse, wouldn't you say, Mr. Goodrich?—fine discourse."

"Uh—" grunted the tradition-bound deacon.

"Just the kind of sermons that's needed, if you ask me," went on Lindsley, who was not a member of the church. "Practical and fearless. I'm glad to have heard the young man. I shall come to your church again." And with that he exited, leaving the disgruntled church leader speechless.

It was not often that a sermon was honored by being discussed at the Goodrich dinner table. Nor indeed was any topic of religion ever mentioned. But the head of the family could not contain himself after what he considered the unheard-of things his pastor had preached that morning.

"I must say it's a pity Cameron hasn't better judgment," he declared, his voice betraying his state of mind. "I thought we really had something when we found him, fresh out of the seminary, good-looking. But now he's turning into a common rabble-rouser with all that nonsense!"

"Nonsense I may grant you," interposed his wife. "But a rabble-rouser, Adam? Is that not going a trifle far?"

"That's where it will lead. Mark my words, no good will come out of this! The man could easily make our church the number-one church in the city if he would only let well enough alone and not be all the time stirring things up. He is a good speaker—certainly as good as French across town everyone's always bragging about—and he carries himself like an aristocrat, and comes from a good family. That's why we liked him at first. We thought he could really make something of Jerusalem. But now that he is forever saying things to jar the best of our people, I begin to doubt our judgment. I'm not alone either; there are others whom I've talked to who fear where this may all lead. The fool might be drawing half again as much salary if only he would put his mind toward the work Jerusalem ought to be doing and try to get those people who are worth something into the church, instead of spending all his energies on the common herd!"

"Perhaps he thinks the common herd worth saving too," suggested his daughter, a beautiful girl of nineteen named Amy, with dark hair and eyes.

"What do you know about it?" shot back the father. "You're getting your head full of ridiculous notions from that Young People's Society of yours. I've no doubt Cameron is filling you with all those ideas of supposedly doing good. Well, I tell you, your friends will soon drop you if you don't pay more attention to your social duties. That's what a Young People's Society is supposed to be about—socializing and having fun. When I was a young man, there was never any talk about our church young people's group doing anything. The common classes are all right, of course, but they can't expect to associate with our kind. Listening to Cameron this morning, I began to wonder if he thinks himself too good for the likes of us. Why, he makes three times as many calls on South Broadway and over by the shops as he does on our street!"

"Perhaps he thinks 'they that are whole have no need of a physician,' " again suggested the young lady.

"Amy," admonished Mrs. Goodrich, "how often have I told you not to always go repeating the Bible. No one does it now. Especially not to contradict your father!"

"You agree with Rev. Cameron perfectly, Mother," put in Frank, the only Goodrich son. "He said this morning that no one used their Bible nowadays."

"It's not necessary to be always throwing your religion at people," commented the father. "And as for Cameron's new-fangled notion about the church being more helpful to those who need help, he'll find out that it won't work. We are the ones who pay his salary, and if he can't preach the things we want to hear, he'll find himself going hungry or forced to dig along with those he is so worried about. I'm a firm believer in the old maxim that God helps those who help themselves! Let him quote *that* scripture! It's in the good book somewhere, I'll be bound. If the lazy men who are forever asking a handout from saps such as Cameron wanted to earn their bread like the rest of us honest hard-working citizens, there's plenty they could find to do. There's no excuse for poverty in this modern age with all its opportunities for advancement. The Bible says as much. There was the man who used his talents to make money, and there was the man who buried it in the ground. And if I know my Scriptures, the Lord himself condemned the lazy fellow who didn't use what he'd been given. I don't find anything in the Bible that tells me to associate with every lowdown person like that in the city, and I guess I'm as good a Christian as anyone in the church."

"Brother Cameron said helping people and associating with them were two different things," Amy reminded them.

"Well, it means the same anyway in the eyes of the world," retorted the father.

"Fancy my walking down the street with that tramp who called at the office last week," Frank remarked. "According to Cameron, you ought to have invited him home and asked him to stay with us until he found a job, Father. I suppose Amy would have liked to meet him and made his visit with us pleasant."

"Who was that, Adam?" inquired the wife.

"Oh, an impudent fellow Frank let into the office the other day. He claimed he was looking for work because of being thrown out of employment by the Kansas City strike. Anyone could see he was a fraud through and through, just Cameron's kind. If I had my way I would give him work he wouldn't want! Such people are getting altogether too numerous. There will be no room for

respectable men if this keeps up. I don't know what we'll come
to if we have many more sermons such as that one this morning."

"A fine thing it will be when the church becomes a home for
every wandering Willie who happens along!" put in Frank.

"Did not Jesus intend His church to be a refuge for the homeless?" asked the sister.

"Amy," interrupted Mrs. Goodrich, "your father is right. You
are getting too filled with those fanciful notions! You will learn in
time that the church is meant to operate on Sundays, not the rest
of the time. The church is no free hotel. The people who know
what is proper in the world leave the goodwill work to the groups
and aid-societies of the lower classes which are established for that
purpose."

Gradually Amy kept her peace, and soon the conversation
around the well-supplied dinner table settled into other channels.

The Goodriches were not unworthy members of the Jerusalem
Church. Their names were on the roll of membership, and even
Frank, in his own way, participated in an occasional activity of the
Young People's Society. Mr. Goodrich contributed liberally (in his
own eyes at least) to the support of the gospel, and gave, now and
then, goodly sums set opposite his name on subscription lists for
various charitable purposes. He was very careful, however, to
make certain that his gifts to God never crippled his business interests, and managed, in religious matters, to make a little go a
long way.

CHAPTER SIX

HITTING A HORNET'S NEST

The pastor of the Jerusalem Church, having been called to attend a funeral, was not present at the following week's meeting of the Boyd City Ministerial Association, and the field was thus left open for his brethren, who assembled in the lecture room of the Zion Church on Monday morning.

After the meeting had been called to order by the chairman, the reports of the work given by the various pastors had been heard, and some unfinished business transacted, good old Father Beason arose, and in his calm, impassioned manner, addressed the rest of his religious colleagues.

"Brethren," he said, "I don't know how you all feel about it, but I would like to know what the association thinks about Rev. Cameron's sermon yesterday—that is, if you've heard any of the same sort of talk I have. Now, I don't want to be misunderstood. I haven't a particle of fault to find with Brother Cameron. I love him as a man, and I believe that whatever he said he meant for the best. But he is a young man yet, and I have heard a good deal of talk about the things he said Sunday morning. Have the rest of you heard anything?"

Seven reverend heads nodded that they had, and the speaker continued.

"Well, I thought probably you would hear of it, and with no harm meant toward our brother, I would like you to express yourselves. I have been in the ministry nearly forty years now, and I have never heard such things as people say he said. But I can't help wondering if there is not some truth in his words."

Slowly shaking his head, the old man took his seat.

The Rev. Jeremiah Wilks was on his feet in an instant, and speaking in a somewhat loud and nervous manner, he said, "Mr. Chairman, I was coming downtown early this morning, and Mrs. Thurston, who runs that little store on Third Street—you know, she's a member of my church, and always gives me things cheaper than I can get them anyplace else because she's a member of my church. She told me that Cameron said that the average church of today was the biggest fraud on earth. What she was doing there instead of in my congregation, I didn't ask her. But she heard him. I don't know, of course, whether he really said those words or not. That is, I don't know if he meant it in that way. But I've heard him myself saying that he didn't think the church was doing all it should. I don't know if he means all churches, or only his own. My people gave fifteen dollars for foreign missions last year, and the Ladies' Aid paid fifty dollars on my salary. Besides that, they bought me a new overcoat last winter, and it will last me through next winter too. They paid eighteen dollars for that, I'm told. And of course they got it cheap because it was for me, you know. And we gave a pound social for Mrs. Grady whose husband died some time ago. It took almost all her money to pay his funeral expenses—she's a member of my church. So was he, poor man. I'm sure I don't know about Cameron's church, but we're doing all we can, and I don't think it's right for him to talk against the work of the Lord."

The reverend gentleman resumed his seat with the self-satisfied air of a schoolboy who has just succeeded in hitting a hornet's nest and devoutly wishes that someone would come along to share the fun.

Little Hugh Cockrell arose and, crossing his hands meekly, spoke out. "Now, brethren, I don't think we ought to be hasty in this matter. I would advise caution. We must give the subject due and careful consideration. We all care about Brother Cameron. Let us not be hasty in condemning him. We don't know what he meant exactly with his 'Church of the Future' sermon. But let us try to find out. I have heard a great many things, for talk is circulating through the town about it. Some say he spoke slightingly of the ministry as a whole, and seemed to think that the church was not practical enough. My wife, for one, is a good deal hurt about some things he said concerning the clergy. But let us be careful. I don't want to believe that our brother would cast a slur in any way upon us or the church. We ought to work in a Christianlike manner, find out by talking with people on the street and in their homes, just what he said, and above all don't let Cameron know how we feel. We ought not to be hasty, brethren, about judging our brother."

There were nods of approval here and there as the minister took his seat, for he was much admired in the association for his piety, and much respected for his judgment. All knew that nothing could possibly harm them if they followed Rev. Cockrell's advice.

Then the Rev. Dr. Frederick Hartzel reared his stoop-shouldered, narrow-chested but commanding figure, and in a most impressive and scholarly manner proceeded to address the association.

"I don't know anything about this matter, brethren; it's all news to me. I am so confined by my studies that I go out on the street very little; and when I do get out, my mind is so full of the deep things of the Scriptures that I find it difficult to retain anything in my thoughts that has to do with the commonplace in life. And inasmuch as the reverend gentleman failed to consult me as to his sermon about the church of the future, I am unable to say at present whether his position is orthodox or not. But, brethren, of one thing I am sure, and I care not what Cameron or any other man thinks, the orthodox church of today is the power of God unto salvation. God intended that we ministers should stand as His representatives on earth, and as such we ought to maintain a keen appreciation of the grandeur and nobility of our calling. After years of study, on the part of myself, and after much consultation with other eminent men, I give it as my opinion that the church of the future will be the same as the church of the past. All denominations—that is, all *evangelical* denominations—are built upon a rock. 'Upon this rock I will build my church,' Matthew 16:18.

"We are secure in our sacred calling, my friends, and even the gates of Hades cannot prevail against us. It is proven by the scholarship of the world that we shall be the same in the future as we have been in the past. Rev. Cameron, whatever may be his opinions, cannot shake or in any way harm so glorious an institution as the church. Why, we represent the learning and culture of the world. Look at our schools and seminaries and missions throughout the world. Look at our churches in every city and town across this great land. No, there will be no change, no undoing of this great church of God, I tell you, for no change is needed. As to the gentleman's remarks about the ministry, I don't think his opinion matters much anyhow. I understand he is not a graduate of any regular theological institution, at least not one of stature, and I'm sure he cannot harm *my* reputation in the least."

Secure in the impregnable position of his own learning and in the scholarship of his church, amid a hush of profound awe and admiration, the learned gentleman took his seat.

Rev. Hartzel's speech practically finished the discussion by the association. Indeed, the learned man nearly always finished whatever discussion he took part in. Rev. French followed with a few remarks about his congregation's recent efforts to help the less fortunate—carried out, however, he added, in moderation and with good taste. One or two of the remaining preachers tried to speak, but gradually the discussion wound down as they caught the eye of the eminent scholar Hartzel fixed upon them. He did not care to have the water clouded by a multitude of words after his having, in his own humble estimation, given the final word of wisdom on a given subject.

After a prayer by the chairman that they might always be able to conduct the Master's business in a manner well pleasing in His sight, and that they might have strength to always grapple boldly with questions concerning the church, ever proving true to the principles of the Christ and following in His footsteps, the meeting of the association was adjourned.

———

While the members of the Boyd City Ministerial Association were thus engaged, the printer George Udell dropped in at the office of Mr. Wicks to make the final payment on a piece of property he had purchased some months before. Mr. Wicks, or as he was more often called, Uncle Bobbie, was an old resident of the county, an elder in the Jerusalem Church, and one of Rev. Cameron's right-hand men.

"Well," he said, as he handed George the proper papers, "that place is yours now. What are you going to do with it?"

"Oh, I don't know," replied Udell. "It's a good building spot, isn't it?"

"You bet," returned the other. "Isn't hardly a better in town. But you must be thinking of marrying to be talking about building."

Udell shook his head.

"Well, you ought to. This is—let's see . . . the third piece of property I've sold you, isn't it?—all good investments too. You're getting a mighty good start for a young man. Doesn't it make you think of the Being that's behind all these blessings? Strikes me that you're too good a young man to be living without any religion. George, why don't you go to church anyway? Don't you know you ought to?"

"Why don't I go to church," replied Udell thoughtfully. "Well, Mr. Wicks, I'll tell you why. Just because I've got too much to do. I make my own way in the world, and it takes all the business sense I have to do it. The dreamy, visionary sort of things I hear at church meetings may be all right for a fellow's soul; but they don't help him much in taking care of his body, and I can't afford to fill my mind with such stuff. I'm living on this side of the grave. I like to hear a good preacher as well as the next man, and I enjoy the music. But their always pretending to be what they are not is what gets me. You take this town right here now," he went on, pushing his hat back on his forehead. "We've got ten or twelve churches, all with preachers saying they are following Christ and professing to exist for the good of men and the glory of God. But what are they actually doing to make this a better place? There's no place in this whole city, besides a saloon, where a man can spend an hour, and not a sign of a place where a fellow down on his luck can stay for a night."

"So what's all that got to do with the churches?" asked Wicks.

"Who else should it have to do with?" returned Udell. "Only last week, an honest enough young fellow, who was out of money through no fault of his own, struck me for a job and before his first day was out had fainted from hunger. And yet the preachers say that Christ told us to feed the hungry. What do these churches in Boyd City have to show for themselves when they spend every cent they can rake and scrape to keep their old machines running and can't feed even one hungry man? Your church members are all right on the believe, trust, hope, pray, and preach; but they're not so much on the do. And I've noticed it's the *do* that counts in this life."

"Getting a little worked up, aren't you?" smiled Uncle Bobbie, though there was something in his sharp old eyes that said he understood and was saddened by the other's words.

"Yes, I am," retorted the printer. "It's enough to get anyone worked up who has a heart to feel and eyes to see the misery in this world, and then to be asked every other day, 'Why don't you go to church?' I don't mean to step on toes, especially yours," he added. "You've proven yourself a Christian to me in ways I'll never forget, Uncle Bobbie. My old mother was a member of the church, and they let her go hungry when I was too little to take care of her. And if it hadn't been for you, she would have died then. But you fed her, and if there's a heaven, she's there, and you'll be there too. But what upsets me is that these fellows who never do anything are just as sure that their 'salvation is secure,' as they say, as one like you who does so much good for others."

"Ah, George," said Wicks, "that help I gave your mother

wasn't anything. Do you think I'd see her suffer? Why, I'd known her when she was a girl."

"I know, Uncle Bobbie, but that's not the point. Why doesn't the church *do* some of the things they are always talking about?"

"Do unbelievers do any more?" asked Mr. Wicks.

"No, they don't," answered George. "But at least they're not going around talking about their righteousness and never doing anything to demonstrate it. Nor do they thank God that Jesus Christ was crucified so that they might get to heaven, while by their actions they seem to remain indifferent to the fate of everyone else."

There was a long pause.

"Well, there's one fellow I didn't feed," said the old man at length, exhaling a sigh. "That same printer called here and I didn't give him anything to do. I've thought of it many a time since, and asked the Lord to forgive me for my carelessness. So he's got a job with you, has he? Well, I'm mighty glad. But say, George, were you at our church yesterday?"

"No," answered Udell. "Why?"

"I only thought from the way you've been preaching Cameron's sermon all over again that you heard him give it, that's all."

CHAPTER SEVEN

WORKING OVERTIME

Within a week from the time the poor outcast had fainted from lack of food, Dick had already become a fixture in the office of Udell's printshop. A shave, clean clothes, food in his stomach, and a purpose once more in his life had made a new man of him.

"There's only one girl in the world for me," he whistled unconsciously as he made a form ready for the press. But had he thought about it, he might have rendered the popular song instead, "There's *not* one girl in the world for me." For from Dick's point of view the latter would have been the more accurate version. Thus far in his life there had come no woman's influence, no loving touch of feminine hand to help in molding his character, no sweet voice bidding him to give away his love, no soft eyes to look to him with affection and thus tug upon the strings of his heart. He had only the memory of his mother.

George Udell was so pleased with Dick's work that he confided to Clara Wilson that he didn't know how he could get along without him, and that he was by long odds the best man he'd ever had. He was quick and sure in his work, and, as George put it, "You don't have to give him a map when you tell him to do anything." With three good meals a day and a comfortable cot in the office for the night, with the privilege of spending his evenings by the fire, and the assurance that there was work for him for many weeks ahead, it was no wonder that Dick whistled as he bent over the stone.

Locking up the form, he carried it to the press and was fixing the guide pins when the door opened and a young lady walked into the shop.

Dick's whistle stopped immediately. His face flushed as he turned, went toward her, offered her a chair, and then went to call Udell, who was in the other room trying to convince the boy that the stove needed a bucket of coal.

"If there ever is one girl in this world for me," said Dick to himself as he went back to the press, "I hope she looks like that one!"

He carefully examined the first impression from the press. "What a smile!" he said to himself, his mind unable to escape the brief memory of the girl's look as he had approached her. He finished his work and went back to the composing case; "—and what eyes!" He turned sideways to empty his stick. "And what hair—"

Trying to read his copy, he reached for the type again. "And the perfect figure of a—"

"Dick," called Udell.

The interruption of his thoughts sent the preoccupied young man to the floor with a crash, landing on top of the overturned stool that had been at his feet.

"Yes, sir," he answered with a very red face as he struggled up.

A merry light danced in the brown eyes, though the girlish countenance was serious enough.

Udell looked at his assistant with mingled wonder and amusement. "What's come over you, Dick?" he asked as Dick came toward him.

"Nothing, sir—I was only—" he replied, then hesitated as he looked around at the overturned stool and spilled type on the floor.

"Yes, I see you were," remarked his employer with a chuckle. "Miss Goodrich, this is my new assistant. Perhaps he can help us out of our difficulty. He is just up from Kansas City," he added, "and is familiar with all the latest developments in printing."

"You see," said Amy, and as she spoke her eyes showed their interest, "we are trying to select a cover design for this little book. Mr. Udell has suggested several, but we cannot come to any decision as to just the proper one. Which would you choose?"

Dick's embarrassment left him at once when a matter of work was to be considered. "This would be my choice," he decided, selecting a design.

"I like that one too," replied the young lady. "But it is not *exactly* what I wanted. And this is such an important matter." Amy Goodrich was one who liked things *just* as she wanted them.

"I'll tell you what," Dick offered. "If you'll let me, and Mr. Udell does not object, I'll set up a cover for you tonight after supper."

"Oh, I would not want you to go to all the extra trouble."

"I would enjoy it," he answered.

"You need your rest after a day's work," she replied. "I wouldn't want you to have to come all the way back down here."

"But we often work after hours, and I—do not live as far away as you might think."

"What do you say, Mr. Udell?"

"I am sure, Miss Goodrich, that my worthy helper would enjoy the work, for we printers have a good bit of pride in that kind of thing, you know; and as he says, we often work after supper. I don't think you need worry about him overworking himself."

After some further talk, the matter was finally settled, and Dick went back to his work. As he picked up his stool, he heard the door close, and then Udell walked up beside him, wearing a broad grin on his face.

"I've seen fellows take a tumble before!" exclaimed his boss, "but hang me if I ever saw a man so completely kerflummused. Great shade of the immortal Benjamin F—! What a sight you were! Aren't you used to seeing beautiful young ladies? Though you seemed all right once you got your feet under you again."

"Who is she?" asked Dick, ignoring the other's laughter.

"Why, I introduced you to her, man. Her name is Amy Goodrich. Her daddy is that old duffer who keeps the hardware store and is so eminently respectable that you can't get near him unless you have a pedigree and a bank account. Amy is the only daughter, but she has a brother who takes after the old man. The girl takes after herself, I reckon."

Dick made no reply and Udell continued.

"The whole family are members of the biggest church in the city, but the girl is the only one who works at it much, active in the Young People's Society and all that." He turned and went off to look after the boy again, who was slowly running off the posters that Dick had made ready on the press.

"What's the matter with him?" the boy asked when his boss approached. "Did he faint again?"

"Don't you worry about him," answered Udell. "You just worry about getting that job finished sometime this week." With the words Udell jerked the lever of the electric motor four notches to the right.

Just before the whistles blew for dinner, he again went back to Dick and stood looking over his shoulder at a bad bit of copy the latter was trying to decipher. "Well, what do you think about it?" he asked.

"She's really something," answered Dick absent-mindedly as he carefully placed a capital *A* upside down.

Udell threw his head back and roared. "Well, you've got it for sure," he said when he could speak.

"Got what?"

"If you don't know, I won't trouble you all the more by telling you," answered Udell. "But let me give you a piece of advice," he added, this time in a very serious tone. "Don't you go thinking about that girl *too* much."

"What girl . . . who's thinking about her?" said Dick quickly. Perhaps a little too quickly. "You need have no fear on that score."

"Whatever you say. Though when a fellow can't even keep his feet, it makes one wonder," George laughed, then removed his apron and left for dinner.

That evening while Miss Goodrich was entertaining a few of her friends at her beautiful home on the avenue, and while George Udell and Clara Wilson were calling on old Mother Gray, whose husband had been injured in the mines, Dick Falkner worked alone in the printshop. The little book, as Amy called it, was a pamphlet issued by the literary club of which she was the secretary, and never had Dick been so bothered over a bit of printing. The large brown eyes and smiling lips of the young woman constantly insisted on coming between him and his work.

In his mind he talked to her of many things, telling her all his plans and ambitions, and watching her eyes light with sympathy. Forgetting the task before him altogether, he grew bolder, and fought life's battles in the light of her smiles, conquering every difficulty, and winning for himself a place and name among men. And then, as he laid his trophies at her feet, her father, the wealthy merchant, appeared, ordering Dick away with a stern look and outstretched arm.

Somehow Dick managed to finish his work at last, and about three o'clock he tumbled onto his cot in the stock room, where he spent the rest of the night trying to rescue Amy from her father, who assumed the shape of a hardware dragon with gold eyes. He had imprisoned the young lady in a log cabin near the river, beneath a hill upon which grew a pine tree tipped with fire, while a lean hound sat at the water's edge and howled.

CHAPTER EIGHT

TALK AROUND THE STOVE

Mr. Robert Wicks pulled down the top of his rolltop desk and heard the lock click with a long sigh of satisfaction. A glance at his large, old-fashioned hunting-case watch told him it was nearly eleven o'clock. It was a dismal, dreary, rainy night—just the sort of night to make a man thank God that he had a home. And those who had homes to go to were already there, except a few businessmen, like Mr. Wicks, who were obliged to be out on work of special importance.

Locking the rear door of the office and getting hastily into his raincoat, the old gentleman took his hat and umbrella from the rack and stepped out into the storm.

As he trudged along through the rainy darkness, his mind still on business, a gleam of light from the window of Udell's printing office caught his eye.

"George is working late tonight," he said to himself. "Guess I'll stop in and see if he's got that last batch of posters ready yet; we'll need them tomorrow morning."

But when he stuck his head into the shop, he was surprised to see Dick rather than George bending over the stone. Though in place of working with the type, at the moment he was playing a game of solitaire.

"Good evening," Dick said, pausing and looking up. "What can I do for you?"

"I see you got yourself a job," remarked Uncle Bobbie.

"Yes," Dick replied as he shuffled the cards. "And a very good one too."

"Looks like you're not overworked at the moment."

"Oh, we quit at six, you know. I'm just working on a bit of a project of my own."

"Strikes me you might find something better to do than fooling around with them dirty cards," said Wicks pointedly.

"They are rather dirty," remarked Dick, examining the queen of hearts, then continuing in a matter-of-fact tone. "But I found them back of the coal box. I guess someone had thrown them away."

"Is that the best you can do with your time?"

"Perhaps you would suggest some more elevating amusement," smiled Dick.

"Well, why don't you read something?"

Dick waved his hand toward a stack of month-old papers and printers journals. "I've gone through that pile three times already."

"Why don't you visit some of your friends?"

"I don't know anyone in the city except Udell," Dick answered. "And even if I did—" He glanced down at his worn clothing.

"Well, go somewhere," tried Wicks again.

"Where? There is only one place open evenings to the likes of me—and that's the saloon. I haven't money for that, and if I had I wouldn't spend it there. So I play solitaire instead. I know I am in good company at least, even if the sport isn't so exciting."

Uncle Bobbie was silent. The rain swished against the windows and roared on the tin roof of the building. The last car of the evening, with one lone passenger, went along Broadway, its lights brightly reflected on the wet pavement. A horse-drawn cab rumbled toward the hotel, the sound of hooves dull and muffled in the mist. A solitary policeman, wrapped in his rubber raincoat, made his way along the almost deserted street.

As Uncle Bobbie stood listening to the lonely sounds and looking at the young man with his pack of dirty cards, he thought of his own cheery fireside and of his waiting wife. A moment more he hesitated, then placed his umbrella in a corner near the door and carefully began removing his coat and hat.

"Where are you from?" he asked as he drew a chair to the stove and seated himself.

"Everywhere," answered Dick. "Been a lot of places."

"Where are you going?" inquired his companion next.

"Nowhere. Got no plans."

"Folks living?"

"No."

"How long they been dead?"

"Since I was a boy."

"You got no relations?"

"One aunt. But I don't need any more like her."

Uncle Bobbie nodded in sympathy.

"How'd you happen to land in this place?"

Dick answered him in three words. "Looking for work."

"Udell's a mighty fine fellow."

"You're right there."

"Not much of a Christian, though." The old man eyed Dick keenly.

"Lucky for me he isn't," replied Dick, his voice betraying a hint of bitterness. "Otherwise he might have been too busy looking down on me to offer me a job."

"Yes . . . I know," nodded Uncle Bobbie. "It's a sad state of affairs when a statement like that has to be agreed to."

"I take it you're not in sympathy with all that religious claptrap then?"

"Religious claptrap? Heavens no! I have no sympathy with that. Christianity, though, that's another matter."

"What's the difference?"

"Between religious talk and living Christianity—all the difference in the world, young man. I may not be religious, but I certainly am a Christian."

"But I thought you said—"

"You thought because I agreed with your assessment a moment ago that I had no sympathy with Christianity, is that it?"

"I suppose that is what I thought," nodded Dick.

"To be sure, I used to look at things like you do. But then I got more sense and learned to see it more clearly. I know there are church members who are meaner than a mule with shoulder galls. They would kick a man's head off quicker than greased lightning. But you think they're the ones going to heaven? Not much they ain't. No more than my dog's going to the legislature. But there's plenty outside the church that's a whole lot worse. It's not Christianity that's to blame for making folks mean and selfish. They're selfish on their own and won't let the Lord make them better like He wants to. But you can't get people looking in from the outside—like yourself, if you don't mind my saying so—to see it that way no more than you can follow a mosquito through a mile of fog. Though I ain't blaming you much for that."

Dick's expression changed. This was not what he expected. When he saw that the old gentleman was waiting for him to reply, he said, "Ever since I can remember, I've been kicked and cuffed and cursed and abused by saint and sinner alike until I can't tell much difference between church members and those they say are in the world—"

"Except that the members of the church do the kicking and cuffing—though in more subtle ways than with their feet and hands—and let the sinners do the cussing," broke in Uncle Bobbie. "You can't tell me nothing about that either."

"I'm not saying anything against the teaching of Christ," returned Dick. "That's all right as far as it goes. But it doesn't seem to go very far. I've not made much of a success in life, but I've worked hard to earn a living and learn my trade, and I don't know but that I am willing to take my chances at the pearly gate alongside some of the church people I have seen."

"To be sure," said Uncle Bobbie. "And I reckon your chance is as good as theirs. But it strikes me that I want to stand in a little better light than most of them fellers. How about the folks who truly *are* Christians? You know there are those who *do* follow the Master's teaching. What about their chances?"

Dick shrugged, but said nothing.

"When I first came out West," continued Uncle Bobbie, settling himself more comfortably in his chair, "I didn't think much about religion neither. My ma and my pa sort of foundered me on it, I reckon. To be sure, I went to Sunday school and church meetings with the rest. My old daddy would have took the hide off me if I hadn't. But I didn't take to it much.

"After a while I came out and got a job punching steers out here in James County. Then I homesteaded a hundred and sixty, and after a spell the railroad came through and I got to buying grain and hogs, and trading in castor-oil beans and managed to get hold of some land here when the town was small. I can't say I ever got rich, though I've got enough to keep me, I reckon. I handle a little real estate, get some rent from my buildings, and loan a little money now and then. But I've worked for every cent too, just like you said."

The old gentleman's voice sank lower and lower as he recalled the years that had flown. As Dick looked at the kind face, seamed and furrowed by the cares of life, and the hair just whitened by the frost of time, he felt his heart warm with sympathy, which he knew was returned full measure by him who had left his Ohio home to battle with life alone in that strange western country.

"But what I wanted to tell you," Uncle Bobbie said, coming suddenly back to the present and speaking in his usual abrupt manner, "was that the day finally came when I discovered the difference between religion as a thing most folks keep stuck between the covers of a dusty book they never read, or keep nicely tucked away in a box on the shelf—between that and living, practical Christianity as lived by the Man who came to the world to teach us how to live. And you'll find out, same as I have, that it don't much matter how the other fellow dabbles in the dirt; you've got to keep your hands clean anyhow. The question ain't whether the other fellow's mean or a hypocrite or not, but am I living square myself? You can find fault with anyone you want to in the world, and we all got a parcel of things wrong. But the other man's faults can't blind you from the truth. Jesus Christ is the Savior of men. I found that out for myself 'cause He saved me. But He can't save them unless they want Him to, no more than I can catch a jackrabbit on foot. Christianity's true all right, but it ain't going to do no good in a man's or a woman's life unless they live it, and there's a heap more to living it than we think. What such fellows as you ought to do is listen to what Christ says and not look at what some little church-goer does who's maybe further from being a true Christian than you are yourself. They ain't worth it. You can't let people like that keep you from seeing what's the real truth in the man Jesus Christ."

Uncle Bobbie fell silent. He had his say.

Dick said nothing, because he could find no words to express himself. He had never heard a gospel quite like that which came out through the simplicity of Uncle Bobbie's words. The older man, seeing how it was, rose to his feet.

"Well, I must be going. My wife'll think I've run out on her. Why don't you come up to the house and see me sometime? I reckon you know you're welcome after what I've been saying."

Dick nodded his thanks, saying he just might do that, and bade Uncle Bobbie good night.

CHAPTER NINE

UNCLE BOBBIE HATCHES A PLAN

"Wife," said Uncle Bobbie the next morning before getting up to build the fire, "I made a discovery last night."

"You were out late enough to discover something," returned Mrs. Wicks with a laugh. "What is it?"

As her husband climbed out of bed and began dressing, he replied slowly, "There's some fellows that go to the devil just because they haven't got no place else to go."

"You mean in Boyd City?"

"In Boyd City, and who knows how many other places just like it. There ain't no place for a young man to go at night. So they go to the saloons and bars and gambling halls, get themselves in trouble with the drink, lose their money, and then all us church folks wonder why they don't come round on Sunday. But the reason's not so hard to see. We're doing nothing to help them in their fight against the enemy."

Later in the day, the old gentleman sat at his desk in his office, tilted back in his swivel chair, his feet up on the desk among the papers where his hands should have been. In his mind revolved many things, not the least of which was that the church ought to be more involved in the lives of those it called "the lost." Also on his mind was Udell's new printing helper.

No one came in to disturb his reverie, for it was still early in the morning, and the only sound was the clicking of a typewriter from his assistant in the next room.

Suddenly the feet came down to their proper place with a bang. Leaning forward, he wrote rapidly for a few moments, then called, "Charlie."

The noise of the typewriter stopped and a young man entered the room. "Charlie," Uncle Bobbie said, "I've been working on a little advertising stuff here. I'd like you to take it over to George Udell's and wait until they fix it up so you can bring me back the proof. You can let those letters of your typewriter rest a spell."

The young man took his hat and umbrella, for it was still raining, and started out on his errand, but his employer stopped him. "Just a minute, Charlie," he called. "Do you remember that young fellow who called here for a job week before last, the time I sold that Johnson property?"

"Said he was a printer from Kansas City?" asked Charlie.

The other nodded.

"Yes, sir, I remember him."

"Well, he's got a job with Udell. I was there last night and had a talk with him. He's got no friends and stays in the office alone nights. I just thought I'd tell you. He's a mite leery of Christians, though, and I think he might have a streak of pride like an old turkey gobbler in the spring. But he strikes me as a good sort; and more than anything else I think he just needs somebody to talk to, that's all."

The old man said no more, then turned back to his papers.

Thus began a budding friendship between the two young men.

Dick was distant at first, and Charlie was wise enough not to force himself upon him. But as Uncle Bobbie found many excuses for sending his young assistant to the printing office frequently, the two slowly grew better acquainted. Eventually the time came when Charlie asked Dick what he did during the evening. Dick answered, "Read and play solitaire."

"I can't play cards," Charlie replied, "but I do like to talk."

"Come by if you'd like," Dick invited. "Though you might

find this a dull place to spend an evening."

Charlie did so the very next evening. The ice once broken, his calls grew more and more frequent until the two met and talked like old friends. Dick also began to think more about his appearance.

"Mr. Udell," Dick asked one Saturday night, as the latter handed him his wages for the week, "where's the best place in town to go for clothing?"

With a pleased look on his face, George directed him to a clothing store on the corner of Fourth and Broadway.

CHAPTER TEN

PHILIPPIANS 4:8

About a month later, the quiet of a Sunday morning in early May lay over the city.

Stores and businesses were closed, except for here and there a market. A group of black loungers sat on the stone steps of the City National Bank. A little farther up the street a company of idle whites sat in front of a restaurant. Farther on, in the doorway of a saloon, a drunkard slept in the sun. Old Dr. Watkins came clattering down the street in his buggy, stopped in front of the Boyd City Drug Store, and a man with his arm in a sling followed him into the building.

Then the church bells rang out their cheery invitation, and the children, neat and clean in their Sunday clothes, trooped along the street to the Sunday schools. An hour later the voices of the bells again floated over the silent city, and men and women were seen making their way to the various places of worship.

In the throng that passed through the door of the Jerusalem Church was a gentleman dressed in gray. It was not difficult to guess from his manner, as he stood awkwardly in the vestibule as though waiting for someone, that he was a stranger in the place. His figure was tall, nearly six feet, well formed, but lithe rather than heavy, giving one the impression not only of strength but of grace as well. The well-set head and clear-cut features, the dark hair and brows overshadowing deep-set, keen gray eyes, the mouth and chin, clean-shaven and finely turned, all combined to carry still further the impression of an inner power that perhaps was still to be realized. Even the most casual observer would know that the man would be both swift and sure in action, while a closer student would say, "Here is one who rules himself, and is sure one day to lead others. He looks to be strong in spirit as well as body, as kind as he is strong, as loving as he is ambitious. This indeed must be a man whom one would love as a friend and be forced to respect as an adversary."

He had indeed taken many strides toward outward respectability—and not a few toward inner maturity as well—since first setting foot in town two months earlier.

Charlie Bowen, one of the ushers, came hurrying up and caught the stranger by the hand. "I'm glad you could come," he whispered. "My, but you look great. Folks will think you're a visiting dignitary for sure in that outfit!"

"Do I take my hat off when I go in?" whispered Dick, who already held his hat in his hand, "or wait till after prayers?"

"Just come along and do what everyone else does," replied Charlie.

"Say, don't rush me way up front, will you?"

"Never you mind that. Come on." And before Dick could say more, the usher was halfway down the aisle.

"Who is that stranger Charlie Bowen is seating?" said old Mrs. Gadsby in a low voice to her neighbor.

The neighbor shook her head.

"Isn't he handsome?" whispered a young schoolteacher to her friend.

Some distinguished stranger's here today, thought the pastor as he glanced over his congregation.

Even Adam Goodrich turned his head just in time to look into the face of the tramp printer, who was being seated in the pew behind him. Miss Goodrich was with her father, and as a result Dick heard nothing of the opening part of the service, only coming to himself when Cameron was well into his discourse.

The preacher's theme was "The Sermon on the Mount," and the first words that caught the young man's ear were: *Blessed are the poor in spirit, for theirs is the kingdom of heaven.* He glanced around at the congregation. Mrs. Gadsby was inspecting the diamonds in the ears of the lady by her side, who was resting her powdered and painted face on the back of the pew in front, as though deep in prayer. In truth, however, she was nearly asleep.

Blessed are they that mourn, for they shall be comforted, read the minister.

Dick thought of the widows and orphans in the city, and of the luxurious homes of the people he saw about him. *Blessed are the meek, for they shall inherit the earth.* Dick looked straight ahead at Adam Goodrich, the very back of whose head showed haughty arrogance and pride. *Blessed are they that do hunger and thirst after righteousness, for they shall be filled.* Dick lifted up his eyes and looked at four members of the choir who were whispering and giggling behind their books, and noted the beautiful frescoed ceiling, the costly stained-glass windows, the soft carpet and carved furniture on the rostrum, and the comfortable, well-cushioned pews.

"Is all this righteousness?" he asked himself. He thought of the boys and girls on the street, of the hungry, shivering, starving, sin-stained creatures he had seen and known. He thought of the homeless and destitute, like he himself had been such a short time before, who would not dare present themselves at the outer door of this temple consecrated to the service of Him who beckoned: "Come unto me and I will give you rest." And then, lest men might be mistaken, added: "Whosoever will may come."

Blessed are the pure in heart, for they shall see God.

Dick's eyes rested on the girl in the next seat. Yes, he thought, Amy was pure in heart. There was no shadow of evil on that beautiful brow. Innocence, purity, and truth were written in every line of the girlish features, and Dick's heart ached as he thought of his own life and the awful barrier between them. Not the barrier of social position or wealth; *that*, he knew, could be overcome.

But the barrier he himself had erected in the reckless, wasted years—the inevitable result of his failure to strive for truth and purity and goodness in his own life.

As he sat reflecting on his past, reflecting on what he had made of his life and what he had *not* done, the strong young man fought a battle in the secret chamber of his own soul—fought with himself over what he would make of his life from this moment on, fought to make real the words falling at that very moment from the preacher's lips.

His struggle with himself made Dick all the more keenly aware of the mockery of the dichotomy between the words of Scripture and the hearts of the so-called worshipers. Suddenly, to him who all his life had been used to looking at things as they really were, without the glasses of conventionalism or early training, the very atmosphere of the place became stifling.

The moment the service was over, he rushed from the building without even a further acknowledgment of Charlie's salutation, drawing in a deep breath when he was safe on the street again. In what struck him as oddly ironic, something in his heart almost rejoiced when at dinner he heard the restaurant keeper curse his wife in the kitchen, and when a moment later a drunken boarder fell from his chair.

"This, at least, is real," Dick mused to himself, "and not like that hollow world of fancy clothes and painted smiles. Oh, what a world this would be if only the Sermon on the Mount were lived, and not merely talked about!"

The Monday following Dick's visit to the church, Charlie Bowen went back to the office in the evening to take care of some unfinished business, forgetting that it was the first Monday of the month, and that the official board of the Jerusalem Church would be holding their regular business meeting there in Uncle Bobbie's office. Charlie's first impulse when Elder Wicks, with Rev. Cameron, entered, followed soon by two or three others, was to leave. But it was necessary that his work be done, and his employer knew he was there and could easily have given him a hint if it would be better for him to retire.

Shrewd old Uncle Bobbie, however, had his own plans for this particular meeting, and it was not a part of them to have his young assistant leave the office. So nothing was said, and the meeting was opened with a prayer by Elder Gardner, the chairman of the board. The pastor, the treasurer, and the different committee chairmen made their reports, some general matters were passed upon, and then the subject of building an addition to their place of worship was introduced. It was not the first time it had been discussed, but certain of the board members had always managed to block the enthusiastic young pastor.

"You know, brothers," began Rev. Cameron, "our house does not begin to hold the people at the regular services, and we must have more Sunday school room. It seems to me that there will be no better time than the present. If we ever expect to enlarge our ministry, the work must begin."

"I know, Brother Cameron," agreed Deacon Godfrey, stating the standard objection, just as it had been stated since the pastor had first broached the subject, "but where do you expect to come up with the money? The members are paying all they can now to keep out of debt, and I don't believe they will do any more."

"The Sunday school is too crowded," added Elder Chambers, "but I too can't see how it's to be done. I'm giving every cent I can now."

"The Lord will provide," said Deacon Wickham, with a pious uplifting of his eyes and a sanctimonious whine in his voice. "I'm ashamed to hear you talk in this doubting manner. Can't you trust the Lord and His precious promises? If we need an addition to the church, let us ask Him. He will provide."

"Yes, the Lord will provide, but we've got to do the hustling," Uncle Bobbie informed them. "He'll provide common sense and expect us to use it."

"Couldn't the womenfolk do something?" timidly suggested another.

"Of course they could!" exclaimed Deacon Sharpe. "They could get up a social or fair or bake sale or entertainment of some kind. They used to do a lot of that kind of thing before Brother

Cameron came. We had a very active Ladies Auxiliary—"

"Yes, and spend twenty-seven cents to make seventeen, and spend all their time at church functions and ladies groups, while their own children run the streets and their husbands darn their own pants," broke in Uncle Bobbie again. "I tell you, I don't believe much in all these ladies activities any more than I believe in men thinking their wives are supposed to take care of church matters. Christ wouldn't run a peanut stand to support the church, nor pave a sinner's way to heaven with popcorn balls and molasses candy."

"Everybody does that kind of thing," remarked Deacon Sharpe, encouraged by the nods of Chambers and Godfrey. "All churches depend upon the women, with their activities and money-making fairs and such, to pay their way. I don't see what's the harm. It gives the women something to do, and keeps us from paying out so much cash."

"Yes, and that's exactly what ails the churches," retorted Wicks. "There's too many of them run like lemonade and ice cream and rummage sale businesses. And as for giving the women something to do, my wife's got her hands full taking care of me and her home. She didn't marry the church, but me. And I'm right content with the arrangement."

"We must all work in the Master's vineyard. None shall lose his reward," said Deacon Wickham again. "We all have our talents and God will hold us responsible for the use we make of them. We all have our work to do."

"And by that do you mean that all the women have our work to do, and we'll get our reward by making them do it?" Wicks shot back scathingly. "I've got no use for a man who lets a woman do his work, even in church. They have enough to do already without us expecting them to make pillows, carpet rags, and mince meat to pay the expenses of the church."

"There is one other way to go about this," proposed the pastor, anxious to prevent the clash between the pious and the sharp old elder from going too far.

"What's that?" asked Chairman Gardner.

"The Young People's Society."

There was a slight rustle and the sound as of a book falling to the floor in the other room where Charlie was listening to the proceedings.

"Humph," uttered Godfrey, "what can *they* do?"

"Have you ever attended one of their meetings?" asked Cameron.

Another *humph* accompanied by a shrug of the shoulders was the only reply.

"They have done more practical Christian work this past year than all the rest of the church put together."

"Better turn the whole church into a Young Folk's Society then," retorted Wickham angrily, "and throw away the Bible and the bank account altogether. How much money do the young people give, I'd like to know? And where in the Bible does it talk about such groups? Christ didn't say, 'Upon this rock I'll build my Young People's Society.' For my part, I won't have nothing to do with it! There is not a single passage of scripture that says we ought to have such things, and until you can show me book, chapter, and verse, I'll fight it."

"I'll give you book, chapter, and verse," offered Uncle Bobbie. "Here it is in three words: Philippians 4:8."

A painful silence followed. Then one of the deacons asked. "Would the young folks help?"

"I think so," replied the pastor.

"We might ask Charlie Bowen about that," suggested Elder Wicks. "Charlie," he called out, "are you almost through with them books?"

"Yes, sir," answered the young man.

"Well, lock them up and come in here."

When a few minutes later they had laid the matter before Charlie, he said, "Yes. I am sure the society would take the matter up, except possibly for one thing. Ever since the pastor's sermon on the Church of the Future, we have been talking among ourselves about how we could be more actively involved in the lives of those in need. And one thing we came up with was the idea of furnishing a reading room somewhere. So it may be that they wouldn't want to give up that idea. Unless, of course, it could be arranged to have a room in the church when the new addition was built, a place that could be open late for those less fortunate to come—either to read or have a cup of coffee or find a friendly face to talk to—then I am sure the society would get behind the project all the way."

Uncle Bobbie's eyes twinkled as he watched his young helper. He had not misjudged his man. This was just what he had expected. But Deacon Wickham was on his feet almost before Charlie finished speaking.

"Brethren, this is entirely out of order. We have no reason to listen to the counsel of this boy. He has not a single qualification, for either a deacon or an elder. He has not been involved in the work of church leadership as we have, and as for the so-called religious work he has been doing, it has not been as part of anything sanctioned by this board. I believe we ought to go according to the Scriptures or not at all. And as for this idea of a reading room in the church, the Bible says nothing about reading rooms and there is no authority for it whatever. If the inspired apostles had wanted reading rooms in the church, they would have said so. Let us stand for the religion of our fathers and let the young people read at home if they want to. Brethren, I am opposed to the whole thing. This boy has no right to speak here. He is not qualified to speak as if he were an elder or a church leader. He will poison the flock with such notions."

Uncle Bobbie whispered to Charlie, "Never you mind him. He's got just so much sputtering to do anyway. I'll fix him in a minute and then he'll wash his hands of the whole matter."

"I think it's a fine plan," he then said aloud to the group.

"So do I," agreed Deacon Sharpe. "Why not let the young folks have a room? We could charge ten cents admission and make a good thing for the church out of it. Why shouldn't we make a little now and then? Paul worked to support himself."

"Make not my Father's house a house of merchandise," reminded Cameron. "I tell you, brethren, this thing must be free. The Young People's Society is not in the business to make money. Am I right, Charlie?"

"Yes, sir," answered the young Christian eagerly. "We wanted to fix up some place where the young men of the town could spend their evenings without going off the deep end into sin. There are lots of them who have no homes, but live in boardinghouses and have no place to go."

"And a pretty crowd you'd have before long," remarked Wickham sarcastically.

"Yes, and if you had to pay the preacher, like we do, then you'd think about renting the room to gain back a little income," added Sharpe.

Cameron's face flushed at the hard words aimed at him.

"Come, come, brethren," soothed the chairman, "what is to be our decision on this matter?"

"I move that we ask the Young People's Society to assist us in building the addition to the church," said Elder Wicks, "and that we give them one of the rooms."

"I second the motion," added Cameron, and it was carried, despite the objections of Wickham, Godfrey, and Sharpe.

Following the usual prayer, the meeting was adjourned.

"Well," responded Wickham, "I wash my hands of the whole matter."

Some time later as Uncle Bobbie walked down the street with his bookkeeper and the pastor, he said, "Poor old Wickham! His heart's all right, but he's got so much Scripture all twisted around in his head that his thinking machine won't work."

"Friends," said Cameron as they paused in front of the parsonage, "I have looked forward to this day for a long time. This step of opening the church to the people of the town, to the needy and unfortunate, will revolutionize our ministry."

"I doubt the people will be any more ready for this than they were for that sermon of yours, Pastor," remarked Charlie.

"You may be right. It's hard to get out of old ruts. But the world has got to have applied and gutsy Christianity. And it has to start somewhere. So it might as well be with us."

"Amen!" agreed Uncle Bobbie heartily, and the three parted with shakes of their hands.

CHAPTER ELEVEN

THE YOUNG PEOPLE'S SOCIETY

Charlie Bowen walked into the printing office not long there-after on his way home to dinner.

"Dick," he said, "it's time you got out of this. I want you to put on your best clothes tonight and come with me to meet some other young people."

Dick carefully spread a pile of letterheads on the drying rack. Then shutting off the power, he stood watching the machine as its movements wound down slower and slower.

"Go where?" he asked.

"The Young People's Society of the church meets tonight."

"Well, I suppose a fellow can't stay alone all the time," mused Dick.

"Of course not," returned Charlie. "You've hidden yourself away long enough. It will do you a world of good to get out."

"But am I not a bit old for such a group? Aren't they mostly teenagers?"

"No. There are a few that are probably seventeen or eighteen. But mostly the group's made up of other young men and women in their twenties, just like us, trying to get a start making it on their own, like you and me."

"Well then, I'll go with you."

"Good! I'll come by at seven-thirty."

When Charlie returned to the office that evening, he found Dick dressed and ready to go, and what a strange contrast he presented to the poorly-clad, half-starved tramp who had walked into Boyd City only two months before. Some thought of this flashed through Dick's mind as he read the admiration in his friend's face, and his own eyes glowed with pleasure.

When the two young men reached the home of Helen Mayfield, where the social was being held, they were met at the door by Clara Wilson.

"Glory," whispered the young lady to herself. "Here comes Charlie Bowen with that tramp printer of George's." But not a hint of her thought found expression in her face. She merely offered her hand in cordial, wholehearted greeting.

The guests gathered quickly, and soon there was a house full of laughing, chattering, joking young people. Dick entered in and was soon talking and laughing with all the rest.

"Who is that tall, handsome man with the dark hair talking to those girls with Nellie Graham and Will Clifton?" whispered Amy Goodrich to Clara, who had been asking her why Frank hadn't come.

"Haven't you met him yet?" asked Clara, secretly amused, for George had told her of the incident involving Amy and Dick at the office. "That's Mr. Falkner, from Kansas City. He's a friend of Charlie's. Come, you must meet him."

She led the way. "Mr. Falkner," she said, skillfully breaking into the group, "I would like to present you to a very dear friend of mine. Miss Goodrich, this is Mr. Falkner."

Dick had, of course, noticed Amy the moment he had walked into the house, but had conspicuously avoided any contact with her, fearing he might stumble over his own feet again. Suddenly finding himself staring into her deep brown eyes, he felt the room spinning around and everybody looking at him as he mumbled over some nonsense about the great honor of having met Miss Goodrich before.

Amy looked at him in astonishment. "I think you must be

mistaken, Mr. Falkner," she replied. "I do not remember having met you. Where was it, here in town?"

With a mighty effort, Dick caught hold of himself and gazed around. In truth, no one was paying the least attention to him. Only Miss Goodrich was looking into his face, still awaiting an answer to his question. Without thinking through the consequences, he jokingly answered with the first words that came to his mind.

"In California, I think it was, year before last," he quipped glibly.

Amy laughed. "But I have never been to California in my life. There—you *are* mistaken after all."

Dick laughed. *No harm done,* he thought to himself, glancing around.

"What is the matter, Mr. Falkner?" Amy asked. "Are you looking for someone?"

"I was wondering where Charlie went," he answered. "He said he wanted me to turn the ice-cream freezer."

"I thought I saw him in the other room," Amy commented. "Let's see."

Dick followed and they walked slowly toward the adjoining room.

"Do you know," Amy remarked after a moment, "I am beginning to feel as if I had met you before too."

"I'm glad of that," Dick returned with a smile.

"You *do* remind me of someone I have seen before. Hmm . . . where could it have been?—I know!" she exclaimed suddenly. "It's that tramp printer of Udell's. That's who you remind me of !"

"What was the fellow's name?" asked Dick, hiding his amusement with this turn of the conversation.

"Oh, I don't know," replied Amy, "but he was very kind to me and offered to work at night to design a cover for a little booklet I was having printed. I never saw him again to thank him though, for he was out when I came the next day. I heard that Mr. Udell had a tramp working for him and I suppose it was he, for he acted very strangely—maybe he had been drinking. There ought to be one of the booklets here." As she spoke she began turning over the materials on a nearby table. "Yes, here it is." She handed Dick the pamphlet that had caused him so much trouble that night in the office.

It is hard to say where the matter would have ended. Dick was at the very point of telling Amy the truth when Miss Jameson appeared, beckoning them to the parlor, where a request had been made for Amy to play the piano.

After the group had listened to several pieces and one or two solos by different girls, one of the young men asked, "Don't you sing, Mr. Falkner?"

"Indeed he does," Charlie broke in, and soon all were calling for a song.

Dick slowly approached the piano, deep in thought, when all at once an inspiration struck him. He sat down, and after a few bars of rollicking introduction, sang out:

> They tell me go work for a living,
> And not round the country to stamp;
> And then when I ask for employment,
> They say there's no work for a tramp.

The song was by no means rendered in a classical style, but the manner in which Dick sang the words made it seem acceptable nonetheless as he continued:

> There's many a true heart beating
> Beneath the old coat of a tramp.

A strange hush fell briefly over the little audience, and when the song was finished a subdued murmur of applause filled the room, while eager voices called for more. Dick responded with another selection and then declared that he had done his share, left the instrument and seated himself by Charlie's side.

"Good show, old man!" Charlie whispered. "But where in the world did you learn all that?"

"Do you really want to know?"

"Of course."

"From dance halls and saloons," whispered Dick with a grin.

"I never thought I'd be airing my accomplishments at a church social!"

Charlie's reply was lost in a call to the dining room, where light refreshments were served to the hungry crowd. After supper came games and more music, while a few of the more serious of the number gathered in a corner to discuss the reading room and continued to refine their plans for its future. Then came a call for everyone to sing, and with Amy at the piano, they sang song after song until it was time to go. Then the bustle of leaving—good night . . . lovely time . . . my house next month . . . nice to have met you . . . wonderful refreshments—and soon Dick found himself walking back toward town with his friend.

"Well," said Charlie, "what do you think?"

"A most pleasant evening," replied Dick. "But I have to tell you, I've never known church people to be so friendly. Even though none of them knew me, they accepted me like a friend. Tell me, do any of them know me—I mean know how I came to town?"

"Some do, some don't. What does it matter?"

"You didn't tell them I was coming, and put them up to being nice?"

"Of course not! What do you take me for, Dick?"

"Forgive me. I ought to have known better. Only, you see my experience with church people has not always been the most pleasant. I've just never met many who accepted a fellow for what he was before. It was downright nice to feel like one of them without having to be ashamed of my past."

They exchanged good nights, and Dick turned down the street toward his humble lodging place, while Charlie went on toward home.

As he walked, Charlie thought to himself, *That's just what's the matter with hundreds like Dick—they don't know what real Christianity is like. They have seen only the sham. But unless I'm mistaken, Dick will find the reality soon enough.*

Meanwhile, Dick had reached the office, and throwing off his coat, he seated himself in the rickety old chair, tilted it back as far as possible, and rested his feet up high against the big Prouty press. For fifteen minutes he sat without moving a muscle. The clanging bell of the eleven-thirty train pulling into the depot sounded in his ear, but still he sat immovable. A night-hawk cab rattled over the brick pavement, and a drunkard yelled beneath the window. Still Dick sat. So motionless was he that a little mouse living behind a wall in one corner of the office crept stealthily out and, glancing curiously with his bead-like eyes at the still figure, ran, with many a pause, to the very legs of Dick's chair.

Suddenly Dick's feet came crashing to the floor. The shaky old piece of furniture almost fell in ruins and the poor frightened mouse fled to cover. Kicking the chair to one side, Dick walked to the window and stood with his hands in his pockets looking into the night.

At length he addressed the lamp that twinkled in the bakery across the street. "I'm a fool," he said sullenly. "I should have told her who I was. She had a right to know she was talking to a tramp. When she and that father of hers find out—"

But with the thought Dick's imagination failed him. He laughed in spite of himself as he thought of the tramp who had applied to Adam Goodrich for work and that evening had chatted away with his beautiful daughter as an equal.

"There'll be a hot time in the Goodrich camp when they learn the truth!" he murmured to himself, and then turned and went to bed.

CHAPTER TWELVE

A MANAGER FOR THE READING ROOM

Throughout the summer months, as construction proceeded on the addition to the Jerusalem Church, the opinions of Rev. Cameron's flock regarding the proposed reading room were numerous and varied.

Adam Goodrich, in pompous manner, gave it as his judgment that Cameron would be running a free lodging house next, as though that were the greatest depth of infamy to which a poor preacher could sink. His wife declared that Cameron's plans would ruin the social influence of the church forever, once homeless tramps and ne'er-do-wells became associated with it. And of course, the social influence of the church, in which she viewed herself as one of the leading members of the congregation, was to Mrs. Goodrich the be-all and end-all of what a church was supposed to be about.

Amy was deeply in favor of the movement, but wisely kept most of her opinions to herself in the presence of her parents. Frank, though he attended most of the meetings of the society and would not openly oppose its efforts for fear of being unpopular, was too much like his father not to think the whole thing worse than ridiculous. His affiliation with the society had as its sole aim the mingling with some of Boyd City's most attractive young women, and this "ministry," as they called it, could be nothing more, in his view, than an interruption to his pursuit of finding a wife. He therefore lost no opportunity to secretly throw stumbling blocks in the way, and made all manner of sneering allusions to the work when he thought it would not come to the ears of the young people most aggressively behind it.

When at last the room was finished and ready to be occupied, a committee was appointed to select someone to manage it during the evening hours. The church, with the usual good judgment shown by churches in such matters, had named as members of this committee two men who were sure to disagree in every facet of the decision, Elder Wicks and Deacon Wickham. The young people had selected Charlie Bowen and two young ladies to represent the society. They met in the new rooms one evening and Deacon Wickham took the floor at once.

"I hope our young friends won't take offense at what I am about to say, but you know I am one of those who always says what he thinks. And what I think is that this business ought to be in the hands of the church board; you young folks have no scriptural rights to speak on the subject at all."

The three young Christians looked at Uncle Bobbie, whose left eye remained closed for just the fraction of a second, and the speaker wondered at the confident smile with which his words were received.

"There's not one of you that has the proper qualifications for an elder or a deacon," he continued. "You girls have no right to have the oversight of a congregation anyway, and Charlie Bowen here is not even the husband of one wife as the Scriptures say an elder must be."

"Give him time, Brother Wickham, give the boy time," broke in Uncle Bobbie with a chuckle, much to the delight of the girls. "You just wait. He may surprise you someday with his qualifications." But the deacon continued with a frown at the interruption. "As far as that goes, the whole thing is unscriptural and I was opposed to it from the first, as Brother Wicks here can tell you."

Uncle Bobbie nodded.

"But you've gone ahead in spite of what I and the Scriptures teach, and you've got your reading room. And now I mean to see to it that you have at the head of it a good brother who is eminently qualified to teach, a good man who is thoroughly grounded in the faith and who has arrived at years of discretion, a workman that needeth not to be ashamed of his handiwork, rightly dividing the word of truth. Such a man could get the young Christians together in the evening and lay out their Bible reading for them, spending an hour or two perhaps each week in explaining the more difficult passages. If I had time I would be glad to do the work myself, for there's nothing I like better than teaching. I don't know, I might possibly find time if the brethren thought it best that I undertake the work. I am always ready to do what the Lord wants me to, and I promise you that I'd teach those young people the Scriptures, and make them interested too. Why, when I was in Bear City, down in Oklahoma, I had a—"

"But, Brother Wickham," interrupted Uncle Bobbie, who knew from experience that if the good deacon ever got started on his days in Oklahoma, they never would get to the business of the evening, "it strikes me that you haven't got the right idea of this at all. It's not to be a Sunday school, nor a place to teach the Bible, though I reckon it's certainly in line with the teachings of Jesus. It is—"

"Not to teach the Bible!" exclaimed the astonished deacon. "What on earth can you teach in the church except the Bible, and what kind of reading room can you have in the Lord's house, I'd like to know, without that?"

"The idea, Brother Wickham," said Uncle Bobbie as gently as he could, "is to furnish some place where the young men of the town can go and spend their time when they're not working. This room will be stocked with books, magazines, and papers. There will be tables with writing materials, and if a fellow wants to write to his girl or his mother, he can. And there will be easy chairs about and sofas for those who want to talk or play games. It seems to me what we want for a manager is some young man who's got good horse sense, who could make things pleasant, even if he doesn't know much Scripture."

"And it's to be free to every loafer who wants to come in and use the place?" asked the deacon sharply.

"Yes, just as free as Christ's invitation to come and be saved," retorted Uncle Bobbie.

"You'll soon find the church filled with a lot of trash who don't know anything about the Bible or the plan of salvation. How can you do it when the Scriptures say, 'Have no fellowship with such'?" continued Deacon Wickham.

"We'll save a few young men who are starting toward hell by way of the saloons and bawdy houses," replied Uncle Bobbie.

"No, you won't. The gospel and the gospel alone is the power of God unto salvation."

"You're right there," chimed in Uncle Bobbie. "The gospel *lived* is a powerful force in men's lives."

"God never ordained that men should be saved by reading rooms and such."

"I believe I know just the man we want," announced Uncle Bobbie, turning to the young people when the deacon had at last subsided into an attitude of sullen protest.

"Who?" asked one of the young ladies.

"That printer of Udell's. He's a clean, strong young fellow, and I believe he would be glad of some such place to spend his evenings. Of course he's not a Christian—"

"Not a Christian!" cried Wickham, starting to his feet again. "You propose to let an alien take charge of the Lord's work? I wash my hands of the whole matter!"

"Do you really think he'll be all right?" asked the other girl.

"Sure," replied Uncle Bobbie, "if he will take it, and I think we can get Charlie here to see to that."

Charlie nodded. "It will be a splendid thing for him." He then told them how Dick was now spending his evenings alone in the office rather than going to the only places open to him.

"Well, let's ask him," suggested Uncle Bobbie. "Brother Wickham," he said, turning to the deacon, "we have decided to ask Richard Falkner to take charge of the room."

"I've nothing more to say about it," answered the pious man. "I know nothing about it. I wash my hands of the whole matter."

And so the work of the reading room at the Jerusalem Church was established.

It took no little power of persuasion on the part of Charlie Bowen to bring his friend to the point of accepting the committee's offer, even when it was endorsed by the entire Young People's Society and a large part of the congregation.

But he finally prevailed and Dick consented to be at the room between the hours of seven and eleven every evening, the time when a strong, tactful man in authority would be most needed.

The room was furnished by friends of the cause and was cheery, comfortable, and homelike, where everyone was made welcome. Many a poor fellow, wandering on the streets, tired of his lonely boardinghouse and sorely tempted by the air of cheerfulness and comfort of the saloons, was led there, where he was able to find good books and good company and hot coffee. What often happened, as was only natural, was that such young men began to attend on Sundays the only church in the city that did not close its doors to them during the week.

CHAPTER THIRTEEN

CONVERSATIONS

Dick enjoyed his work at the reading room.

In a short time he had many friends among the young men who frequented the place. He treated everybody in the same kindly, courteous manner—whether well dressed or resembling his own state when first he chanced into Udell's printshop. To more than one he told his own story, offering what encouragement he could to those in need.

He was always ready to recommend a book, to introduce an acquaintance, or to enter into conversation with a stranger. Before long many from the Young People's Society were befriending the less fortunate, taking Dick's lead; and the reading room became an actively thriving place most evenings. Everyone said its success was due to Dick Falkner's accepting and friendly disposition, which was willing to make anyone his friend. Indeed, he soon grew so popular among the young folk of the church, and the tramps of the city, that George Udell told Clara it seemed as though he had always lived in Boyd City, for he knew so many people, and so many knew him.

"I told you so, George," Clara answered. "Didn't I say that he was no common tramp? I know a man when I see him."

The two were driving in George's buggy in the evening of a

warm autumn, on the road that led south from town, down a hill, across the bridge, and along the creek where the trees bent far over to dip the tips of their branches in the water; and the flowers growing wild along the edges nodded lazily at their own faces reflected in the quiet pools and eddies.

"You may know a man when you see him," replied George, letting the horse take his own time beneath the overhanging boughs, "but you take precious good care that you don't see too much of one that I could name."

"Whom do you mean, George—not Mr. Falkner?" replied Clara with a provoking smile as she tried in vain to catch one of the tall weeds that grew close to the side of the road.

"You know whom I mean, Clara," returned Udell impatiently. "What's the use of you and me pretending? Haven't I told you since I was ten years old that I loved you and would have no one else to be my wife? And haven't you always understood it that way, and by your manners and your behavior toward me given unspoken assent?"

The girl looked straight ahead at the horse's head as she answered slowly, "If my manner has led you to have false hopes, George, it is very easy to change it. And if accepting your company gives assent to all the foolish things you may have said when you were ten years old, you'd better seek less dangerous society."

"Forgive me. I spoke hastily," George apologized softly. "But it's mighty hard to have you always just within reach and yet always just beyond."

"You know how it is, George. I can't do more with you believing as you do."

The sun had gone down behind the ridge. The timbers of an old mining shaft and the limbs and twigs of a leafless tree showed black against the tinted sky.

A faint breath of air rustled the dry leaves of the big sycamores and pawpaw bushes, and the birds called sleepily to each other as they settled themselves for the coming night. A sparrow hawk darted past on silent wings, a rabbit hopped across the road, while far away an evening train whistled for a crossing, and nearer a farm boy called to his cattle.

After a long silence, George spoke again, this time with a note of manly dignity that made his fair companion's heart beat quicker.

"Clara, look at me," he said. "I want to see your eyes."

She turned her face toward him.

"Clara, if you can say that you do not love me as a woman ought to love her husband, I will promise you, on my honor, never to mention the subject of marriage again. Can you say it?"

She tried to turn her head and hide the telltale color in her cheeks, but he would not permit it.

"Answer me," he insisted. "Say you do not love me, and I will never bother you again."

At last she lifted her eyes, and in their light George read his answer.

"All right," he said, picking up the rein. "I knew you could not lie. You do love me, and I'll never stop asking you to be my wife."

He turned the horse's head back toward the city.

———

Meanwhile, Adam Goodrich, with his family and two or three neighbors, sat on the veranda of his home enjoying the beauty of that same evening and passing the time in social chat. In the course of the conversation someone mentioned the new room that had been added to the Jerusalem Church.

"What a splendid thing it is for the young men of the city," remarked one of the lady callers. "I don't see why more of the churches don't do something similar. I wish ours would."

Their host grunted, but held his peace.

"Yes," chimed in another, "and isn't that Mr. Falkner who has charge of the room in the evening a nice fellow? My brother speaks of him so highly, and all the young men seem to think a great deal of him."

"Where is he from, St. Louis, is it?" asked the first lady.

"Kansas City," replied Frank Goodrich. "At least that's what *he* says. He bummed his way into town last spring and got a job in that non-Christian Udell's printing office. That's all anybody knows of him."

"Except that he has never shown himself to be anything but a perfect gentleman," added his sister.

"Amy," admonished Mrs. Goodrich, a note of warning in her voice.

"It's the truth, Mama. What if he *was* out of money and hungry and ragged when he came to town? He was willing to work and Mr. Udell says he is a fine workman, and—"

"What of it?" her father interrupted. "No one knows anything about his family or how he lived before he came here. He's only a tramp, and you can't make anything else out of him. Some folks are never satisfied unless they are trying to make gentlemen out of gutter snipes. But you know what the good book says about wolves in sheep's clothing. If we let such fellows get a foothold, there won't be any respectable society left. It will be all stable boys and boot-blacks."

Later that night, after the visitors had bid good night and Amy and her mother had entered the house, Frank said in a subdued tone, "Father, I'll tell you one thing about that man Falkner, you've got to watch him."

"What do you mean?" asked Adam.

"I mean Amy," replied the son, moving his chair nearer his father and speaking in a guarded voice. "He takes every chance he can to talk with her, and she is altogether too willing to listen."

"Pshaw," grunted the older man. "She never sees him."

"That's where you are mistaken, Father. They first met last spring in the printing office. Afterward, when he had gotten in with that soft fool, Charlie Bowen, they met again at the Young People's social. He was all dressed up in a new suit of clothes and Amy didn't recognize him. They were together all that evening, and he never confided to her who he was, pulled a real charade on her."

"Why, the nerve of the young blackguard!" muttered Adam, half rising from his chair.

"Since then, of course, she has found out who he is, yet she persists in talking to him at every opportunity. She doesn't seem to mind in the least that he is a homeless tramp. They meet at the Young People's group, at church, at picnics and parties, and more often than you would like at the printing office. I tell you, you'd better watch him. He's doing his level best to win her over, and just look how he's working his wiles on everybody else. Half the town thinks he's the greatest."

Low spoken as were Frank's words, Amy heard every one. For she had not retired as her brother supposed, but was lying on a couch just inside the doorway of the darkened parlor.

With red cheeks burning in anger, she rose cautiously and tip-toed silently out of the room. She made her way upstairs, entered her own room, closed and locked the door, and then threw herself on the floor by the low seat of an open window and rested her head on her arm while she looked up at the stars, which were now shining clear and bright. Recalling her brother's words, her eyes filled with angry tears.

But in a few moments she grew calm again, and soon the girlish face was worthy again of a master's brush as she gazed reverently into the beautiful heavens, her lips moving in a whispered prayer—a softly whispered prayer for Dick.

As she prayed, unseen by her, a man walked slowly down the street in the shadow of the trees. Reaching the corner, he turned and strolled past the house again. Crossing the street, he passed once more on the opposite side, paused a moment at the corner, and then started hurriedly away toward the business portion of the city.

CHAPTER FOURTEEN

THE POUCH IN THE SNOW

November, with its whispered promises of winter fun, passed, and the Christmas month, with snow and ice, was ushered in.

Usually in the latitude of Boyd City, a degree or two south of St. Louis, the weather remained clear and not terribly cold until the first of the new year. But this particular winter was one of those exceptions which are met with in every climate. The result was that the first of December brought with it zero weather.

Indeed, it had been unusually cold for several weeks. To make matters worse, a genuine western blizzard came howling across the prairie from the northwest regions of South Dakota and Nebraska, whistling and screaming about the streets, from which it had driven everything that could find a place of shelter. The stores on Broadway were deserted except for a few shivering clerks. In offices throughout town, men sat with their feet on their stoves recalling in their minds the biggest storms they had ever known, while streetcars stood motionless and railway trains, covered with ice and snow, came puffing into the station of Boyd City three or four hours behind time.

In spite of the severe weather, George Udell spent the evening of December second at the Wilson home on the east side. He had not seen Clara for nearly two weeks, and it was rather late when he at last rose from his chair to prepare for the long, cold walk back to his boardinghouse.

"Good night, Clara," he said as he stepped out into the storm. With heavy heart, Clara stood at the window watching long after his form had vanished into the night.

The wind was blustery and the snow cut Udell's face like tiny needles, while he was forced again and again to turn his back to the blast in order to breathe. In spite of his heavy clothing and overcoat, he was chilled to the bone before he had gone three blocks.

On Broadway he passed saloon after saloon, brilliant with glittering chandeliers and attractive with merry music, inviting all the world to share the good fellowship and cheer within. He thought of the rooms of his tiny apartment, how cold and lonely they would be, and had half a mind to stop at the hotel for the night.

For an instant he hesitated, then shook his head in defiance of the storm.

"No, I won't do it," he muttered to himself. "I won't try to find comfort that way."

He struggled on, fighting every inch of the way, with head down and body braced to the task. The contrast of the warm lights falling across his path from the windows of the many cozy homes seemed to make him feel the cold all the more keenly.

Then through the storm he saw a church, dark, grim, and forbidding, half hidden in the swirling snow, the steps and entrance barricaded with heavy drifts, the stained-glass windows reflecting only the black of the night, the doors locked, the inside lifeless, reminding George of a gigantic tomb.

A smile of sarcasm curled his lip. "How appropriate," he mumbled to himself. "What a fine monument to the religious activity of the followers of Christ—cold and dark and empty, and locked to any who might seek refuge there." He almost laughed aloud when he remembered that the sermon delivered there the Sunday before was from the text, "I was a stranger and ye took me not in." He had read the announcement of the service and topic of the guest evangelist in last Saturday's paper, but had hardly thought of it again until now. "I only hope Dick's doing more good with that reading room of his this winter than is this empty building," he said to himself as he began to make his way forward again.

Suddenly he stopped and peered through the storm.

In the light of an electric lamp that sizzled and sputtered on the corner, he spied what looked to be a dark form barely visible in the snow piled about the doorway of the deserted house of worship.

He approached, stepped closer, reached out and touched it with his foot, then bent down. A look of horror spread over his face.

It was the body of a man!

Falling to his knee, George tried desperately to arouse the fallen man. He put his hand under the lifeless shoulder and attempted to lift him to his feet, but all his efforts met only with failure.

What should he do?

He glanced around, thinking desperately. His eyes caught a gleam of light from a house down the street. "Of course!" he cried. "Uncle Bobbie Wicks!" Stooping again, he gathered the man in his arms, and with a supreme effort, slowly and painfully made his way across the street and along the sidewalk to the Wicks' home.

Uncle Bobbie was sitting in front of the fire, dozing over a book in his hands. The sound of heavy feet on the porch aroused him. A strange knock followed, as though someone was kicking at the door. Quickly he leaped up and threw it open. Udell, with his heavy burden, staggered into the room.

"Found him on the church steps . . . just down the street," he gasped out of breath as he laid the stranger on a couch. "I'll go for the doctor," he added, then turned and rushed back out into the storm.

He returned some twenty minutes later with Dr. James at his heels. They found Uncle Bobbie, who had done all that was possible, sitting beside the still form on the couch. "It's too late, Doc," he said. "The poor chap was dead before George left the house."

The physician made his examination.

"You're right, Mr. Wicks," he answered; "we can do nothing here. Frozen to death. Must have died early in the evening."

Dr. James returned to his home to get what sleep he could before another call should break his rest, and all that night the Christian and the heathen sat together, keeping watch over the dead body of the unknown man.

The next morning the coroner was summoned. The verdict was swift: death by exposure. On the body was found a church statement showing that there had been paid to the current expense fund, for the quarter ending August first, the sum of three dollars, but the name written with lead pencil was illegible. Besides this there was a prayer-meeting topic card, soiled and worn, and a small dog-eared Testament, but no money. A cheap pin in the sign of the cross, such as were often given to visitors, was fastened to the ragged vest. There was nothing to identify the man or furnish a clue as to where he was from. The face and form were that of a young man, and though his frame was thin and his face careworn, they showed no marks of dissipation. The right hand was marked by a long scar across the back and the loss of the little finger. The clothing was very poor.

Among those who viewed the body in the undertaking room where it lay for identification was Dick Falkner. Udell, who was with him, thought he seemed strangely moved as he bent over the casket. George called his attention to the disfigured hand, but Dick only nodded. Then, as they drew back to make room for others, he asked in a whisper, "Did they search thoroughly for letters or papers? Sometimes people hide important documents in their clothing, you know."

"No, there was nothing," answered George. "We even ripped out the linings."

When they again reached the open air, Dick drew in a long breath. "I must hurry back to the office," he said. "I suppose you'll not be down today."

"No, I'll have to help arrange for the funeral. You can get along I guess."

"Don't worry about that; I'll get along," he replied, and the young man started off down the street. But at the corner he turned and walked rapidly in the other direction, reaching a few moments later the church where the body of the stranger had been found.

The steps and walks had been carefully cleaned, and the snow about the place was packed hard by the feet of the curious crowd that had visited the scene earlier in the morning.

Dick glanced up and down the street. There was no one in sight.

Stepping swiftly to the pile of snow that the church janitor had made with his shovel and broom, he began kicking it around with his feet.

Suddenly he stopped. With an exclamation he glanced quickly about again. Then stooping, he brushed away a top layer of snow and his fingers clutched a long leather pocketbook. He stood, turned, and walked hurriedly away to the office, holding the pouch tightly.

The body was held for some days. But when nothing could be learned of the poor fellow's identity, he was buried in the city plot, with George Udell bearing all the funeral expenses. When Uncle Bobbie asked to help him with the finances, George answered, "No, this is my work. I found him. Let me do this, for the poor man's mother's sake."

The funeral was held in the undertaker's room. Dick Falkner, Uncle Bobbie Wicks and his wife, and Clara Wilson, with George Udell, followed the hearse to the cemetery.

To this very day, the visitor to Mt. Olive can read the inscription on a single stone, bearing no name, telling the story of the young man's death, and concluding with these words: "I was a stranger and ye took me not in."

The church people of the town protested loudly when it was known how the grave was to be marked. But George Udell answered that he wanted something from the Bible because the young man was evidently a Christian, and that the text he had selected was the only appropriate one he could find.

The evening after the funeral, Charlie Bowen and Dick sat alone in the reading room. The hour was late and all the night's visitors had left. Charlie was talking about the burial. "I tell you," he said, "it is mighty hard to see a man laid away by strangers who do not even know his name. And after dying all alone in the snow like a poor dog. And to think that perhaps a mother is watching somewhere, waiting for him to come home. And the hardest part is that he is only one of many. In a cold winter like this, the amount of suffering among the poor and outcast is something terrible."

Dick made no reply, but sat staring moodily into the fire.

"Why is it that people are so indifferent to the suffering about them?" continued Charlie. "Is Udell right when he says that church members, by their own teaching, prove themselves to be the biggest frauds in the world?"

"He is, so far as the church goes," replied Dick, "but not as regards Christianity. The neglect and indifference comes from a *lack* of Christ's teaching, or rather from a lack of the application of His teaching, and from *too much* teaching of the church. The trouble is that people follow the church and not Christ. They become church members, but not Christians."

"Do you mean to say that the church ought to furnish a lodging place for every stranger who comes to town?" asked Charlie.

"I mean just this," answered Dick, "and I've had a chance to think about it a good deal here, now that I am, in a sense, working as part of the church ministry, though I'm not even a member and can't say with any certainty yet exactly what I believe."

He rose to his feet and began walking slowly back and forth across the room. "But I do know this," he said at length; "there is plenty of food in this world to give every man, woman, and child enough to eat, and it is contrary to God's law that the helpless should go hungry. There is enough material to clothe every man, woman, and child, and God never intended that the needy should go naked. There is enough wealth to house and keep warm every creature tonight, and every night, for God never meant that men should freeze in such weather as this. And Christ surely teaches, both by words and example, that the hungry should be fed, the naked clothed, and the homeless housed. Is it not the Christian's duty to carry out His teaching? It is an awful comment on the policy of the church when a young man, bearing on his body the evidence of Christianity and proof even that he supported the church, dies of cold and hunger at the locked door of the house of God. And in a city where there are ten or twelve denominations, paying at least that many thousands of dollars for preachers' salaries alone every year."

"But we couldn't do all those things you suggest," said Charlie.

"Other agencies do," replied Dick. "There is more than enough wealth spent in the churches in this city for useless, gaudy, self-promoting display, and in trying to get ahead of some other denomination, that could be used to clothe every naked child in warmth in the city tonight. You claim—I should say the church claims—to be God's stewards; but then you spend His goods on yourselves, while Jesus, in the person of that boy in the cemetery, is crying for food and clothing and companionship. And you wonder why George Udell and I, who have suffered these things, don't unite with the church. The wonder to me is that such honest men as you and Mr. Wicks and Rev. Cameron can remain connected with such an organization when men like Goodrich and Wickham and many other deacons and elders work so hard to keep your voices of truth from being heard."

"How would you do all you suggest?" asked Charlie. "That has been the great problem of the church for years."

"No, Charlie. It has *not* been the problem of the church. If the church's leaders and pastors and ministers and elders had spent one-fourth the time studying this question, and in trying to *fulfill* the teaching of Christ, that they had wasted in quarreling over one another's opinions, or in tickling the ears of their wealthy members, or in trying to preserve their positions of power, or in keeping voices from being heard which conflicted with their own pious viewpoints, then this problem would have been solved years ago. But the church is mostly preoccupied doing nothing but talking to itself. The world is not listening because the world can see the false standard. But I tell you, the homelessness and want and hunger and loneliness in the world *could* be largely ministered to if the church was serious about Christ's words. Different localities would require different plans, but the purpose must always be the same: to make it possible for those in need to receive aid without compromising their self-respect or making beggars of them. In other words, *living* the gospel, not merely debating its meaning."

For some minutes the silence in the room that followed Dick's impassioned speech was broken only by the steady sound of his feet as he continued to walk back and forth.

"Dick," said Charlie at last, "do you believe anything could be done here?"

Dick stopped, turned, and looked at his companion.

"Of course," he replied. "Of course it could. Any church, any group of people, no matter how small, could begin a movement that could turn the world upside down if they truly lived Christ's words—really *lived* them day and night. Of course this church could do something—something significant—something great!—if only they would go about it in a practical, businesslike way."

Charlie shook his head. "But you know what a difficult time it was just to get this reading room passed. Brother Cameron has preached again and again on these things, on practical, daily, applied Christian living, and yet most of the leaders oppose him at every turn. I won't be surprised if they ask for his resignation one day. The elders, that is, except for Uncle Bobbie, don't want their comfortable world upset with disquieting notions."

"But has your pastor presented any definite plan for work?" asked Dick. "It's one thing to preach about it and another thing to present a plan that will begin to set about meeting the need."

"I think he's tried to be practical. But he's faced such stiff opposition from the staid old members who were in control long before he came."

"But has there ever been a real plan presented? If there were, I have no doubt there would be some members at least who would take it up. That's the great trouble. They're all the time preaching about Christianity—and I don't mean Brother Cameron especially; I think he genuinely wants to move the people forward. But so often all the talk is sentimental, when of all things in the world

Christianity is the most practical, or it is nothing at all."

"The young folks would get behind a plan, I'm sure," said Charlie. "We're always talking about how to live our faith more practically. Why don't you suggest something to the society?"

"I'm like the rest," Dick answered with a half smile. "I'm preaching when I have no cure to offer. Remember, I don't even claim to be a Christian myself."

"To hear you talk, I'd say you were miles closer to the true meaning of the word than most of those who sit in the pews of the church every Sunday."

"Well, I don't know about that," replied Dick as he began locking up for the night. "But if there's anything that can be done, I would be glad to do my part."

Nothing more was said on the subject until the Saturday before the regular monthly business meeting of the Young People's Society. Then Charlie brought up the matter to Dick as they walked down the street together at the close of the day.

"No," said Dick, "I have not forgotten our earlier talk, and I've been thinking a great deal about it. In fact, I think I might have a plan that would help considerably, at least in the case of Boyd City."

"Would you go before the Young People's Society at their meeting next Tuesday night and explain your scheme?"

Dick hesitated.

"I'm afraid they would not listen to me, Charlie," he replied at last. He paused, thinking for a long moment. Then he rested his hand on the other's shoulder and added, "You see, old man, people here don't look at me as you do. They can't forget the way I came to town, and I fear they would not attach much weight to my opinion, even if they should consent to hear me."

"That's where you are wrong, Dick. I know there are some who continue to look at things in that light, but they wouldn't do anything if Paul himself were to get up and teach them. However, there are many others, sincere people, who are only looking for someone to lead the way. They are willing, even eager, but don't know what to do. Take myself, for instance. I realize what's needed, and I honestly want to do something. But I don't know how to go at it. If this problem is ever to be solved, and if the church people are ever to get moving in helping people, it will be from someone who knows from actual experience, not from occasional slumming expeditions, what's needed. It will be from someone whose heart is filled with love for men, not religious jargon, who is absolutely free from ecclesiastical chains, who holds no position in the church, and who is a follower of no creed but Christ, a believer in no particular denomination—that's where the leadership must come from, not from the organized church boards of deacons and elders. They are too wrapped up in their own little world to hear the cries of need out on the street. Even if you don't claim to be a Christian, you have lived on the street. Your heart hears the cries."

Dick smiled at his friend's long talk.

"You too have been thinking about this," he commented. "But has this thought also come to you—that the person to take a leading role ought to be a Christian?"

"Yes," answered Charlie, "a Christian so far as he is a believer in the truths that Jesus Christ teaches, but not necessarily in the generally accepted use of that word, which is that a man or woman can't be a Christian without hitching himself up in some denominational harness, after being baptized in *that* particular denomination's water and according to its *own* method, and then involving himself in *that* church's activities. It is never asked, 'Are you doing the work of Christ?' but only. 'What church do you belong to?' So on that score, yes I think the person ought to be a Christian. But who cares if he is an active church member?"

"If you believe all that, why do you wear the badge?" asked Dick dryly.

"You mean, why am *I* a church member?"

Dick nodded.

"I don't believe there is anything inherently *wrong* in being a church member. In fact, it's a decent and good thing to be. What's wrong is if that's the sole foundation upon which you base your allegiance to Christ. Church membership means *nothing* if that's all there is. But if that allegiance to the church is a means to help you more actively *live* the commands of Christ, then it is a very good thing."

"Well put," stated Dick. "I see your distinction."

"I hope you will one day come to see that the church, even with all its shortcomings and mistakes and the hypocrisy of many of its members, nevertheless *is* of divine origin. She needs men to help lead her back to the simplicity of Christ's life and teaching. But that's not the immediate question," Charlie continued. "The question is: Will you go before the Young People's Society next Tuesday night and share your plan for doing the Lord's work here in this city? You won't be going before the whole church, only other young men and women such as you and me who want to make their lives count. And I will give you an introduction that will leave no question of a mistaken notion as to your presence."

The two walked on in silence until they reached the door of the restaurant where Dick took his meals.

"Will you come in and have something to eat with me?" asked Dick.

"I must get home," answered Charlie; "that is, unless you need some additional urging."

Dick laughed. "No, you've made your point. I'll do it."

CHAPTER FIFTEEN

DICK'S PLAN

Charlie Bowen, who was president of the Young People's Society at this time, took particular care to notify each member that there would be a matter of unusual importance to discuss at the next meeting. Thus, when he called the meeting to order at eight o'clock on the following Tuesday evening, the lecture room of the church was nearly filled to capacity.

After the regular routine business had been disposed of, Charlie stated that he wished to introduce a matter of great importance, which he felt certain would interest every Christian present. Before doing so, he called to their minds some of the teachings they had heard recently from their pastor regarding ministry and the practical living of their faith. He went on to mention briefly the condition of things in Boyd City, asking if they would not like to do more to help in the remedying of such evils. The nodding heads and earnest faces told Charlie of their interest.

After recalling the death of the young man found by George Udell, he told of his conversation with Dick. "I am well aware that Mr. Falkner makes no profession of Christianity," he told them. "But you have come to know him, as I have, and you need no word from me to tell you of the strength of his character and the compassion of his heart toward the less fortunate." He explained how he had asked Dick to speak to them, and after delicately stating Dick's objections with respect to his own background, he asked if they would receive him and listen to his ideas of Christian work.

At the close of Charlie's talk, Rev. Cameron rose to his feet and, in a voice full of emotion, said, "My dear young people, my heart is moved more than I can say by what I am hearing. Before we hear from Mr. Falkner, let us bow our heads in prayer that we may be guided by the Holy Spirit in listening to the things the young man may have to put before us."

A deep hush fell on the band of young people. It seemed as if a wonderful presence filled the room. In simple words Cameron voiced the prayer in the hearts of all, then sat down, while Charlie escorted Dick to the front. He was greeted by smiling faces, nods of encouragement, and just a faint ripple of applause, which sprang from a desire on the part of those present to let him know they were glad to welcome him and ready to give him their attention.

"What I have to say to you," began Dick openly, "is nothing new or startling. I claim no originality here, but have simply found myself convinced lately that it should be possible . . . *is* possible for people such as yourselves to meet certain needs of the people of this particular city. I do not speak to you as a Christian, but rather from the standpoint of one to whom has been given opportunities to see a side of life perhaps many of you are unfamiliar with.

"As I understand it, the problem we have to consider is how to apply Christ's teaching in our own city; how to help people in need.

"Of course there have always been welfare agencies and missions that give assistance to those in need. But oftentimes it strikes me that their efforts do nothing to permanently relieve the situation. What I would like to see is some means whereby those in unfortunate straits could be given, not just a handout, but assistance in helping them to stand on their own feet and begin working to provide for themselves.

"In this city, as in every city, there are two classes of people

CHOICE BOOKS

Choice Books
9920 Rosedale MC Rd.
Irwin, OH 43029
614•857•1368

WE WELCOME YOUR RESPONSE

who present themselves as in need of assistance. At the risk of oversimplifying the problem, I would classify them as the deserving and the undeserving, the idle and those who want to earn their bread, those whose need is a fraud and those whose need is genuine. The only test that can possibly succeed in distinguishing between these two classes is the test of work.

"Thus, my plan in short is this: to provide a place and a means where men can be given food and shelter in exchange for work, with the end in view, not merely of giving a handout but rather of helping men to find both work and self-respect, so that they might eventually be able to begin supporting themselves.

"The first thing necessary would be a suitable building. It should have sleeping rooms, dining rooms, a sitting room, kitchen, storeroom, and bathroom. There should also be a large yard with an open shed in the rear. It would seem to me best for the sleeping rooms to be small, and a single cot in each, for you know it is sometimes good for a man to be alone. It ought not to be hard to find twenty-five people in the church who would each underwrite the cost of furnishing a room at a cost of say a few dollars. The reading room supplies could be donated by friends who would be glad to give their papers and magazines when they were through with them, just as the present reading room is supplied.

"As to what sort of work we could provide these men when they come, if you stop to think about it, this is a mining town where everyone burns coal, and everyone has need of kindling wood. There ought to be ways we could find to generate a small kindling business in which the men could take a share, and thus, in a sense, earn their keep. I believe the merchants would be glad to give away their old packing crates, boxes, and barrels. These could be collected and hauled to the yard, and there worked up into kindling and delivered to our customers.

"The whole establishment should be under the supervision of some man who, with his family, could live in the house. But all the work of the place—the kitchen, the dining room, the care of the sleeping rooms, and all the maintenance—would have to be done by the men themselves. When a man applied for help he would be received on these conditions: that his time belonged entirely to the house, to contribute toward the wood business or the upkeep of the house itself, and that he receive for his work only food and bed, with the privilege of course of bath and reading room. If he refused to comply with these simple conditions, or to conform to the rules of the house, it would be obvious that he was of the class I mentioned earlier, the idle and undeserving, and to such no food would be given, nor would he be admitted.

"This briefly is my plan. I would be glad to have you ask questions and make objections or suggestions."

Dick paused and one by one the young people began to ask questions.

"What would the storeroom be for?"

"Let people of the community contribute clothing," answered Dick, "which could be kept and issued by the superintendent in charge. I said storeroom, that the material might always be on hand when needed."

"Would women be received?"

"No. Certainly there are women also who need ministering to, but they would require a separate institution with a different kind of employment."

"Wouldn't women be needed to do the housework?"

"No. Everything could be done by the men under the direction of the superintendent's wife."

"Would the townspeople contribute boxes enough to actually keep a small kindling business going?"

"That," replied Dick with a smile, "would be a matter for the society to see to. The workers at the house would gather them up and haul them to the yard. Old sidewalks, fences, and tumbled-down buildings could all be used, so the supply need not run short, and the city would be much improved if these things were gathered up and put to use."

"Do you really think there would be enough people to buy the kindling wood to make it pay?"

"That again would be the business of the society. Every member should be a salesman for the enterprise. The kindling would be put up in bundles of uniform size, warranted to be dry and satisfactory. It should of course be delivered by the workers. It ought not to be difficult for you to get a sufficient number of regular customers to insure the success of the business. You see, it is not a church-begging scheme, for it benefits every person connected with it, and everyone pays for what he gets. The citizens would have the satisfaction of feeling they were assisting only the worthy and hard working among the poor, and the sense that they were receiving their money's worth."

"But would the modest income be sufficient to pay all bills?" asked Cameron.

"The food, of course, would be of the plainest, and could be bought in quantities. Twenty cents will feed a man a day. It is possible to live on less," Dick added with a whimsical smile, which was met with answering smiles from the company of young people. "I can attest to that. But to answer the question, suppose you had for a start one hundred regular customers who would each pay ten cents per week for their kindling. That would bring you ten dollars per week, which would feed seven people. Not a large thing I grant you, but a start in the right direction, and much more than the church is doing now. And who knows, it is possible other similar businesses could be established in time that would bring in additional money—maintenance, grounds keeping, odd jobs. But most of the other expenses of the house would not be large, and I am confident that the institution could become self-supporting. But bear in mind that the society must own the grounds and the building so that there would be no rent. *That* must be the gift of the people to the poor."

"How would the superintendent and his wife be paid?"

"They would receive their rent, provisions, and a small weekly salary, paid either by the society, the church, or the institution. There are many men and women who would be glad to do such work of ministry. And once other sorts of income-producing ventures suggested themselves, I do not think finances would be a problem."

"But what about men who worked just enough to get their

food and yet remained idle the rest of the time?"

"That," answered Dick, "is the greatest danger. But I believe the men would have to be kept busy at the housework, scrubbing and cleaning when not out in the yard or making deliveries of wood. When the time came that they began to be hired out to do odd jobs for the townspeople, all the wages would go to the house. Thus, if every man was kept busy eight hours each day and received only his food and a place to sleep, there would be no temptation to remain longer than necessary. The institution would also act as an employment agency, and when a man was offered work of any kind, he would no longer be permitted to remain in the house. Much of this would necessarily be left to the discretion of the managers and directors. And the superintendent would have to be a strong man in order to deal with would-be freeloaders, as you suggested."

This question seemed to bring the matter to a close, and Dick thanked them all for their attention and resumed his seat.

A lively discussion followed. Several spoke enthusiastically in favor of the scheme. One or two thought it very good, but feared it would be impossible because of the expense of the building needed. A few offered suggestions. In the end a committee was appointed to continue looking into the matter.

As the meeting broke up, the young people crowded about Dick, shaking his hand, thanking him, and asking more questions. To Charlie's delight, Dick seemed to forget himself and talked and laughed with the rest about *our* house and the things *we* would do.

Suddenly in the midst of the good-natured talk, however, his manner abruptly changed. He made his way quickly to Charlie's side and whispered, "Good night, old man. I have to go."

"So soon?" asked his friend in a tone of surprise.

"Yes," replied Dick hurriedly.

He turned and walked out, leaving Charlie wondering at the look of pain on his face, which a moment earlier had been so bright.

Charlie did not know that Dick had overheard Frank Goodrich

say to his sister, "Come, we must go home. We mustn't associate with the schemes of that tramp any longer," and that he had seen Amy leaving the room on her brother's arm without even acknowledging Dick's presence by so much as a glance.

CHAPTER SIXTEEN

REACTIONS

The next morning bright and early, Deacon Wickham knocked on the door of the parsonage.

"Why, good morning, brother!" cried Cameron, throwing wide the door and extending his hand. "What good fortune has brought you out so early? Come in, come in."

"No good fortune," replied the deacon. And seating himself very stiffly on the edge of the straightest-backed chair in the room, he glared with stern eyes at the pastor, who threw himself carelessly into an easy rocker. "No good fortune, sir," he repeated. "I came to inquire if it is true that you are encouraging that unscriptural organization in their foolish and worldly-wise plans."

A puzzled look spread over Cameron's face. "What organization, and what plans?" he asked.

"There," said the good deacon with a sigh of great relief. "I told Sister Jones there must be some mistake, for though you and I don't always agree, and lock horns sometimes on certain passages of the Scriptures, I did not believe that you could have been so far from the teaching of the Word as that."

"As what?" asked Cameron again, but this time with a faint glimmer of understanding in his voice. "Please explain, Brother Wickham."

"Why, Sister Jones came over to my house early this morning and told me that at the meeting of the Young People's Society last night, the young upstart Falkner laid down plans for doing church work, and that you were there and approved of them. That rattle-headed boy of hers is all carried away with enthusiasm over the project."

"Well?" the preacher nodded.

"I could not believe it, of course, but she said, as near as I could gather, that you were going to have the church buy a house and keep all the tramps who come to Boyd City. A more unscriptural thing I never heard of. Were you at the meeting last night?"

"Yes, I was there," answered Cameron.

The official frowned again as he said sharply, "You'll do more for the cause, Brother Cameron, if you spend your time calling on the members. Deacon Godfrey's wife hasn't been out to ser-vices for three months because you haven't been to see her. And now you're ruining the church with your teaching. You've got to build on a scriptural foundation if you want your work to last. All these people you've been getting into the church these last two years don't know a thing about first principles."

The minister tried to explain. "The plan suggested last night by Mr. Falkner, who was there, I might add, by the invitation of the society, was simply for an institution that would permit a man who was homeless, cold, and hungry to pay for food and lodging until he could do better. In short, it is a plan to prevent deaths like that of the young man found frozen a few weeks ago."

"You don't know anything about that fellow," argued the dea-con. "If he had followed the teaching of the Scriptures, he wouldn't have been in that fix. The Word says plainly: 'He that provideth not for his own is worse than an infidel.' You don't know whether he was a Christian or not. He may never have been baptized. Indeed, I am ready to prove that he never was, for the Scripture says that the righteous are never forsaken, nor their seed begging for bread. I've lived for fifty years now, and I never went hungry and never slept out-of-doors either."

Cameron sat silently biting his lip. Then looking his parishioner straight in the eye, he said, "Brother Wickham, I cannot harmonize your teaching with Christ's life and character."

"My teaching is the Scripture, sir! I'll give you book, chapter, and verse!" snapped the deacon.

"I'm sure you could. But Jesus lived and taught a doctrine of love and compassion and helpfulness toward all men, especially enemies and the downtrodden," replied Cameron. "When I remember how He pointed out the hungry and naked and homeless, and then said, 'Inasmuch as ye did it not unto one of the least of these, ye did it not unto me,' I cannot help but feel sure in my heart that what the young people have proposed is a right and scriptural thing to do. I must tell you that Mr. Falkner's plan for doing just that work is the most practical and common sense one I have ever heard. The only thing I find to wonder at is the stupidity of the church and myself that we did not think of some such plan to put into effect long ago."

"Then am I to understand that you support and encourage this unscriptural way of doing things?"

"I most certainly have given my support, and as far as possible I will encourage the young people and help them however I can in their labor of love."

"Labor of love, fiddlesticks!" retorted the deacon. "Labor of foolishness! You'll find, sir, that it will be better to take my advice and the advice of the sacred writers instead of going off after the strange teaching of an outcast and a begging heathen!"

"Stop!" cried Cameron, springing to his feet and speaking in a tone that good Deacon Wickham had never before heard him use. "Do not go too far. Whatever his religious convictions may be, Mr. Falkner is neither an outcast nor a beggar. And although I am only your pastor, it might be well for you to remember that I am also a gentleman, and I will allow no man to speak of my friends in any such language."

"Well," whined Wickham, "I meant no harm. But I must reemphasize my objection to the whole thing. I want you to know, however, that I bear you no ill-will whatever. But I warn you, I wash my hands of the whole matter. I don't want to know anything about it." He extended his hand dutifully.

Cameron took it and replied, "That's the best thing you can do, Brother Wickham. You have discharged your duty faithfully as you have seen fit as an officer in the church, and you are released from all responsibility whatever."

"Yes, yes," replied the other as he stood on the porch to leave. "And don't let them call on me for any money. I wash my hands of the whole thing. How much did you say it would cost?"

"I don't know yet exactly."

"Well, you know I can't give anyway. I'm already doing more than my share in a scriptural way, and I must wash my hands of this."

"Yes," murmured Cameron to himself as he shut the door. "A certain Roman governor washed his hands once upon a time as well." But even as he said the words, the young pastor took himself to task for his uncharitable spirit toward the blind old pious deacon.

Later in the day, Rev. Cameron had another visitor, old Father Beason, whose hair had grown white in the Master's service. He had been with his congregation over twenty years and they would not give him up. For while his sermons may have lost some of their youthful fire, they were riper for the preacher's long experience, and sweeter for his nearness to the Source of love.

The old man met Cameron's outstretched hand of welcome with a smile that in itself was a benediction. Though pastor of a church of a different denomination, he was a close friend to the head of the Jerusalem Church, and always stood ready to draw from his wealth of experience for the benefit of his younger brother. When they were seated in Cameron's cozy den with a basket of fruit between them, Father Beason began:

"Brother Jim, what's this about the proposed work of your young people? I've heard a good many things today, and I thought I'd come over and get the straight of it, if you don't mind telling me."

Cameron laughed as he carefully selected a rosy-cheeked apple.

"You're the second caller I've had today who needed straightening out. I've been hoping to see you. This work is right along the lines you and I have talked over many times." And then he told the whole story.

When Cameron had finished, the older man asked a few questions, slowly nodded his head, and repeated softly: "Thy kingdom come, thy will be done on earth as it is in heaven."

He then lifted his head and turned to his young friend. "Brother Cameron," he began, "you know that I belong to a church that is noted for its conservative spirit. But I have been preaching more years than you have lived, and have been at it too long to be bound by the particular belief of any particular people. And I want to say to you that if I were a younger man, I would take exactly the course you have taken. People will oppose you, your own most faithful church leaders and friends will turn against you, but that is often the price we must pay for speaking our minds and standing up for what we feel is the truth. Brother Jim, there is no use in our flinching or dodging the question. The church is not meeting the problems of the day, and it's high time something were done. We mustn't just keep sitting in our warm comfortable churches and talking to ourselves. I have tried to do my small part through the years, but I'm too old to get involved in the battle much longer. Now, you are young, my boy. Go on in this fight, go on to win, and may God's richest blessings rest upon you. You'll stir this city as it never was stirred before. I only wish I were twenty years younger to stand by you. But be assured, I am behind your efforts one hundred percent!"

He rose to his feet, and grasping Cameron's hand, said, "Good day, Brother Jim. Hang on to that which is committed to you, and don't be sidetracked by the opinions of men. The victory will be yours, through Jesus Christ, our Lord. I thank God for this day!"

CHAPTER SEVENTEEN

Rival Games and Their Stakes

The sun sank into the prairie and tinted the sky all red and green and gold where it shone through the rents in the ragged clouds of purple black.

The glowing colors touching dull, weather-beaten steeples and factory smokestacks changed them to objects of interest and beauty. The poisonous smoke from smelter and engine hanging over the town like a heavy veil shot through with the brilliant rays became a sea of color that drifted here and there, tumbled and tossed by the wind, while above, the ball of the newly painted flagstaff on the courthouse tower gleamed like a signal lamp from another world.

Through it all, the light reflected from a hundred windows flashed and blazed in wondrous glory until the city seemed a dream of unearthly splendor and fairy loveliness.

Only for a moment it lasted. Then a heavy cloud curtain was drawn hurriedly across the west as though the previous scene was too sacred for the gaze of men whose souls were dwarfed by baser visions. For an instant a single star gleamed above the curtain in the soft green of the upper sky. Then it too vanished, blotted out by the flying forerunners of the coming storm.

The wind came on, and quickly night descended.

About nine o'clock, when the first wild fury of the gale had passed, a young man muffled in a heavy coat and with a soft hat pulled low over his face made his way along the deserted streets. In front of the Goodrich hardware store he stopped and looked carefully about as though afraid of some observer. Then taking a key from his pocket, he unlocked the door and entered.

Walking quickly through the store to the office, as though familiar with the place, he knelt before the big safe, his hand upon the knob that worked the combination. A moment later the heavy door yielded to his hand.

Taking a bunch of keys from his pocket, without hesitation, he selected one and applied it to the cash box that sat inside the safe. It opened, revealing a large sum of money. He reached out, grabbed a packet of bills, stuffed it into his side coat pocket, locked the cash box again, and was closing the safe when he paused as though struck with a sudden thought.

The storm outside seemed to be renewing its strength. The dashing of sleet and snow against the windows, the howling of the wind, the weird singing of the wires, and the sharp banging and swinging of signs and shutters carried terror to the heart of the young man kneeling in the dimly lit office.

"My God—what am I doing!" he said to himself.

Again there came a sudden lull in the storm. Everything grew hushed and still, almost as if the very spirit of the night waited breathlessly for the result of the battle being fought in the heart of the tempted man. Slowly he swung back the heavy doors and once more unlocked the cash box, reaching out to replace the packet of bills.

But then with a sudden exclamation, he said, "No—I won't fail this time. I can't keep losing! This *has* to be my night!"

Quickly he closed the safe, and with the money in his pocket, he sprang to his feet and hurried out of the building, where the storm met him in all its fury. But with set face and clenched fists, he pushed into the gale, and a few minutes later knocked at the door of a room on the top floor of a big hotel. He was admitted and greeted cordially by two men who were drinking. A haze of smoke from numerous cigars and cigarettes hung in the air.

"Hello, Frank!" exclaimed one. "We thought you had skipped out on us for sure this time. What makes you so late? It's nearly ten."

"Oh, the old man had some work for me. Where's Whitley?"

He tried to speak as if he hadn't a care, but his eyes wavered about nervously, and his hands trembled as he unbuttoned his heavy coat.

"You're right, this storm's a ripper. Jim will be back in a minute. He just stepped down to the drugstore to see a man. Here he is now," he added, as another low knock sounded on the door, and the fourth man entered, shaking the snow from his fur-trimmed coat.

"Pile out of your duds, boys, and have a drink," said the other man who was already seated. "Good liquor hits the spot on a night like this."

Whitley eagerly grasped the glass that was held out to him and emptied it without a word, but Frank refused.

"You know I don't drink," he said. "Take it yourself if you need it, and let's get to work." He drew a chair to the table in the center of the room.

The others laughed as they took their places. One said as he shuffled a deck of cards, "We forgot you were a church member."

"Maybe you'd like to open the services with a song and a prayer," sneered the other.

"You shut up and mind your own business," retorted the young Goodrich angrily. "I'll show you tonight that you can't always have your own way with me. Did you bring my papers?"

The others nodded. "Whitley here told us you wanted a chance to win them back before we were obliged to collect," stated one.

"It's to be cash tonight, though," added the other; "good cold cash against the notes we hold."

"Shut up and play," growled Frank in reply. "I guess there's cash enough," and he laid the package of bills on the table.

Four eyes gleamed in triumph. Whitley looked at the young

man keenly and paused with the cards in his hands. Then he dealt and the game began.

———

Meanwhile, Adam Goodrich and his wife were entertaining the bridge club at its regular weekly meeting, a club of which they were enthusiastic members. And though the weather was rough, not a few of the devoted lovers of the game were present.

In the conversation that preceded the play, the Young People's Society and Dick Falkner's plan of work was mentioned. Nearly all of the guests, being members of different churches, expressed themselves quite freely, with a variety of opinions, until the host, with annoyance plainly expressed on his proud face, said in his hard, cold voice, "You must not think that because I and my family are members of the Jerusalem Church that we agree with Rev. Cameron in his outlandish ideas. We have never been accustomed to associating with such low characters as he delights in forcing us to meet in the congregation; and if he does not change his tack, he will either drive all the best people to other churches or force us to consider the appointment of a pulpit committee. As for that tramp printer, I can tell you that *my* children shall have nothing to do with his notions. It's just such stuff that causes all the discontent among the lower classes."

The other guests all nodded emphatic approval.

Amy's face flushed slightly, and she lifted her head as if to speak. But Mrs. Goodrich silenced her with a look and skillfully changed the subject.

"It's too bad Frank won't be here tonight," she said. "He so enjoys these evenings. But he and Mr. Whitley are spending the evening with a sick friend. And Mr. Whitley will miss the game too, and Amy loses a strong partner."

The company talked of other things until the all-absorbing game began.

And so, while the son played with his friend Whitley and the two professional gamblers at the hotel—played with fear in his face and a curse in his heart to save himself from sure disgrace—

his fond parents and beautiful sister at home forgot his absence in their eager efforts to win with the cards the petty prize of the evening: a silver-mounted loving cup.

One, two, three hours passed.

The storm had spent its strength. Mr. Goodrich had won the coveted prize, and the guests of the evening had returned to their homes.

––––––

The last of the pile of bills in front of Frank was placed in the center of the table. The silence was unbroken except for the sound of the shuffling of the cards and the clink of a whiskey glass as one of the men helped himself to a drink.

Suddenly young Goodrich leaped to his feet with a wild exclamation: "Tom Wharton, you're a liar and a cheat!"

As he spoke, he grabbed up a heavy chair, spun it above his head, and let it fall with a crashing blow upon the man who sat at his right. Instantly all was confusion. The table was overturned, while the cards, money, and glasses flew scattering throughout the room.

Whitley and the other gambler stood in blank astonishment at the sudden outburst. Frank leaped at his prostrate victim, then raised the chair to strike again, the intent of murder shining out of his glittering eyes. But just in time, Whitley caught his arm, while the other drew a knife and stepped between the crazed man and his victim.

"Stop, you fool!" cried Whitley. "And you, Jack, put away that knife and look after Tom. Let's don't make this a worse mess than it already is."

The gambler did as he was told, but Frank struggled in his friend's grasp. "Let me go, Jim! Let me at him! I'm ruined anyway, and I'll finish the man that did it before I go myself."

But Whitley was the stronger and forced him backward while the other man was busy with his fallen partner.

"Ruined, nothing!" said Whitley in Frank's ear in a harsh whisper. "I'll stand by you. You get out of here quick. Go to my room.

I'll come when I've settled with these two."

He unlocked the door and pushed Frank into the hall just as the man on the floor struggled to his feet.

The two gamblers turned on Whitley in a rage when they saw that Frank had escaped. Standing with his back to the door, he let them curse at him a few minutes and then said calmly, "Now, if you feel better, let's have a drink and talk this over."

When he had them quieted down, he continued in a matter-of-fact tone. "Suppose you fellows raise a ruckus about this, what will you gain?"

"We'll teach that young fool a lesson he won't soon forget," snarled the one who had fallen.

"Yes, and you'll pay handsomely for the lesson," replied Whitley quietly.

"What do you mean?" asked Wharton.

"I mean that if this gets out, young Goodrich will be ruined. His father will probably disown him, and you won't get a cent on the paper you hold."

Wharton's friend nodded. "That's straight, Tom," he agreed.

"Well, what of it?" growled the other. "The old man won't pay it anyway."

"Yes, he will," returned Jim quickly, "if nothing was made public. He'll do anything to save his own reputation. But I don't happen to want him to know about this little deal."

"What's it to you?" said Wharton.

"Never mind what it is to me. I know what I'm doing, and I don't want this to get out," replied Whitley.

"How will you help it?" Tom retorted.

"This way." Whitley took a checkbook from his pocket. "Make the notes over to me and I'll add two hundred to the amount. Go after Frank and you get nothing. Go to the old man and you'll probably get paid, but not a cent more than the paper calls for. Keep your mouth shut and sell me the notes and you get an extra hundred apiece. What do you say?"

"I say yes!" exclaimed Jack with an oath. "I'm no fool."

The other grumbled a surly, "All right. But I'd like to get one crack at that kid's head."

"You'll have to pass that little pleasure this time," commented the other with a laugh. "Write your check, Whitley, and let us get out of here."

When Whitley reached his room after settling with the two gamblers, he found Frank pacing the floor, his face white and haggard.

"Sit down, sit down," said Whitley, "and take things easy. You're all right. Look here." He drew the notes from his pocket.

Frank sank into a chair. "How did you get hold of those?" he gasped.

Whitley laughed. "Just invested a little of my spare cash, that's all," he replied.

"But I'm ruined, I tell you," moaned Frank. "I can't pay a third of that in six years."

"Maybe you won't have to," said Whitley.

"What do you mean?" asked Frank with a puzzled look.

"I mean Amy," the other replied coolly.

Frank continued to stare at him with blank expression.

"You poor idiot, can't you see!" Whitley cried. "I can't afford to have you disgraced before the whole world. If I wasn't involved with you, I'd let you go to thunder and it'd serve you right. But a fine chance I'd have to marry your sister if she finds out about this business tonight. If it wasn't for her, I'd let you hang your fool self before I'd spend a dollar on your worthless carcass. But I've said that I would marry that girl and I will, if it costs me every cent I've got. And you'll help me." Frank was silent for a time, cowed by the contempt in the other's voice and too frightened to protest. At last he managed to say, "There's more than those notes."

"I know that too," returned Whitley with an oath. "How much did you steal from your father's safe tonight?"

"What—how do you know about that?" stammered Frank.

"I saw you," replied Whitley, and then added as Frank rose to his feet and began walking the floor again, "Oh, for heaven's sake

quit wallowing in your tragedy and sit down. You make me tired.
You're not cut out to be either a gambler or a thief. You haven't
the nerve."

Frank was silent, while the other went to a small cupboard and
leisurely helped himself to a glass of whiskey and then lit a fresh
cigar.

"What can I do?" ventured Frank at last, his voice barely above
a whisper.

Whitley crossed the room, unlocked a drawer in his desk, and
returned with a handful of bills, which he handed toward his
friend.

"You can put that money back in the safe before morning and
keep your mouth shut."

When Frank attempted to grasp his hand while stammering
words of gratitude, Whitley added, "No thanks," while placing
his own hands behind his back. "You be a good boy, Frankie.
Listen to your pastor's sermons. Keep your Young People's Society pledge. Read your Bible and pray every day, and go to all
the meetings. And when I marry your sister I'll make you a present
of these papers. But, oh my, what a good brother-in-law you're
going to make!"

He laughed, then asked in a disgusted tone, "How much did
you say?"

Frank muttered the amount he had stolen.

Whitley quickly counted it out and threw the bills on the table.
"There you are. Now you better go quickly before you slop over
again and I kick you."

Turning his back he poured himself another glass of liquor
while Frank, with the money in his hand, sneaked from the room
like a well-whipped cur.

The storm was gone, and over his head, as he crept stealthily
down the street toward his father's store, the stars shone clear and
cold in their pure, calm beauty, while the last of the clouds passed
out of sight on the far horizon.

CHAPTER EIGHTEEN

THE GIFT OF AN UNBELIEVER

The committee appointed by the society called on Uncle Bobbie at his office, and found him absorbed in a letter to an old lady whose small business affairs he was trying to straighten out.

He dropped the matter at once when they entered. He shook hands with each one as though he had not seen them for years, then said, "Now tell me what's on your mind. To be sure, Charlie here has had some talk with me, but I want to know your thoughts on the matter."

"Our brightest idea, I think," said the leader with a smile, "is to get your help."

Uncle Bobbie laughed heartily. "I reckoned you'd be around," he replied. "I'm generally kept posted by the young folks when there's anything to do. It's true, I ain't got much education, except in money matters and real estate, but I don't know—I reckon education is only the trimmings anyhow. It's the horse sense that counts. I've seen some college fellows that were just like the pies a stingy old landlady of mine used to make—they was all outside. Now, tell me what you want."

When the young people had detailed to him Dick's plan, and he had questioned them on some points, the old gentleman leaned back in his chair and thoughtfully stroked his face. Then he said,

"I'll tell you what you do. Maybe I can handle the property end of this the best. To be sure, folks would talk with me when they might not listen to you, 'cause they'd be watching for a chance to get me into a deal, you see. For business is a sort of catch-as-catch-can proposition anyhow you fix it. So just let me work on that end, and you drum up the storekeepers to find out if they'll let you have their barrels and boxes. Then go to the townspeople and see how many will buy kindling wood. Tell them about what it will cost—say, ten cents a week for one stove. You might find that some will use more than others, but give them an idea. After that we'll all come together again and swap reports, and see what we've got."

For the next few days the young people went from store to store and house to house, telling people their plan and asking for support. Some turned them away with rudeness, some listened and smiled, some said they couldn't afford it, and some gave them encouragement by entering heartily into the scheme. With but few exceptions, the merchants promised the greater part of their boxes and barrels, and one man even gave them the ruins of an old cow shed, which he said he would be glad to have cleared away.

Meanwhile, Uncle Bobbie interviewed the businessmen, both members of the church and others who were not. He studied plans, consulted architects and contractors, and talked to many influential men in the city, but nowhere could he find anyone with the least interest in helping the young people. When the society met again in the church two Wednesday nights later, Uncle Bobbie wished he had a better report to make. The weather was cold and stormy, but, as at the previous meeting, nearly every member was present. When the committee had made its report and it was known that a good number of storekeepers and townspeople would support the plan by patronage and contributions, enthusiasm in the room ran high.

When Uncle Bobbie rose to speak, however, his face betrayed dejection. "I didn't want to meet with you tonight," he confessed, "for I was ashamed to come without good news. And now I find myself ashamed that I didn't want to. I should have known better.

For I can see right now as I look into your faces that what I have to tell you won't make a difference." A hush fell over the company of young people. "To be sure, we may have to wait a bit," he went on, "but God will show a way, and we'll conquer this old devil of indifference yet."

He paused and drew in a deep breath. "Well, the long and the short of it is just this: I haven't found anyone of means in this town who's the least interested in helping us with a building. I went to every church member I could think of, and I have to admit it's plumb discouraging to listen to them say no with their self-satisfied airs. But there may be hope yet. I did find a big house for sale. Just the kind of place we need, if it could be bought and fixed up in first-class shape for about nine hundred dollars. I just sold the property myself to Mr. Udell for fifteen hundred about a year ago. I just talked to Mr. Udell yesterday, and I want to tell you, that whether he's a Christian or not, and it's not for me to say one way or the other—that's the Lord's business—but as I said, whatever he be, he is one of the most selfless men in this city." He then went on to say that of all the men he had interviewed, only Udell had met him halfway and had agreed to donate the lot if they would raise the money to pay for the house.

"Just think," continued Uncle Bobbie, "that among all the church members in this city, I couldn't raise two hundred dollars for such a cause of helping our fellowman. One of them said no because he's just bought a new span of carriage horses. I told him he might ride to hell behind fine horses, but he'd not feel any better when he got there. Another said he'd just put five hundred dollars into the new lodge temple and that he couldn't spend any more. I asked him if Jesus was a member of his lodge, and he said he reckoned not. I said, well, we want to build a home for Christ, and you say you can't. Seems to me if I was you I wouldn't call Jesus my Lord and redeemer in prayer meeting so much. You know what Christ said to those who called Him Lord but didn't feed the hungry and clothe the naked. Another of them had just put in a new inventory of goods into his business, and so with all of them. Every one had some excuse handy, and I don't know what to do. We've got the material to work up, we've got the people to buy the goods, we've got the lot; and there we're stuck, for we can't get the house. We're just like a boy that went fishing, had a big basket to carry home his fish, a nice new jointed pole with reel and fixings, a good strong line, and a nice bait box full of big fat worms; but when he got to the river he had no hook, and the fish just swam around under his nose and laughed at him 'cause he couldn't touch them. As for me, I still believe that God will show us the way."

After a long silence, one or two offered suggestions, but nothing to change matters presented itself. Rev. Cameron was called for and tried to speak encouragingly, but it was hard work, and it seemed that the plans were about to come to an inglorious end when Clara Wilson sprang to her feet.

"I'm not surprised at this," she said. "Why should the businessmen back such a scheme? They haven't faith that it will succeed. It isn't so much that they don't have the money or don't want to help, but they don't trust the church. They've seen so many things started, and they've been asked to support so many projects that no real good comes out of in the end. They're willing to put money into their lodges because they see the results there. There has been more wealth put into churches than has ever been put into lodges and clubs, but all we've got to show for it is fine organs, pretty windows, and flowery talk, while the lodges take less money and do practical work with it. We can't expect folks to get behind our plan until we show what we are going to do. We are starting at the wrong end. *We* haven't done anything yet."

"We've gone around and drummed up some potential business," said one young man. "What more can we do without the house?"

"There's plenty more we could do if we were serious," replied Clara. "Why, there's enough jewelry here tonight to raise more than half the amount. We've come this far; we can't give up now. Let's have a big meeting—invite the whole town if we can—and tell what has been done, and see how much more we can raise."

Cameron jumped to his feet. "A wonderful idea!" he exclaimed. "And I can't think of a better person to put in charge of the program than Clara Wilson!"

A chorus of ayes was followed by prolonged applause. By the time the meeting was over they were trooping from the building, out into the storm, with warm hearts and merry voices.

CHAPTER NINETEEN

DICK TAKES A STAND

The night came when the young people had planned to hold their special meeting in hopes of widening support for the new movement. Clara Wilson had worked incessantly, and when at last the evening arrived she was well satisfied that she had done her best.

The incident—still so fresh in the minds of the people of the town—of the man found frozen to death on the steps of the church, the rumors flying about Dick's visit to the society, and the plans of the young people—all combined to arouse public curiosity to such a height that the place of the meeting was crowded, and many were forced to stand in the rear of the room.

After a brief opening, in which the purpose of the society and the proposed plan of work were fully explained, Uncle Bobbie rose and told, in his simple way, of the work that had been done, how the young people had called on him, how they had gone from house to house, through the cold and snow, and how he had interviewed the businessmen, many of whom he saw in the audience.

"To be sure," he said, "I don't suppose you understand the matter fully or you would have been glad to help, but we'll give you another chance in a minute."

Then he told of the last meeting, how they were encouraged when the reports came in that the townspeople had responded so liberally, and how he had been forced to tell them he had met with nothing but failure in his attempt to raise the finances necessary to secure a house. "I tell you, it made my old heart ache to see our young folks trying to do some practical work for Christ and to come up against a roadblock of money like that. I wish you all could have seen them and heard them pray."

The old gentleman finished amid a silence that was almost painful. His words seemed to have taken profound hold, and many were eagerly leaning forward in their seats. The audience was impressed by the scheme and by the thought of a work so practical. This was no theory, no doctrine of men, no denominational dogma—this was a Christlike helping of brothers in need.

The pastor of the Jerusalem Church stepped to the front of the rostrum and raised his hand. Without a word the people bowed their heads. After a moment of silence, the minister prayed sincerely, "God, help us to help others."

Then he began to speak, in simple but clear tones. He recalled to their minds the Savior of men as He walked and talked in Galilee. He pictured Jesus feeding the hungry and healing the sick. He made the audience hear again the voice that spoke as never a man had spoken before, giving forth the Sermon on the Mount and pronouncing His blessing on the poor and merciful. They felt as if they stood with the Master when He wept at the grave of Lazarus, and sat with Him at the last supper. They walked with Him across the brook Kidron and entered the shadows of the olive trees, where they heard Him pray while His disciples slept: "If it be possible, let this cup pass from me. Nevertheless, not my will, but thine be done." And then they stood with the Jewish mob, clamoring for His blood, and later at the foot of the cross, where they heard that wonderful testimony of His undying love: "Father forgive them, for they know not what they do."

Then under the spell of Cameron's speech, they looked into the empty tomb and felt their hearts throb as the full meaning of that silent vault burst upon them. Looking up they saw their risen

Lord seated at the right hand of the Father. And then they looked where the Master pointed, to the starving, shivering, naked ones of earth, and heard with new understanding those too-familiar but too-infrequently-heeded words: "Inasmuch as ye have done it unto one of the least of these my brethren, ye have done it unto me."

"Brothers and sisters," cried the pastor, stretching out his arms in the earnestness of his appeal, "what shall we do? Shall there be no place in all this city where the least of these may find help in the name of our common Master? Must our brothers perish with cold and hunger because we close the doors of the Savior's church against them? These young people, led by a deep desire to do God's will, have gone as far as they can go alone. Their plan has been carefully studied by good businessmen and pronounced practical in every way. They have the promised support of merchants in supplying material. They have the promised patronage of many of your friends and neighbors of the town. And a man, not a professed Christian, but with a heart that feels for suffering humanity, has given the land. In the name of Jesus, to help the least of these, won't you all contribute together to help buy the house?"

The deacons, with the baskets and paper and pencils, started through the congregation.

After a moment Mr. Godfrey walked up to Rev. Cameron and placed something in his hand. The pastor, after listening a moment to the whispered words of his officer, turned to the audience and said, "At our last meeting, one of the young people made the remark that there were enough jewels on the persons of those present to pay half the amount needed. Brother Godfrey has just handed me this diamond ring, worth, I should say, between forty and fifty dollars. It was dropped into the basket by one of the young women of the Young People's Society. Friends, do you need any more proof that these young folks are in earnest?"

At last the offering was taken. The deacons reported one thousand and twenty dollars in cash and pledges. "And perhaps," said the leader, "I ought to say, in jewelry also." And he held up to the gaze of the audience a handful of finger rings, scarf pins, earrings and ornaments, and a gold watch, in the case of which was set a tiny diamond.

Again for a moment a deep hush fell over the congregation. Then the minister raised his voice in a prayer that God would bless the offering and use it in His service, and the audience was dismissed.

Dick did not sleep well that night.

Something Cameron had said in his talk, together with the remarkable gifts of the young people and others from the town, had impressed him. He had gone to the meeting more from curiosity than anything, to see what would become of his plan. He had come away with an unexpected feeling of respect for Christians who were serious about their faith. It was completely new to him.

As he thought of the jewelry, given without the display of name or show of hands, he said to himself, "Surely these people are in earnest." He suddenly realized that he had always dismissed church people in a lump together, as if all were hypocrites. Now he saw that he had allowed himself to view only one segment of the whole. But for every hypocrite, he said to himself, perhaps there is one serious Christian for whom the words of Jesus *do* mean something about how one is to live.

Under the spell of Cameron's talk, he saw before him the figure of Jesus as He lived His life of sacrifice and love, and heard Him speak the simple words of command: "Follow me."

He realized that he had seen, without even realizing it, people doing just that thing: following Him, doing as He did. Along with the Adam Goodriches, there were Bobbie Udells and Charlie Bowens who *did* live the words taught by the Master. As he sat there, new and strange thoughts tumbling through his awakening brain and opening heart, young Dick Falkner found himself facing questions inside he had never paused to consider before.

Therefore, when he went to the office the following morning and found Udell strangely silent, he was not in the least surprised.

"What's the matter, George?" he asked. "Didn't you sleep well last night either? Or did the thought of having been so generous with your property keep you awake?"

"The property has nothing to do with it," answered Udell.

"It's what that preacher said. Well, maybe it's not even that either. I guess it's what those young people *did*. I've been thinking ever since about that handful of jewelry. If I hadn't seen it I wouldn't have believed it! Do you know that a few sermons like those gold trinkets would do more to convert the world than all the theological seminaries that ever bewildered the brains of poor preachers! If they'd *do* it instead of trying to understand and talk about it, why, the world would beat a path to the door of every church in the land clamoring to get a piece of such practical truth."

"I think you're right, George, but is it true?" questioned Dick.

"Is what true?"

"What Cameron said about Jesus Christ being the Savior of men, and all that," replied Dick.

Udell paused in his work. "What do *you* say?" he asked at last without answering Dick's question.

Dick thought several long moments before replying.

"For several years," he finally said slowly, "I tried hard to make an unbeliever of myself. I couldn't stand the way the church did things, and didn't care much for most of the church people I met. I suppose I never really stopped to consider the truth of Christianity, because all I could see was the falsehood of the people representing it. But now all at once I'm realizing that perhaps the two are in fact not the same."

"What do you mean?"

"Well, that meeting last night was different—or at least my response to it. In spite of myself, I was forced to the conclusion that Cameron spoke the truth and that maybe Jesus is exactly what He claimed to be, the Son of God and the Savior of mankind. Is it possible Jesus is the truth and we are bound to follow Him in spite of the fact that many of His so-called followers don't follow His example in the way they live their lives?"

"You've got me there," responded Udell, smiling thoughtfully. "Like you, I've spent a lifetime battling a reputation as an infidel for that very reason."

"I am sure of this," continued Dick; "something inside me has always wished that it were true. I have always believed that the

Christian life—I mean the *true* Christian life, you know, as Christ taught it, not the dreary sort practiced by most churches—would be the happiest life possible on earth."

"What life do you mean, exactly?"

"The life of living for others, of course," replied Dick, "as Jesus did. You remember His words about doing it for the least of these, for the people in need—the hungry, the sick, the outcast. To give your life in such a cause I think would be a wonderful life."

"But like you said, the churches aren't doing that."

"Most churches have become nothing more than giant social clubs—an endless string of activities promoting their own inner relationships and finances and projects, but with very little impact outside their own tight little circles. Even all their Bible studies and prayer meetings are directed inward, not outward."

"I've always felt that way myself," said Udell. "That's why I never joined the church."

"But don't you see—there's the rub," Dick pointed out in an agitated tone. "If the words of Jesus are true, then where can a fellow go to live the life He taught if it's not being lived in the churches? And you and I can hardly claim to be living it any better than the people with their names on the church books.

"If I want to come to terms with this because it is the truth, must I join a company of canting hypocrites in order to get to heaven?"

"Those are pretty strong words," cautioned Udell. "You yourself said not everyone in the church was such. What about Cameron? And wasn't your reaction last night exactly because of those who tried to do something to live it by putting up their rings and money?"

"You are right, George," returned Dick. "I spoke harshly. I know there are earnest ones in the church. And last night was indeed an indication of it, as is the whole Young People's Society and its desire to practically live the gospel. But I don't see how they stand it when so many others care only about the social and intellectual side of the church. But you're dodging my question.

Do you believe that Jesus Christ is the Son of God and the Savior of men?"

"Folks say I'm a heathen," answered George.

"I don't care what folks say," argued Dick. "I want to know what *you* think about it."

"I don't know," he replied. "I've found myself thinking about it since last night too. When I listen to the preachers, I usually get so befuddled that there's nothing but a big pile of chaff, with now and then a few stray grains of truth; and the parson keeps the air so full of the dust and dirt that you'd rather he wouldn't hunt for the grain of truth at all. At times like that I'm an unbeliever. But then something like the meeting last night will come along and I think the gospel must be true. And then I think of Clara, and another part of me is afraid to believe because I fear it's the girl and not the truth I'm after. You see, I want to believe, but I don't want to believe for the wrong reasons, and I'm afraid I'll talk myself into believing something I don't really believe. There! That's my statement of belief and unbelief all mixed together. You can untangle that while you run off the batch of flyers for that politician. It's half past eight and we haven't done a blessed thing this morning."

And with that George turned resolutely to his task of setting up another job.

About two hours later, Dick came to Udell and asked, "George, what in the world does this mean?" He held in his hand a proof sheet he had just taken from the form George had placed on the stone. "When Patrick Henry said, 'Give me liberty or give me Clara,' he voiced a sentiment of every American church member."

George flushed at his mistake.

"Guess you'd better set up the rest of this," he said gruffly. "I'll run the press a while."

He laid down his stick and put the composing case between himself and Dick.

For the remainder of the week Dick could not keep his mind from fastening itself on the question: Is Jesus Christ indeed the Son of God and Savior of men? If so, what was supposed to be his response?

At intervals during working hours at the office, he discussed and argued the question with Udell, who after his seeming openness during their previous discussion followed by his strange rendering of the great statesman's famous speech, had relapsed into infidelity; and with all the strength of his mind, he opposed Dick in his growing belief. Dick spent his evenings with Charlie Bowen discussing the same question.

At such times, then, it was Charlie who assumed the affirmative and Dick who stoutly championed Udell's position. Thus Dick looked at and investigated the question from every possible angle, determined to take no one's word for anything but to think through the implications of the matter himself as honestly and forthrightly as he could.

At last, one day when Dick had argued his employer into a corner, the latter ended the debate by saying, "Well, if I believed it all as strongly as you do, I'd stand up like a man and say so. No matter what anyone else believed, did, or said, if Jesus Christ is all you say He is, then I'd stand by Him, dead or alive."

That same evening Charlie clinched the matter. After Dick had been taking the opposite side of the very argument he had pursued so passionately earlier that day with Udell, Charlie said, "Dick, if I thought you really believed the arguments you are putting forth, I wouldn't talk with you five minutes, for the doctrine you are proposing is the most hopeless thing on earth. I can't help feeling that if you were as honest with yourself as you are with others, you wouldn't take that side of the question. Suppose you preach a while from your favorite Shakespeare:

> " 'This above all:
> To thine own self be true,
> And it must follow as the night the day,
> Thou canst not then be false to any man.' "

There were no more arguments after that.

Over and over Dick thought about his experiences of the past, of the professed Christians he had seen and known whose lives proved untrue to their Christ. He looked at the church, proud and cold, standing in the very midst of sin and suffering but maintaining a pious distance from the world's needs. He remembered his first evening in Boyd City and his reception at the church he had stumbled into. Yet at the same time he remembered the meeting of the young people and the unmistakable evidence of their love, and the words of Uncle Bobbie in the printing office that rainy night: "You'll find out, same as I have, that it don't much matter how the other fellow dabbles in the dirt, you've got to keep your hands clean anyhow. The question ain't whether the other fellow's mean or a hypocrite, but am I living square myself?"

And so it was that when he went to church the next Sunday evening, his heart was torn with conflicting emotions. He slipped into a seat in the rear of the building, when the ushers were all busy, so that even Charlie did not know he was there.

Cameron's sermon was from the text, "What is that to thee? Follow thou me."

As he went on with his sermon, pointing out the evils of the church, saying many of the very things Dick had been saying to himself, he continually called the minds of his listeners back to the words of Jesus: "What is that to thee? Follow thou me."

One by one Dick felt his objections vanish as the great truth emerged. The minister brought his talk to a close with an earnest appeal for those who recognized the wrongs that existed in the church because it was not following Jesus as closely as it ought, to come and help right them. Slowly Dick left his seat and walked forward. He took Cameron's outstretched hand and, while the congregation sang the final hymn, he said to him, "I am finally ready to make Him my Savior. I am ready to follow wherever He leads."

As he stood there the audience was forgotten. The past, with all its mistakes and suffering, its doubt, its loneliness, came before his mind's eye for an instant, then vanished. His heart leaped for joy, because he knew that the heartache of the past was gone forever. And the future, made all at once beautiful and exciting, stretched away as a path leading ever upward until it was lost in the words of his new Master: "Follow me."

CHAPTER TWENTY

ADAM GOODRICH ALSO TAKES A STAND

George was busy in the stockroom getting out some paper for a printing of circulars that Dick had just finished setting up when the door opened and Amy Goodrich entered.

"Good morning, Mr. Falkner," she said as Dick left his work and went forward to greet her. "I need some new calling cards. You have the plate here in the office, I believe."

"Yes," responded Dick. "The plate is here. We ought to be able to have them for you this afternoon."

"And, Mr. Falkner," Amy continued, "I want to tell you how proud I was when you took the stand you did Sunday night."

Dick's face flushed and he looked at her keenly.

"I have thought for a long time," she went on, "that, if I can say this, you were the sort of person who *should* be a Christian. The church needs young men who are firm in their convictions, and you can do so much good."

"You are very kind," replied Dick politely.

"I mean it," insisted Amy. "I have always felt that you exerted a powerful influence over all with whom you came in touch. Let me make a prophecy—you will one day be a preacher of the gospel."

"Not me!" exclaimed Dick.

"Mark my words," laughed Amy.

"I'm sure that if I truly came to believe such to be my work, I would not refuse," said Dick soberly. "But I can hardly imagine it. I suppose it's a question only time can answer. Do you remember the first time we met?"

"Indeed I do," the girl replied, laughing again. "It was right here, and you met with an accident at the same time."

Dick's face reddened slightly. "I should say I did. I acted like a frightened fool."

"Oh, but you redeemed yourself beautifully," Amy replied. "I still have one of those little books. I shall always keep it, and when you get to be a famous preacher, I'll exhibit my treasure and tell how the Rev. Richard Falkner sat up late one night to design the cover for me when he was only a poor printer."

"Yes," rejoined Dick, "and I'll tell the world how I went to my first church social, and what a charming young lady I met, who told me how much I reminded her of someone she knew."

It was Amy's turn to blush now, and she did so very prettily as she hurriedly said, "Let's change the subject. I ought not to be keeping you from your work. Mr. Udell will ask me to stay away."

"Oh, we're not rushed today," Dick told her, "and I'll soon make up for lost time."

"So you consider this lost time, do you?" quipped Amy with a mischievous grin. "Then I know I should be going."

"No, please," hastened Dick. "You know I did not mean that. But tell me, I can't help noticing that you haven't been so much at the meetings of the society as you used to, and that—well—you don't seem—somehow—to take the interest you once did. Is anything wrong?"

A shadow crossed her beautiful face. But then she said, "Why—why, no."

Her tone, however, lacked conviction.

"And I heard you had given up the class you had been teaching down at the South Broadway Mission."

"How do you know that?" asked Amy.

"I asked Rev. Cameron if there was any place for me out there, besides the reading room, where I might help people, and he told me your class was without a teacher now," Dick replied.

"So you are to have my children at the mission. Oh, I am so glad." Her eyes filled with tears. "Please, Mr. Falkner, don't let them forget me altogether."

"But why won't you come back and teach them?"

"So, you do not understand. I must give it up," said Amy, her voice filled with pain. "But you'll do better than I anyway. You can get closer to them. You understand the life they come from."

"Yes," agreed Dick soberly, "I do understand that life very well indeed."

"Forgive me, I didn't mean to remind you of the past."

"It's nothing."

She laid her hand timidly on his arm. "I admire you so much for what you have overcome," she said, "and that's what makes me say that you can do a great deal, now that you have come out of it."

She hesitated, drawing back her hand. Neither said anything for a few moments. Suddenly she extended her hand again, this time in a parting shake.

"Mr. Falkner," she asked, and as she spoke Dick discerned anxiety in her tone, "won't you please pray for me that I may be worthy of your friendship? For I too have my battles to fight." She smiled, and with a quick "goodbye," she turned and left the office. Suddenly the room drew dark around him, and Dick turned slowly back to his work.

———

Adam Goodrich was just coming out of the express office across the street when he saw his daughter leave Udell's Print Shop. For the rest of the day the incident persisted in forcing itself upon his mind, and that night, after the younger members of the family had retired and he and his wife were alone, he laid aside his evening paper and asked, "What was Amy doing at Udell's place today?"

"She went to have some calling cards printed," replied Mrs. Goodrich. "Why do you ask?"

"Oh, nothing. I saw her coming from the building and wondered what she was doing there, that's all."

He picked up his paper again, but in a moment laid it down once more. "That fellow Falkner joined the church last Sunday night."

"So Frank told me," returned Mrs. Goodrich. "I do wish Rev. Cameron would be more selective. He lets so many characters into the church. Why can't he keep them out at the mission where they belong and not force them to associate with us?"

"I suppose he will be active in the Young People's Society," said Mr. Goodrich. "Does Amy still take as much interest in it as she did?"

"Not so much," replied his wife. "I have tried to show her that it is not her place to mix in that kind of work, and she's beginning to understand her position. She will outgrow it in time, I am sure. She's taking up some of her social duties. We are to make some calls tomorrow, and Thursday night she has accepted an invitation to the card party at Mrs. Lansdown's. Also, Mr. Whitley has been calling on her frequently this past month. I have great hopes, for she seems to be quite interested in him."

"Yes," agreed Adam, "Whitley's a good man and of a good family. It wouldn't surprise me if he's the richest man in Boyd City. It's time he was thinking about a wife too. He must be well on toward forty."

"Oh, dear no. He couldn't be more than thirty-five," replied Mrs. Goodrich. "He was quite young when he went overseas, and you remember that was only five years ago."

"Well, it doesn't matter; he's young enough. But does she see much of that printer of Udell's?" Adam asked.

"Why, of course not. What a question! She would have nothing to do with him," replied Mrs. Goodrich indignantly.

"She has met him at the society's functions," argued Adam. "And you never know how young people are going to think. He could almost pose as a sort of hero, for he was the one who suggested that fool plan Cameron is working on; and now that he has joined the church, she must see more or less of him. I tell you, he's a sharp fellow. Can't you see how he has been quietly worming his way into decent society, first with that reading room, and now joining the church. There is no knowing what such a man will do, and Amy naturally would be a good mark for him."

"I'm doing the best for her I can," said Mrs. Goodrich. "But if you are so concerned, perhaps you'd better talk to her yourself. With Mr. Whitley so interested, we must be careful. I do wish she would be more like Frank. He has never given us a moment's trouble."

"Yes," agreed the father, with no little pride manifest in his voice and manner. "Frank is a Goodrich through and through."

The next day, after dinner, Mr. Goodrich found his daughter alone in the library. "Frank tells me that Mr. Falkner has joined the church," he remarked nonchalantly.

"Yes," Amy responded. "I am glad of it too. The church needs such young men, I think."

"He is quite a shrewd fellow, isn't he?" continued her father.

"He's very intelligent, I'm sure," said Amy. "You know it was he who proposed the plan for a house to help those who are out of work, and Mr. Wicks and Rev. Cameron think it is a very fine plan."

"I understand that," continued her father cunningly. "Does he use good language and proper English in his conversation?"

"Oh yes. He is a most interesting talker," replied Amy. "He has traveled so much and read almost everything. I tell him I think he ought to preach."

"Where did he live before he came here?" persisted Adam.

"In nearly all the big cities. He was in Kansas City last."

"And what did his father do?" queried Adam.

"His mother died when he was a little boy, and his father drank himself to death, or something," answered Amy with frank innocence. "He won't talk about his family much. He did say, though, that his father was a mechanic. I believe he tells Mr. Udell more about his past than anyone."

"And did Udell tell you all this?" asked her father in seeming surprise.

"No," responded Amy, suddenly aware of what was coming.

"How do you know so much about him?" he asked.

"He told me," she answered.

"Indeed," he said. "You seem to be on very friendly terms with this hero. How long were you at the printing office yesterday? I saw you leaving the building."

Amy was silent, but her burning cheeks convinced her father that he had cause to be alarmed.

"Did you talk with him when you were there?" he pressed.

"Yes, sir," replied Amy. "He waited on me."

"And do you think it is a credit to your family to be so intimate with a tramp who was kicked out of my place of business?" asked Adam harshly.

"Oh, Father, that is not true—I mean, you don't understand. Mr. Falkner is not a tramp. He was out of work and applied to you for a job. Surely that is not dishonest. And that he wanted to work for you ought not to be used against him."

In her excitement she spoke rapidly, and continued on with hardly a pause. "He has never shown himself to be anything but a gentleman, and is more modest and intelligent than many of the young men in Boyd City who come from fine homes. Surely he is not to be blamed because he has had to fight his own way in the world instead of always having things brought to him. If you knew him better, you wouldn't think of him as a tramp."

"You seem to know him very well when you champion him so strongly that you call your own father a liar!" Mr. Goodrich responded angrily.

"Oh, Papa!" cried Amy, now in tears, "I did not mean to say that. I only meant that you are mistaken because you do not really know him. I cannot help talking to Mr. Falkner when I meet him in the Young People's Society. I have not been anywhere in his company, and only just speak a few words when we do meet. You wouldn't have me refuse to recognize him in the church, would you? Surely Christ wants us to be kind to others, doesn't He?"

"Christ has nothing to do with this," retorted Adam. "I simply will not have my daughter associating with such characters. And another thing, you must give up that mission business. I believe that's where you get these strange ideas. Work such as that with the lower classes is meant to be carried out, but—by other sorts than ourselves."

"I have already given up my work there," murmured Amy sadly. "Mr. Falkner is going to take my class."

"Which is just the place for him," continued her father, still angry. "But don't you go there again. And if you have any printing that must be done at Udell's, send it by Frank or your mother. Do you understand? I forbid you to have any conversation whatever with that man Falkner. He's no good, I tell you. And I won't let any such fellows work themselves into my family!"

Amy's face grew crimson again. "You must learn," went on the wrathful man, "that the church is a place for you to listen to a sermon and nothing more. It's the preacher's business to tend to those other details; that's what we hire him for. Let him get people from the lower classes to do his dirty work; he shall *not* have my daughter. Christianity is all right, and I trust I'm as good a Christian as anyone; but a man need not make a fool of himself to get to heaven. After all, I'm only looking out for my own family's interest. I wish you would follow Frank's example. He is a good church member, but he doesn't let it interfere with his best interests. He has plenty of friends and he chooses his associates from among the best families in the city. *He* doesn't think it necessary to take up with every vagabond Cameron chooses to drag into the church. But as for you, these habits of yours must stop!"

And with that, the wise, concerned Christian father turned away, caught up his hat, and left for the establishment on Broadway, where on the shelves and behind the counters of his hardware store he kept the god that was really the object of his worship.

CHAPTER TWENTY-ONE

GOING IN OPPOSITE DIRECTIONS

The year following Dick's decision, there were many changes that occurred. The house of ministry was established by the Young People's Society, and, with a modest beginning, gradually came to be accepted by the community both as an acceptable and a worthwhile endeavor.

Dick grew rapidly in his new faith, became closer friends than ever with Charlie Bowen and Rev. Cameron, and continued to work for George Udell as well as discuss matters of religious conviction with him. He did not see Amy except from a distance across the pews on Sunday mornings. And even those occasions grew less and less frequent.

The year passed and summer came. On a certain evening in August, a small party of young men and ladies were walking through the park near West Fourth Street, attracting no little notice from other passers-by. The men had clearly had too much to drink, as had a couple of the ladies; one of the men carried a bottle of wine as he walked tipsily along. They were not, however, common drunks, as could be discerned from their expensive clothes. They were apparently on their way home from the theater.

Singing and excited, they made a boisterous show as they walked along. After about a block, one of the girls and her companion, who was well more than half intoxicated, dropped a little behind the others. Before long they turned down a side street.

"This is not the way, Jim," she said in a tone of laughing protest.

"Oh, yesh it is. I know where'm goin'." And he caught her by the arm. "Jusht a nice place down here where we can stop and resht," he slurred as he staggered against her.

"I want to go home, Jim," protested the girl, her laughing tone changing to one of earnestness. "Father will be looking for me."

"Hang your father," he responded. "The ol' man won't know. Come on, I tell you." He tried to put his arm about her waist.

The girl was now thoroughly frightened. "Stop—please, Jim."

"Whash the matter m' dear?" stammered her drunken escort. "I'll take care you all right—the ol' man will never know." Again he clutched her arm.

At last realizing her danger, the girl gave the drunken man a push, which sent him tumbling into the gutter, where cursing fiercely he struggled to regain his feet. The frightened girl, without pausing to see his condition and hardly hearing his calls and threats, fled down the street. When her companion had at last managed to stagger to the sidewalk and was able to look around by clinging to the fence, he could see no sign of her. He called two or three times, and then swearing vilely, started in pursuit, reeling from side to side as he struggled to keep his feet under his spinning head. The terrified girl ran on and on, paying no heed to her direction; and as she turned corner after corner, her only thought was to escape from her drunken and enraged escort.

Meanwhile, Dick Falkner was making his way slowly home after a delightful evening at the parsonage, where he had talked with Cameron on the veranda until it was quite late.

As he was walking leisurely along through the quiet streets, past the dark houses, enjoying the coolness of the evening and thinking of the things he and Cameron had been discussing, his musings were suddenly interrupted by a strange sound. The cry seemed to come from inside a half-finished house on North Catalpa Street near the railroad.

He paused a moment and listened.

Surely he was not mistaken . . . there it was again! The sound of someone sobbing.

He stepped cautiously closer. Peering into the shadow, he saw a figure crouching behind a pile of lumber. It was a woman.

"I beg your pardon, but can I be of any help to you?" he asked.

She started to her feet with a little cry.

"Don't be frightened," Dick said calmly. "I am a gentleman. I won't hurt you. Come, let me help." Stepping into the shadow, he extended his hand and gently led her out toward the light, where she stood trembling before him. "Tell me what—Oh, no!—Amy! What are you doing here, Miss Goodrich?"

"Oh, Mr. Falkner," sobbed the poor girl, almost beside herself with fear. "Don't let that man come near me. I want to go home. Oh, please, take me home."

"There," said Dick, controlling himself and speaking in a steady, matter-of-fact tone. "Of course I'll see you home. Take my arm. You needn't be afraid. You know I'll protect you."

Calmed by his voice and manner, the girl ceased her sobbing and walked quietly down the street by his side.

Dick's mind was in a whirl. How could she possibly have come to be here at such an hour? Who was she afraid of? By her dress she had been to a party or social event of some kind. But as they walked on together he voiced none of his questions, and no word was spoken.

"Oh no!" exclaimed Amy as they turned east on Sixth Street, "there he is again! Oh, Mr. Falkner, what shall I do? Let me go." She turned to run once more.

Dick laid his hand on her arm. "Miss Goodrich, don't you know you are safe with me? Be calm and tell me why you are afraid."

Something in his touch brought Amy to herself again. "Do you see that man standing there by the light?" she whispered, pointing to a figure leaning against a telephone pole.

"Yes, I see him," answered Dick. "But he won't hurt you."

"Oh, but you don't understand. I ran away from him. He is

drunk and threatened me!" she explained excitedly.

Dick's form straightened and his face grew hard and cold. "Ran away from him? Do you mean that fellow tried to hurt you, Miss Goodrich?"

"I—I—was with him—and—he—frightened me . . ." faltered Amy. "Let's go back the other way."

But they were too late.

Whitley had seen them, and now with uncertain steps he approached. "Oh, here you are," he said, his mind having cleared somewhat. "I thought I'd find you, my beauty."

Dick whispered to Amy in a tone that compelled obedience, "Stand right where you are. Don't move. You might just watch that star over there." He deftly turned her so that she was facing away from the drunkard. "You see, isn't it a beautiful one?"

Then with three long steps, he placed himself in the way of the alcohol-benumbed man.

"Who are you?" asked the fellow with an oath.

"None of your business," replied Dick curtly. "I'm that girl's friend. And as such, I ask you to move to the other side of the street."

"Ho, I know you now!" cried the other. "You're that bum printer of Udell's. Get outta my way! That girl's a lady and I'm a gentleman. Furthermore, I am her escort for the evening, and she doesn't go in for tramps. I'll see her home myself."

Dick spoke again. "You may be a gentleman, but you are in no condition to see anybody home. I'll tell you just once more—cross to the other side of the street."

The fellow's only answer was another string of vile oaths.

Fearing for Dick's safety, Amy turned just in time to see a revolver glisten in the light of the electric lamp. But before Whitley had a chance to aim it, Dick's fist crashed forward. The owner of the gun rolled senseless into the gutter.

"Miss Goodrich, I told you to watch that star." Dick's voice was calm, with just a suggestion of mild reproach.

"I was so worried when I heard him cursing you. Oh, Mr. Falkner, have you killed him?"

"No, nothing of the kind. Come." He led her quickly away from the place where the self-styled gentleman lay. "Just a moment," he said, then turned back and briefly examined the fallen man. "He'll have a sore head for a few days, that's all. I'll send a cab to pick him up when we get downtown."

"Mr. Falkner," Amy began after they had walked some distance in silence, "I don't know what you think of finding me here at this hour, but I don't want you to judge me worse than I am."

She then told him the whole story.

"Oh, what must you think of me?" she exclaimed when she was finished, nearly breaking down again.

"I think just as I always have," Dick replied simply, "that you are my friend and someone who means a great deal to me." Then to occupy her mind, he told her of the work the Young People's Society was doing and how they missed her.

"But don't you find such things rather tiresome, you know?" she asked. "There's not much life in those meetings, it seems to me. I wonder now how I ever stood them."

"You are very busy then?" Dick questioned, hiding the pain her words caused him.

"Oh yes, with our bridge club, box parties, dances and dinners, I'm so tired when Sunday comes I just want to sleep all day," replied Amy. "One must look after social duties, you know—that is, if you want to be somebody. And our set is such a jolly crowd that there's always something going on."

Dick remained silent, thinking to himself, *Can it be possible that this is the same girl who was such a worker in the church?*

But the moment the question came to him, he reflected on the great changes in his own life in the same period of time, a change fully as great, though in another direction. "It doesn't take long to go either way if one only has help enough," he said, half aloud.

"What are you saying, Mr. Falkner?" asked Amy.

"It's not far home now," answered Dick, and they fell into silence again.

As they neared the large Goodrich home, Amy clasped Dick's arm with both her hands. "Mr. Falkner," she begged, "promise me that you will never speak to a living soul about this evening."

Dick looked her straight in the eyes. "I am a gentleman, Miss Goodrich," was all he said.

As they reached the steps of the house, she held out her hand.

"I thank you for your kindness," she said, "—and please don't think of me too harshly. I know I am not the same young girl I was a year ago, but I—do you remember our talk at the printing office?"

"Every word."

"Well, has my prophecy come true?"

"About my preaching? No, not yet."

Amy was silent a moment, then spoke again. "Do you—really—value my friendship, as you said a while ago?" she asked.

Dick hesitated.

"The truth, please," she pressed. "I want to know."

"Miss Goodrich," Dick began, "I don't know how I can make you understand." He paused a moment, thinking, then continued. "You know my whole life has changed in the last year."

"Yes," she replied.

"But my feelings toward you can never change. I value your friendship. More than that, I value you as the person I once knew, and the person you are meant to be, for I know that your present life does not—cannot—satisfy you, and that you are untrue to your best self in living it."

Amy drew herself up haughtily. "Indeed, you are fast becoming a very proficient preacher," she retorted coldly.

"Wait a moment, please," Dick said hurriedly. "You urged me to tell the truth. I desire your friendship because I know the beautiful life you could live and because you—you—could help me—" His voice broke.

Amy held out her hand again.

"Forgive me, please," she murmured. "You are a true friend, and I shall never forget you. Oh, Mr. Falkner, pray for me before it is too late. Good night."

She turned and went quickly inside, unaware that her brother Frank was coming up the walk.

Young Goodrich stopped short when he saw Dick, then sprang up the steps and into the house just in time to see his sister disappear up the stairway toward her room.

CHAPTER TWENTY-TWO

AMY'S FLIGHT

The next day Frank Goodrich had a long interview with his father, which resulted in Adam calling his daughter into his library that evening.

Without any preface, he began. "I understand, Amy, that you have disobeyed my express command with regard to that tramp printer," he admonished angrily, "and that you have been with him again, and late at night besides. Now I have simply to tell you that you must choose between him and your home. I will *not* have a child of mine keeping such company. You must either give him up or go."

"But, Father, you do not know the circumstances or you would not say such a thing," Amy protested.

"No circumstances can excuse your conduct! I know you were with him, and that is enough."

"I did not disobey you, Father. You don't understand. I was in Mr. Falkner's company only by accident, and—"

"Stop. Don't add a lie to your conduct. I understand quite enough," interrupted Adam, beside himself with rage. "Your own brother saw you bidding him an affectionate good night at one o'clock on my doorstep. Such things do not happen by accident. I wonder how you can dare look me in the face after roaming the streets at that time of night with such a disreputable character!"

"Father, I tell you, you are mistaken," insisted Amy, almost in tears. "Won't you please let me explain?"

But the angry man only replied. "No explanation can be made. Frank himself saw you and that's enough. No excuse can justify such conduct. I have only to repeat that I will not own you as my daughter if you persist in keeping such company."

Amy tried to speak again, but he interrupted her.

"Silence!" he shouted. "I don't want to hear a word from you. Go to your room!"

But the woman in his daughter asserted herself. There were no tears this time as she said, in a respectful but firm voice, "Father, you *shall* hear me. I am not guilty of what you are accusing me of. I was in other company—company of your own choosing; and to save myself from insult, and possible injury, I was forced to appeal to Mr. Falkner for help, and he brought me safely home. He is far more a gentleman than the man I was with, even though my original escort is welcome at this home and Mr. Falkner is not. I—"

Goodrich turned fairly green with rage.

"You ungrateful, disobedient girl! How dare you say that this miserable vagabond is a fit associate for you and more worthy than the guests of my house! You cannot deceive me and clear yourself by some trumped-up lie of his teaching. You may have your tramp, but don't call me father. You are no daughter of mine!"

He turned and strode passionately from the room.

It is astonishing how little the proud man knew of the real nature of his child, a nature that rightfully understood and influenced was capable of any sacrifice or hardship for the one she loved, but misunderstood or falsely condemned was just as capable of reckless folly or despair. A nature that would never prove false to a trust, but if unjustly suspected would turn to the very thing of which it stood accused.

The next morning Amy did not appear at breakfast.

The mother went to her daughter's room, while Mr. Goodrich,

impatient at the delay, stood with angry eyes awaiting their appearance.

Frank came in.

"Good morning, Father," he said, glancing around with an amused expression of surprise. "Where are Amy and Mother? I thought I heard the bell for breakfast."

Adam grunted some reply and the son picked up a week-old newspaper and pretended to be deeply interested.

Suddenly a piercing scream reached their ears, and a sound as of someone falling. With an exclamation of alarm, Adam Goodrich, followed by his son, hurried from the dining room and ran upstairs.

The door of Amy's room was open, and just inside, prone upon the floor, lay Mrs. Goodrich, holding in her hand a piece of paper. With the help of his son, Adam lifted his wife and laid her upon the bed, which they noticed had not been occupied during the night. For an instant the two stood looking into each other's faces without a word, and then the older man said, "We must take care of Mother first. Call Dr. Gleason."

Under the advice of the physician, who came immediately in answer to Frank's telephone call, Mrs. Goodrich was carried to her own room, and in a short time regained consciousness. But she instantly fell to moaning and sobbing. "Oh, Amy—Amy—my poor child—my baby girl—what have you done? I never thought you would do a thing like this! Oh, my beautiful girl—come back—come back—"

And then when she became calmer, they told her what she already knew, that the daughter's room was undisturbed, and that a note addressed only to the mother had been found on the dressing table containing the simplest of farewell messages.

"There, there, wife, she's gone," Adam consoled, clumsily trying to soothe the mother's anguish, but finding that a tongue long accustomed to expressions of haughty pride and bigotry could but poorly lend itself to softer words of comfort. "There, there, don't cry, let her go. That scoundrel printer is at the bottom of it all. You must not make yourself sick over this."

Mrs. Goodrich, accustomed to obeying, with a great effort ceased the open expression of her grief.

"There can be no doubt but that she has gone off with that tramp," continued Adam. "I shall do what I can to find her and give her one more chance. If she acknowledges her fault and promises to do better, she may come home. If not, she shall never darken these doors again."

"Oh, please, Adam, don't say such a thing," lamented the mother. "Think of the poor child out on the streets alone. Perhaps you are mistaken."

"*What!*" shouted Goodrich. "Am I to understand that you take her part against me?"

"No, no," murmured the frightened woman.

"I tell you, there can be no mistake," he affirmed. "You saw them, Frank, did you not?"

"Yes, sir," answered the dutiful son.

"You hear that, Mrs. Goodrich? You will oblige me by not mentioning this matter again."

Hurriedly leaving the room, Adam went to his own private quarter, where, after he had locked the door, he paced back and forth. He fought back a host of emotions with which he was by no means intimately acquainted, as well as did battle against a rising sensation in the region of his eyes, a sensation he could in no wise properly interpret.

But in a few moments, while he made his preparations for going down the street to the store, thoughts of the curious faces he would be likely to meet aroused the old pride and hardened his heart again. So that when he left his home, not a trace of his worthier feelings showed on his cold, proper countenance—except that to the keen observer, he looked a little older perhaps, and a trifle less self-satisfied.

He spent his first hour at the store going over his correspondence, interviewing the head clerk, and issuing his orders for the day. Then taking his hat and cane, he left for Udell's printing office.

The boy was away on an errand, and George had stepped out

for a few moments, so that Dick was alone when Mr. Goodrich entered. Thinking that it was Udell who had returned, he did not look up from his work until he was startled by the angry voice of his visitor.

"Well, sir, I suppose you are satisfied at last! Where is my daughter?" demanded the red-faced businessman.

"Your daughter?" said Dick, glancing up. "I don't know. She is not at home?"

"Don't lie to me, you scoundrel!" shouted Adam, losing all control of himself. "You were with her last! You have been trying ever since you came here to worm your way into the society of your betters. Tell me what you have done with her!"

"Mr. Goodrich," Dick replied, forcing himself to remain calm, "it is true that I escorted your daughter home two nights ago, but—"

He hesitated. Should he explain how he had found Amy?

"—but," he went on slowly, "I left her safely at your door and have not seen her since." Then he asked, "Is she not at home?"

Adam only glared at him. "She did not sleep at home last night," he growled through clenched teeth.

For an instant Dick's voice failed him. "Then she must be staying with some friend," he suggested after a moment. "Surely there is no need for alarm."

"I tell you, she's gone!" cried the other furiously. "She left a letter. You are to blame for this!"

He shook his fist at the young man.

"If you have hidden her anywhere, I'll have your life, you miserable, low-down vagabond. You have schemed and schemed until you have succeeded in stealing her heart from her home, and in disgracing me."

"Adam Goodrich, you are completely mistaken," protested Dick, pale with mingled anxiety for Amy, yet angry that he should be thus accused. "Do you understand me? What you say is—is— nothing short of a lie. In fact, your whole life is a lie."

He spoke in a low tone, but there was something underlying the quiet of his voice and manner that contrasted strangely with the loud bluster of the older man. This was a new experience for

Adam, and the awful words resounding in his shocked consciousness almost caused him to tremble. Something in the manly face of the one who uttered this unthinkable pronouncement against him could not help but startle and frighten him.

"You have forced your daughter to drop her church work," continued Dick. "You have goaded her into the society of people whose only claim to respectability is their wealth and perhaps their standing in the church but not the way they live their lives. You value your position in the world more than your daughter's character. And you yourself are to blame for this. I tell you again, sir, you are grievously in error, both about your daughter and me. I do not know where your daughter is, but if she is on the earth I will find her and bring her back to your home. Not for your sake, but for hers. Now go. The very air is foul with the hypocrisy of your so-called love for your daughter, which is no love at all."

"Whew!" whistled George Udell a moment later as he stepped into the shop, having passed the proprietor of the local hardware store just outside the door, "what's the matter with him! He looks like he has been in a boiler explosion."

His expression immediately changed when Dick told him of the interview and apologized for driving a good customer from the office.

"Good customer!" repeated Udell with a laugh. "After what he's done to his daughter? Good customer, indeed! I say you'd better apologize for not throwing him into the street!"

For many days thereafter Dick searched for Amy, bringing to bear all his painfully acquired knowledge of life and the crooked ways of the world. Though unknown to Mr. Goodrich, the detective Dick employed was an old companion, and to him only did he confide the full story of Amy's experience the night he found her hiding from Whitley.

The only fact they could learn was that she had boarded the twelve-forty Kansas City Southern for Jonesville, and that a woman answering to her description had stopped there until nearly noon the next day, when she was seen in conversation with a man whose face was badly bruised on the under left side of the chin.

The two had taken the same train east on the "Frisco."

They found also that her erstwhile companion Jim Whitley had hurriedly left Boyd City on the morning "Frisco" to Jonesville and that he had not returned, nor could his whereabouts be discovered. It was given out to the public, among the society items of the newspaper, that Whitley had suddenly been called to the bedside of a sick friend.

Gradually interest on the part of the townspeople subsided, and the detective returned to other matters demanding his attention. Adam Goodrich refused to talk of the matter, and gave no sign of sorrow, other than an added sternness in his manner. But the mother's health was broken. And Frank, declaring that he could not stand the disgrace, went for a long visit to a friend in a neighboring city.

Finally Dick himself was forced to give up the search. But though baffled for a time, he declared to Udell and his pastor that he would yet bring Amy home as he had promised her father. And while he went about his work as usual, it was with a heavy heart and a look on his face that caused his friends who knew him best to be concerned for him.

CHAPTER TWENTY-THREE

WHAT THE POUCH REVEALED

The summer passed and again the catalpa trees shed their broad leaves, while the prairie grass took on the reddish brown of fall.

One day Jim Whitley unexpectedly returned to Boyd City, and Dick by chance encountered him at the post office. Not a word passed between them, but an hour later a note was put into Whitley's hand by a ragged shoeshine boy.

"George," said Dick later that afternoon as they were locking up, "if you don't mind, I'd like to sleep in my old bed in the office tonight."

Udell looked at his employee in astonishment. "What in the world?" he began.

"I can't explain now," Dick went on, "but please let me have my way and say nothing about it to anyone, not even to Clara."

"Why sure," George agreed heartily. He paused, then in an anxious tone added, "Dick, I know it's hard to change your way of life, and you've been putting up a great fight. But you're not going to let it go now, are you, after you've come so far?"

"No, no, it's nothing like that," laughed Dick. But the smile lasted only a brief moment. "I'll explain someday," he promised, and something in his face assured his friend that whatever it was that prompted his strange request, Dick was still master of himself.

Late that night, as Udell passed the office on his way home after spending the evening with Clara Wilson, he was surprised to see Jim Whitley entering the building. He stood watching for a moment, then fearing possible danger to Dick, he ran lightly toward the door. But as he reached out his hand to lay on the latch, he heard a key turn in the lock and his friend's voice saying, "I thought you would come."

George paused, and then with a shrug of his shoulder and an odd smile on his rugged face, he turned and went softly off down the street again.

Dick and his visitor faced each other in the dimly lighted office.

"Well," snapped Whitley, swearing hatefully, "what do you want?"

"I want you to take your hand out of your pocket first," flashed Dick. "That gun won't help you tonight," and with a quick motion of his host's hand, Whitley found a revolver pointing directly at his heart. He instantly granted the request and pulled out both hands where Dick could see them.

"Now walk into the other room," commanded Dick.

They passed into the stockroom, which was well lighted. The windows were covered with heavy paper. The long table was cleared and moved out from its place near the wall.

Dick closed the door and pointed to the table. "Lay your gun there," he said. "And be careful about it," he added as Whitley drew out the revolver.

Whitley glanced at the determined eyes and steady hand of his master, then sullenly obeyed.

"Now sit down," demanded Dick.

Crossing the room, Whitley seated himself in the chair indicated, which placed him in the full glare of the light. Dick took the other chair facing him, with the long table between them. He placed his weapon beside that of Whitley, within easy reach of his hand, then rested his elbows on the table and looked long and steadily at the man before him.

Whitley grew uneasy under the unrelenting scrutiny.

"Well," he said at last, when he could bear the silence no longer. "I hope you like my looks."

"Your figure is somewhat heavier, but shaving off your beard has made you appear some years younger," replied Dick dryly.

The other jumped to his feet.

"Don't be so nervous," Dick warned softly, resting his hand on one of the revolvers. "Stay in your seat please."

"I never wore a beard," the man retorted, dropping back in his chair. "You are mistaken."

"Then how did you know the meaning of my note, and why did you answer it in person?" asked Dick. "If you were not the right man, you should have sent the man who was."

Whitley realized he had betrayed himself, but made one more effort.

"I came out of curiosity," he muttered.

Dick laughed—a laugh that was not good to hear.

"I can easily satisfy you," he said. "Permit me to tell you a little story. You will soon know that you are not the only young man to have traveled at some length, though some travel in search of employment, while others travel merely to exercise their leisure, which, as you will see, can never be the best of motives."

Whitley's only response was a disinterested grunt.

"The story commences in a little manufacturing town a few miles from Liverpool, England, just four years ago today," Dick began. Beneath the unwavering eyes of the man leaning on the table, Whitley's face suddenly grew ghastly white and he shifted uncomfortably in his chair. "An old man and his wife, with their two orphaned grandsons, lived in a little cottage on the outskirts of the town. The older of the boys was a strong man of twenty, the other a sickly lad of eight. The old people earned a slender income by cultivating small fruits. This was helped by the wages of the older brother, who was a machinist in one of the big factories. They were a quiet and unpretentious little family, devout Christians, and very much attached to one another.

"One afternoon a wealthy American, who was staying at a large resort a few miles from the village, hired a carriage and went for a drive along the road leading past their home. As he was passing, the little boy, who was playing just outside the yard, unintentionally frightened the horses and they shied quickly. At the same moment, the American's silk hat fell in the dust. The driver stopped the team, and the frightened lad picked up the hat and ran with it toward the carriage, stammering an apology for what he had done.

"Instead of accepting the boy's excuse, the man, beside himself with anger and slightly under the influence of wine, sprang from the carriage, seized the lad, and began kicking him brutally.

"The grandfather, who was working in his garden, saw the incident and hurried as fast as he could to the rescue of the small boy. At the same time the hired driver jumped from his seat to protect the child, but before they could reach the spot, the boy was lying bruised and senseless in the dust.

"The old man rushed at the bearded American in impotent rage, and the driver, fearing for the grandfather's safety, caught him by the arm and tried to separate them, saying, 'You look after the boy. Let me settle with him.'

"But the old man, who was deaf and could not understand, mistakenly thought that the driver, also an American, was assisting his employer. In truth, the two men did not even know each other. In the struggle, the American suddenly drew a knife, and in spite of the driver's effort to prevent it, struck twice at his feeble opponent, who fell back into the arms of his would-be protector.

"It so happened that the older brother was just getting home from work, and now rushed upon the scene. The American leaped into the carriage and snatched up the reins. The young machinist sprang after him, and as he caught hold of the seat in his attempt to climb in, the knife flashed again, cutting a long gash in his arm and hand and severing the little finger. With the other hand, he caught the wrist of the American, but a heavy blow in the face knocked him beneath the wheels, and the horses dashed away down the road.

"The driver was bending over the old man, trying to stop the flow of blood when several workmen, attracted by the cries of the helpless grandmother, who had witnessed the scene from the porch, came running up. ' 'E's one of 'em—'e's one of 'em!' cried the old lady. ' 'E 'eld my man while t'other 'it 'im.'

"The driver perceived at once the mistake the woman was making and realized his danger. He ran down the street and escaped as the workmen carried the body of the old man into the house. Two days later, the driver read in a Liverpool paper that both the grandfather and boy were dead, and that the dying statement of the old man and the testimony of the grandmother and the brother was that both the strangers were guilty.

"How the wealthy American made his escape you know best. The driver shipped aboard a vessel bound for Australia, and later made his way home to the United States."

When Dick had finished his story, Whitley's face was drawn and haggard. He leaped to his feet, but Dick's revolver motioned him back. "What fiend told you all this?" he gasped hoarsely. "Who are you?"

"I am the driver," replied Dick coolly.

Whitley sank back in his chair. Then suddenly he broke into a harsh laugh.

"You are a crazy fool. Who would believe you? You have no proof!"

"There is another chapter to my story," replied Dick calmly. "Less than a year after the tragedy, the invalid grandmother died, and the young machinist was free to enter upon the great work of his life: the bringing to justice of his little brother's murderer, or, as *he* believed, murderers. He could find no clue as to the identity of the obscure driver of the carriage, but with the wealthy American it was different, and he succeeded at last in tracing him to his home in this city. Unfortunately, though, the long search had left the young man without means, and he arrived in Boyd City in a penniless and starving condition, the night of the great storm winter before last. You are no doubt familiar with the finding of his body on the church steps."

Again Whitley sprang to his feet and with an awful oath exclaimed, "How do you know all this?"

Dick drew forth a long leather pocketbook, opened it, and took out a package of papers, which he laid on the table between the two revolvers. "There is the story, written by his own hand, together with the testimony of his grandfather and grandmother, his own sworn statement, and all the evidence he had so carefully gathered."

Whitley sprang forward. But before he could cross the room, both revolvers were aimed directly at his chest.

"Stop!" cried Dick. The voice was calm and steady, but full of deadly menace.

Whitley crouched like an animal at bay. The hands that held the weapons never trembled; the gray eyes looking at him from above the shining barrels never wavered. Slowly Whitley drew back.

"Name your price," he said sullenly. "I am a wealthy man."

"You do not have money enough to pay my price," replied Dick in a firm voice.

Whitley sank back in his seat. "You blamed fool, put down those guns and tell me what you want!"

"I want to know where you left Miss Goodrich."

"And if I refuse to tell?"

Dick laid a pair of handcuffs on the table.

A cunning gleam crept into Whitley's eyes. "You'll put them on yourself at the same time. The evidence is just as strong against you."

"If it were not, I would have turned you over to the law long ago," retorted Dick.

"But you idiot!" yelled Whitley; "they'll hang you."

"That won't save you, and you'll answer to God for the murder," threatened Dick.

"You'd have to kill me to put those cuffs on me."

"Be that as it may," Dick replied calmly.

"You wouldn't dare do it. You haven't the guts!"

"We shall see. In the meantime, I am innocent; you are the coward."

Whitley paused a moment, revolved the situation in his mind once more, and finally, with a look of resolution on his face, he seemed to give up the fight. He told how he had met Amy in

Jonesville and had taken her east to Buffalo, where he had left her just before returning to Boyd City.

"Did you marry her?" asked Dick.

"I am not looking for a wife," replied Whitley with a shrug of his shoulders.

"There was no ceremony of any kind?" persisted Dick.

"None was necessary. I did not harm her."

"Why did you leave so soon?"

"I had business of importance at home," Whitley sneered.

Dick asked no further questions. Slowly he rose to his feet, his hands clinching and unclinching in agitation. Cautiously he reached out and picked up the two guns from the table. Whitley sat motionless at the far end, his face livid with fear. For a full minute no word was spoken as Dick stood with the weapons in his hand. At length he spoke.

"Jim Whitley," he said, his voice strangely quiet, "if I were not a Christian, I doubt you would live past this night." He paused, then added, "Now go, get out of here!"

Slowly Whitley rose from his chair and left the room. Dick followed him, watched him leave the building and walk down the sidewalk. Then he returned, locked the door again, and threw himself on the bed, where he wept as only a strong man can, with great sobs, until, utterly exhausted, he fell into a stupor, where George Udell found him the next morning.

Dick told his employer the whole story, and took the first train east.

That same day, Whitley left the city.

CHAPTER TWENTY-FOUR

A STIRRING OF THE MINISTERS

The matter of Amy's strange disappearance came up at the next meeting of the Ministerial Association, which led to a general discussion of the low standard of morality in Boyd City.

Old Father Beason stated, "Brethren, I tell you things are getting worse, not better. And what are we doing? I don't believe one thing. It costs all we can scrape and dig just to keep the churches running, and so far as I know, only Brother Cameron here has even attempted any aggressive outreach work. I think it's high time we put our heads together to formulate some plan that would stir this town and save our boys and girls from the snares that are open to them from every side in the world."

"What we need is something like a YMCA," suggested Hugh Cockrell.

"That's all right," said big Brother Howell. "The association's a good thing. I'd like to see one started here. But a dozen YMCA's won't meet the needs of this place. We need something that will really reach out to the fallen and degraded men and women, not merely those who could afford to pay to come."

Father Beason nodded emphatic approval.

"I don't know how you plan to raise the money for all this," remarked the Rev. Jeremiah Wilks. "I'm doing all I can now trying to clear off the debt on our organ, and I've got to raise our benevolence yet. And besides this, my own salary is behind. I'm doing more work than any three preachers in the city. I tell you, the men who have got the money are going to hang on to it. I met Mr. Richmond on the street yesterday. He's got lots of money, you know, so I asked him for a donation. He just looked at me with a peculiar look on his face and then said, 'I always like to know what returns I may expect for the money I invest. I'm no church member and I have no money to throw away.' But when I told him about the organ and my salary, he just laughed. 'When you can show me that my money is doing some actual good among the poor people in this city,' he stated, 'then come to me and I'll invest. Until then, I'll keep my money, for I think I can make better use of it than paying off your organ, and you can keep your prayers.' "

The Rev. Jeremiah sat down with an air of mingled triumph and suffering, as if to say, "See how gladly I bear persecution for the Lord."

"I understand that Mr. Richmond came to Cameron's church, though," Howell remarked.

"Yes," replied Cameron. "He gave one hundred dollars unsolicited for the ministry of our house for the unemployed, and promised more if it were needed."

There was silence for a moment; then the chairman asked, "Brother Cameron, would you mind telling us a little more about how your work is conducted? I for one would like to know more about it. Perhaps there are similar programs the rest of us could work toward. What would you suggest we do?"

"As far as our work goes, both with the house and the reading room at the church, we have hardly begun to touch the need yet," replied Cameron. "There are so many people in unfortunate circumstances. There is room for every church in town to be involved. I am convinced that a united effort of—"

"Brethren," interrupted the Rev. Dr. Frederick Hartzel, "I must beg that we refrain from going any further in this useless discussion. My time is altogether too valuable to waste in such foolish talk as this. I endeavor to put some thought into *my* sermons, and I cannot take this valuable time from my studies. If the association persists in taking up the time of the meetings with such subjects, instead of discussing some of the recent theological themes that are attracting the attention of the clergy everywhere, I will be forced to change my attendance pattern to optional at best. These notions of uneducated young men may be all right for some, but you can't expect such learned men as I to listen to them. I move that we adjourn."

"Brother Cameron has the floor and I think the rest of the brothers would like to hear him out," suggested the chairman.

"Brother Chairman," began Cameron calmly before others could speak, for he saw the light of righteous indignation creeping into the eyes of some, and the fight of intractableness on the faces of others; and above all things he wished to avoid a bitter argument in the cause of Christ. "If any of the brethren wish to talk with me about our work," he went on, "they know they are always welcome at my home. I will be glad, even eager, to discuss any plan for reaching the lost for whom our Savior died. I have some ideas that I think might be useful for the rest of your churches. Unfortunately, I do not think this is the best place to present them. Therefore, I second Rev. Hartzel's motion to adjourn."

And the meeting was dismissed with prayer as usual, that God would fill their hearts with love, and help them to do their Master's work as He would have it done, and that many souls might be added to their number.

That evening, lost in troubled thought, the young pastor of the Jerusalem Church sat alone in front of the fire in his little study. At length his wife came in. "James," she said, "it's time you're going to bed."

He nodded, but she knew what the look in his face meant. He had many things to wrestle through in his mind.

Finally, well after midnight, with the fire burning low, he made his way to his room, where he fell asleep as a man tired out from a hard day's work.

All the next day he was silent and moody, saying but little, and the following evening, he sat once more alone in his study, thinking, thinking, thinking, until again the fire went out and he was cold.

Then the next afternoon, the reservoir of his thoughts overflowed its bounds and he began to speak.

"It's the do-nothing policy of the church," he said as he entered the kitchen and put his arm about his wife where she stood at the table busy with her baking. "That's why so many people go wrong—because of the kind of so-called Christians who think more of their social position than they do the souls of their children or the purity of their characters."

"James, you shouldn't say such things."

"But you know it's true."

"Are you thinking of Amy?"

"Of course Amy, poor girl."

"Mr. Goodrich might be able to look at these things as you do perhaps if his own background were different. We must remember his early training."

"Early training, bosh," answered the minister. "*Lack* of early training would be more like it. I tell you, the true man, whether he's a Christian or not, values character more than position and appearance. Background and training give no man or woman an excuse to behave selfishly, or to hurt others."

"I have the feeling an impromptu sermon is coming on," smiled his wife, with a twinkle in her eye.

"I can't help it," he replied excitedly. "It's the truth. And the ministers in this city are the worst of it. They not only allow such mistaken priorities to flourish in their churches, they actually lead people into such falsehood by their own misrepresentation of the true gospel message. If the ministers in this city cared half as much for the salvation of souls and the living out of the teaching of Christ as they do for their own little theories and doctrines and personally derived insights into this or that scripture, our congregations would not be filled with churchified hypocrites, putting on their religion like their Sunday suit of clothes, then taking it off again once services are past. You can walk down Fourth Street or East

Third and see the results—egotism, self-righteousness, and man-made doctrines flowing out of the pulpit, while saloons and brothels, pain and loneliness fill the streets; church doors closed over a mawkish sentimentality, while men and women are dying without shelter and without God."

By now the once silent, thoughtful young man had become again the Rev. James Cameron, tramping up and down the kitchen, speaking with all the excitement of a political spellbinder.

"Truly we need a preacher," he went on, "with a wilderness training like John the Baptist who will show us the way of the Lord, rather than a thousand theological, hothouse posies, who will show us only the opinions of the authorities while they read to us from the infallible Matthew Henry!"

None of his fellow clergymen took up his offer to visit his home and discuss further what work might be done in Boyd City. But James Cameron remained a good deal worked up by the ministerial meeting and his subsequent thought and talk with his wife. He cared not in the least for the Rev. Dr. Hartzel, D.D.'s opinion of himself. He did care, however, for the work itself, and his heart burned within him to see that more be done.

Thus, with his heart full and his mind stirred, when the following Sunday came and he rose to take his place behind the pulpit, the subject of his sermon was what he called "Applied Christianity."

The growth of Cameron's reputation through the town had, over the course of the past year, caused attendance to gradually increase, and on this particular day the church was crowded with an interesting mix of young men and woman, business and professional persons, and not a few from the ranks of the poor and unemployed who had been helped through one of the church's ministries.

Still wrought up, Cameron's face was aglow as he introduced his subject by showing the purpose and duty of the church: that it was not a social club, not a place to have fellowship with other Christians, not simply a place to see and be seen, not a musical organization nor talent show, not a forum for different kinds of entertainment, and not an intellectual greenhouse or battlefield.

It was instead, he said, a body of believers whose sole purpose was to nurture and build Christlike characters. The church had no excuse for existing at all unless it preached Christ's gospel, did His work, and cultivated attitudes and practical behavior in all of its members that reflected the attitudes and perspectives and actions of Jesus Christ. Our responsibility, he went on, is to be men and women who are *like* Jesus—like Him in how we think, in our behavior toward others, in our attitudes, in how we order our lives, how we run our businesses, in how we treat our friends and husbands and wives and employees and employers, and in the compassion we show to those less fortunate whom God brings into our path. *That*, and nothing else, is what the church is to be about.

"Is the church doing this? Is that what is on our minds when we walk through these doors on Sundays? Are we asking ourselves: 'How can I be more like Jesus today, in the next five minutes, toward the next person who crosses my path?' Is that what we are trying to accomplish by being part of this congregation?

"I ask again: Is the church doing this? Look around you. Look at all the magnificent buildings in this town, the expensive organs, the talented choirs, the large-salaried preachers, the steeples, the stained-glass windows. Look at the efforts we expend to put on a wonderful 'show' every Sunday, and the efforts we preachers expend during the week devising sermons that demonstrate our keen intellectual prowess and our superb insight into the Scriptures. And all the while, what is this effort accomplishing? What difference does it all make when in this same city hundreds and thousands of men and women are on their way to eternal ruin, and in our well-dressed, attentive, self-satisfied congregations hundreds and thousands of pious church members are no closer to reflecting the character of Jesus Christ than they were the day they joined the church? So I ask again: What is all our effort accomplishing?"

He went on to show that the reason why more people were not Christians and why the church felt it so often had to struggle to make inroads in the community was that Christianity had become, not a work and a way of life and a wonderful behavior-modifying reality, but a mere belief. It had grown to be, not a *life*, but a sentiment. "The church," he said, "must prove herself by her works as did Christ, and her work must be the same as Christ's. But Jesus never sang a solo, never put on a Sunday-school program, never funded a drive, never tried to intellectually dissect the Scriptures. The church has no impact in the world because it exists to make its members feel good once a week rather than to do the work of Christ. Is it any wonder the world is hardly listening?"

His sermon caused a great deal of talk throughout the town. He was roundly scored by a number of his brethren in the ministry, and accused of all sorts of sensationalism. The young preacher bore it all without a word of response, except to say, "I am glad if I can even stir you up enough so that you will condemn me, though I cannot help but think that if you would spend the same energy in trying to remedy the evils of the world, you would do more for Christ and your fellowmen."

To his wife he confided, "I am convinced that if we Christians are ever to have a major impact in helping people, it will come from the laity and not from the pastorate. I think the world really wants to believe in Jesus, but has lost confidence in the church."

"Well," replied his wife, "I think I know one preacher who will have a hand in it anyway."

"You know," mused Cameron, "I am scheduled to speak next month at a joint meeting of the youth and young adult groups of the various churches."

"Yes, I remember," she said.

"Well, I just have half a mind to speak out that night and see what might come of it! I think the practicality of what we have done with our house and the reading room is being noticed around Boyd City. People are realizing the value of such work. The time is ripe for larger things!"

It was a custom of the Young People's Societies and other young adult groups of the churches of the city to meet for a joint service every two months, at which time one of the pastors was invited to speak on some topic of particular interest to young Christians. This happened to be Cameron's turn to deliver the address, and the subject that had been given him was "Reaching the Masses." The young pastor was a favorite generally, in spite of his standing with the theologians; so when it was announced that he would speak, and that the subject was one upon which he was known to have strong ideas, the public looked forward to the meeting with more than usual interest. When the time came, Zion Church, which was the largest in the city, was crowded to its utmost capacity, with many more interested persons than merely the members of the various young adult groups.

Cameron began by reading from the twenty-fifth chapter of Matthew: "Inasmuch as ye have done it unto one of the least of these my brethren, ye have done it unto me."

He followed the Scripture reading by saying that his talk was in no way meant to be a sermon. He felt himself free to give his thoughts more liberty perhaps than he would if delivering a pulpit discourse, and that he would discuss the question not simply from the standpoint of Christianity, but from that of good citizenship, and of the best interests of the people as well.

The audience settled itself at these words, and waited.

Rev. Cameron then laid down the proposition that the question of reaching the masses was not the responsibility of only those who called themselves Christians, but with all society, all business, all government—in fact, with all that touched mankind. He showed how the conditions of the least of these gave rise to bad conditions everywhere—from poverty to crime—and corrupted the physical, moral, and intellectual life of all men. Then he took his listeners from street to street in their own city, bidding them look upon the young men and women on the corners, in the saloons, and asked, without any reference to Christianity in any way, "What will be the legitimate fruit of all this? What influence are we throwing about our boys and girls, and upon what foundation are we building our social, business, and city life?"

Then turning to Christians, he reviewed the grand work that the church had done in the past in molding the lives of men and nations, and pleaded that she prove true to the past by rising to the present and meeting the problems of today. He called upon them in the name of their Master, to put their energies to work to find practical ways to carry out the example and words of Jesus. At the same time he urged that those standing outside the church with idle hands, content to criticize and condemn, examine themselves also. "I can see no difference," he said, "between an idle church member and a do-nothing man of the world. They both stand on the same plane, and that plane is the plane of death."

After an earnest appeal that the teaching of Jesus be applied, that the worth of souls be judged by the price paid on Calvary, and that all men, inside and outside the church, unite in common cause, he turned quickly to the chairman of the meeting and said, "I propose that each youth and young adult group in this union appoint a committee of three from their membership, and that each of these committees adds to itself one good businessman who believes in the practical teaching of Christ but is not a member of any church. After this has been done I suggest that the large joint committee made up of all the smaller ones meet in council for the purpose of formulating some plan to aid the needy of this city along the lines of our subject this evening."

At this strange and unexpected ending of Cameron's address, the audience sat astonished. Then, from all over the house, voices were heard murmuring approval of the plan.

Rev. Jeremiah Wilks was the first to speak. "I'm heartily in favor of the suggestion," he said. "It will get some of our moneyed men interested in the church, which will do them good. I've often told our people that something like this ought to be done, and I know the preachers of the city will be glad to take hold of the matter and help to push it along. I'll bring it before our Ministerial Association."

"But, Mr. Chairman," asked another gentleman when Wilks had resumed his seat, "is it the idea of Rev. Cameron that the movement be managed by the ministers?"

A painful hush fell over the audience.

The chairman turned to Cameron, who answered, "It is certainly not my idea that this matter be placed in the hands of the ministers. Whatever part they have in it must simply be as Christian citizens of this community, without regard for their profession."

The audience smiled. Rev. Dr. Frederick Hartzel was on his feet instantly.

"Ladies and gentlemen, I must protest," he said. "I do not doubt that your young brother here means well. But perhaps some of us with more experience, and with more mature thought, are better able to handle this great question. Such a plan as he has proposed is preposterous. A committee without an ordained minister on it, thinking to start any movement in harmony with the teaching of Christ, is utter folly. It is a direct insult to the clergy, who, as you know, compose the finest body of men, intellectually and morally, in the country. I must insist that the regularly ordained ministers of the city be recognized on this committee."

Rev. Hugh Cockrell agreed with Hartzel, in a short speech, and then Uncle Bobbie Wicks rose out of his chair.

"I don't reckon there's much danger of Brother Hartzel's amendment going through, but I just want a word anyhow. To be sure, you all know me, and I'm a pretty good friend to preachers."

The audience laughed.

"I ain't got a thing in the world against them. To be sure, I reckon a preacher is as good as any other fellow, so long as he behaves himself. But seeing as how they've been trying for about two thousand years to fix this business, and ain't done nothing yet, I think it's a mighty good idea to give the poor fellows a rest, and let the Christians try it for a spell."

"You've got to recognize the church, sir!" cried Hartzel.

"Well, if we recognize Christ," Uncle Bobbie retorted, "the church will come out all right, I reckon."

Which sentiment so pleased the people that Cameron's suggestion was immediately adopted.

CHAPTER TWENTY-FIVE

THE TESTING OF AMY GOODRICH

On the night of her flight from Boyd City when Amy Goodrich went to her room after the scene with her bigoted father, she was filled with wounded pride, anger at his injustice, and reckless defiance at his demands.

Mrs. Goodrich had heard the harsh words and quickly followed her daughter, but Amy's door was locked. When she called softly for admittance, Amy only answered between her sobs, "No, Mama, please . . . go away. I want to be alone."

But the girl did not spend much time in weeping.

With a look of growing determination gradually coming over her tear-stained face, Amy caught up a daily paper lying where she had dropped it that morning. Carefully studying the railway schedule, she decided she just might make the night train to Jonesville.

Removing as far as possible the evidence of her grief, she changed her dress for a more simple and serviceable one, then gathered together a few necessary articles, and packed them, with some jewelry, in a small satchel. She had finished her simple preparations and was just writing the last word of her brief farewell message when Mrs. Goodrich came quietly to the door again.

Amy started to her feet in alarm when she heard the low knock, and then as she listened to her mother's voice softly calling her name, the hot tears filled her eyes once more, and she moved as though to destroy the note in her hand. But as she hesitated, her father's words came back: "You may have your tramp, but don't call me father. You are no daughter of mine!" The cruel ultimatum raised a like response in her heart, arresting her better impulse, forcing her to remain silent.

Mrs. Goodrich, when she received no answer to her call, thought her daughter was sleeping, and with a sigh of relief, went to her own room. A little later, the father came upstairs and retired. Then Frank returned home, and the trembling listener heard the servants locking up the house. When all was still, and her watch told her that it was a few minutes past midnight, she carefully opened the door, and with her satchel in hand, stole cautiously down the stairs, unlocked the door and slipped out of the house. Hurrying as fast as she could to Broadway, she found a cab and was driven to the depot on the east side.

As Amy stepped from the vehicle beneath the electric light and paused a moment to give the driver his fare, a man came out of a saloon on the corner nearby. It was Jim Whitley.

He recognized the girl instantly and sprang to one side, drew back into the shadow of the building, and waited until she went to the ticket office. Then going quickly to the open window of the waiting room, he heard her ask for a ticket to Jonesville. After the train had pulled in and he had watched her board, he went to the cab that had brought her to the station, and was driven home.

The next morning Whitley was the first to learn from Frank Goodrich of Amy's quarrel with her father, and the reason. Without a word of what he had seen, he made hurried preparations and followed her on the next train.

At Jonesville, with little delay, he made the rounds of the hotels and carefully examined the registers, but Amy's name was on none of them. Concluding that she must be at the home of some friend, he had placed his own name on the last book he examined, and had seated himself to think over the situation when he heard a bellboy say to the clerk, "That girl in number sixteen wants a 'Frisco' timetable."

Whitley lounged carelessly up to the counter and again glanced over the register. Number sixteen was occupied by a Miss Anderson. Catching the eye of the clerk, he placed his finger on the name and winked. "When did she get in?" he asked in a low tone, at the same time slipping a coin beneath the open page.

"On the two-thirty from the west, last night," the clerk replied, using the same cautious manner as he whirled the book toward himself and deftly transferred the coin to his own pocket, all without attracting the attention of the hotel's owner who stood not far off.

"I believe I'll go to my room and clean up," said Whitley a moment later.

"Show this gentleman to number fifteen," promptly called the clerk, and Whitley mounted the stairs, following the boy who had answered Miss Anderson's call.

When the boy had placed the heavy grip on the floor, he turned to see Whitley holding out a dollar bill.

"Did you get a look at the lady in sixteen when you went up with that timetable?" he asked.

" 'Course I did," replied the bellboy.

"Can you describe her?" Whitley continued.

"You bet, mister. She's a daisy too." And as he folded the bill and carefully placed it in his vest pocket, he gave an accurate description of Amy.

Whitley dismissed the boy and seated himself to watch, through the half-closed door, the room across the hall.

He had not long to wait. Amy stepped out into the corridor and started toward the stairway. In an instant Whitley was by her side. The girl gave a start of surprise and uttered a frightened exclamation as he said, "Don't be frightened, Miss Goodrich. I have very important news for you from home. Step into my parlor, please."

Too bewildered to do otherwise, she followed him.

"I have been searching for you all day," he said as he conducted her to a seat in the far corner of the empty room.

Amy tried to look indignant and started to reply, but he interrupted her.

"Wait a moment, please, Miss Goodrich, and hear me first. When your father discovered this morning that you had left home, he came at once to me and told me the whole story. I tried to explain to him that it was I, and not Falkner, who had been with you, but he would not listen. And in spite of my pleading, he declared that you should never enter his home again. I am sorry, but he is very angry and I fear will keep his word, for a time at least. He even accused me of telling falsehoods to shield you, and insisted that I should forget you forever and never mention your name in his hearing again. I learned at the depot that you had purchased a ticket to this city, so I took the first train, hoping to find you and offer you any assistance that might be in my power to give. A girl in your position needs a friend, for you cannot go home just now."

In spite of herself, Amy was touched by the words spoken with such seeming truth and earnestness, but her heart was filled with anger at her father, and her face was hard and set as she replied coldly, "I thank you, but you might have saved yourself the trouble. I have no wish to go home."

"Indeed, I do not see how you can feel differently under the circumstances," admitted Whitley with apparent reluctance. "But have you thought of the future? What can you do? You have never been dependent upon yourself. You know nothing of the world."

Amy's face grew white. Seeing his advantage, Whitley continued, drawing a dark picture of a young woman without friends or means of support. At last, as he talked, Amy began to cry. Then his voice grew tender. "Miss Goodrich . . . Amy—come to me. Be my wife. I have long loved you. I will teach you to love me. Let me comfort and protect you."

The girl lifted her head. "You dare ask that after what happened the other night?"

"God knows how I regret that awful mistake," he replied earnestly. "But you know I was not myself. I am no worse than other men, and—"

He hesitated briefly before going on. "—I was never intoxicated before. Won't you forgive me this once and let me devote my life to righting the wrong?"

Amy's eyes fell. The seeming sincerity of his words impressed her.

Again the man saw his advantage and talked to her of the life his wealth would help her to live. She would be free from every care. They would travel abroad until her father had forgotten his wrath, and there could be no doubt that all would be well when she returned as his wife.

Amy hesitated, and again he pointed out the awful danger of her trying to live alone. As he spoke, the girl's utter helplessness overcame her, and rising to her feet, she faltered. "Give me time to think. I will come back to you here in an hour."

She went. Whitley remained in the room. An hour later she was back.

When she returned she said, "Mr. Whitley, I will marry you. But my people must not know until later."

Whitley started toward her eagerly, but she stepped back.

"Not now . . . wait. We will go east on the evening train and take every precaution to hide our course. We will travel in separate cars as strangers, and while stopping at hotels we will register under assumed names and not even show when we meet that we recognize one another. When we reach New York, I will become your wife."

Whitley could scarcely conceal his triumph. That she should so fully play into his hand was to him the greatest possible good fortune.

With many expressions of love he agreed to everything, but when he would embrace her she stepped back again.

"Not until we are married," she said, and he was compelled to be satisfied.

They talked for a while longer, completing their plans. Then he drew out his pocketbook, saying, "You will need money."

But she shook her head. "Not until I have the right to call it mine. But now—here are my jewels. Sell them for me."

He protested, laughing at her scruples.

But she insisted. At last he took the valuables and left the hotel. Going to a bank where he was known, he drew out a large sum of money, then returned, placing a roll of bills in her hand. Thinking it was the price of her rings, she accepted it without the slightest question.

That night he bought a ticket for Chicago, over the "Frisco" via the Wabash from St. Louis, taking a chair car, while she purchased one and traveled in a sleeper. They remained at St. Louis two days, staying at an agreed-upon hotel, but as strangers. On reaching Chicago they again purchased tickets for different stations, over another road, but stopped at Detroit. It was here that Amy's suspicions were first aroused.

She was sitting at dinner when Whitley entered the dining room with two traveling men who seemed well acquainted with him. The trio, laughing and talking boisterously, seated themselves at a table behind her. Recognizing Whitley's voice, she lifted her eyes to a mirror on the opposite wall, and to her horror, distinctly saw him point her out to his friends.

Amy's dinner remained untouched, for she did not understand this sudden change after many days of Whitley's showing her every thoughtfulness. She hid her confusion as best she could, but when she rose to leave the room, as she passed the table where Whitley and the men were eating, his companions looked at her in such a way that the color rushed to her pale cheeks in a crimson flame. Later, at the depot, she saw them again, and was sure from Whitley's manner that he had been drinking.

Once more aboard the train, Amy found herself overcome by troubling thoughts. Worn out by the long journey under such trying circumstances, and the lonely hours among strangers at the hotels, and now thoroughly frightened about Whitley's motives and the possible outcome when they reached New York, the poor child worried herself into such a state that when they left the train at Buffalo, she was thoroughly ill. Whitley became concerned, and in spite of her protests, registered at the hotel as her brother and called in a physician.

The doctor at once insisted that she should be taken to a boardinghouse where she could have perfect rest and quiet. She was nearly exhausted, he said, though he could not at once determine whether the condition was serious. With his help such a place was found and Whitley, still posing as her brother, made all the arrangements.

Once having collapsed, the balance of Amy's system gave way altogether. The emotional uncertainty, along with the physical strain, exacted a terrible toll. For three weeks she hovered between life and death, and strangely enough, in her delirium, called not once for father or mother or brother, but always for Dick, and always begged him to save her from some great danger. Whitley came to the place every day and procured her every attention that money could buy. But when at last she began to mend, something in her eyes as she looked at him made him curse beneath his breath.

Day after day she put him off when he urged marriage, saying, "When we get to New York."

But at last the time came when she could offer no excuse for longer delay, and in a few firm words she told him that she could not keep her promise, telling him why and begging his forgiveness if she had wronged him.

Then the man's true nature showed itself.

He cursed her for being a fool, taunted her with using his money, and swore that he would force her to come to him.

That afternoon the landlady came to her room, placed a letter in her hand, and asked, "Will you please be kind enough to explain this?"

Amy read the note, which informed the lady of the house that her boarder was a woman of questionable character, and that the man who was paying her bills was not her brother. With a sinking heart, Amy saw that the writing was Jim Whitley's.

Her face flushed painfully. "I did not know that he was paying my bills," she answered slowly.

"Then it is true?" exclaimed the woman. "He is not your brother?"

Amy was silent. She could find no words to explain.

"You must leave this house instantly," commanded the landlady. "If it were not for the publicity, I would hand you over to the police."

Amy gathered her few things, left the place, and went to a cheap but respectable hotel; and the next morning, Whitley, who had not lost sight of her, managed to force an interview.

"Will you come to me now?" he asked. "You see what you may expect from the world."

"I would take my own life before I would trust it in your hands," she replied.

Knowing that she spoke the truth, he left her and returned to Boyd City. When he arrived home he wrote a letter to the proprietor, explaining the character of the woman calling herself Miss Wheeler. He had just dropped it in the box that same day when he met Dick inside the post office.

It was not many days thereafter when Dick Falkner stepped off the train at Buffalo and hurried through the depot toward the cab that bore the name of the hotel where Whitley had left Amy. He did not notice that the girl he had come so far to find was standing at the window of the ticket office. Thus while the proprietor of the hotel was explaining to Dick why Miss Wheeler had left his house, the westbound train was carrying Amy toward Cleveland.

With the aid of the Buffalo police, Dick searched long and carefully for the missing girl, but with no results. At last, his small savings nearly exhausted, he was forced to return to Boyd City.

———

In Cleveland Amy sought out a cheap lodging house, for she realized that her means were limited. She then began a weary search for some kind of employment.

Day after day she went from place to place answering advertisements for positions she thought she might be able to fill. Walking all she could, she took a car only when her strength failed, but always met with the same result—a cold dismissal because she could give no references and had no job history. Never was there so much as a kind look, an encouraging word, or a helpful smile. As the days went by, her face grew hard and her eyes had a hopeless, defiant look that lessened her chances of success all the more—

even giving some cause for the suspicious glances she encountered on every hand, though her features showed that under better circumstances she would be beautiful.

One evening as she stood on the street corner, tired out, shivering in the sharp wind, confused by the rush and roar of the city, and in doubt as to the streetcar she should take, a tall, beautifully dressed woman stopped by her side, also waiting for a car.

Trembling slightly, Amy asked the lady for directions. The lady looked at her keenly as she gave the needed information, and then added kindly, "You are evidently not acquainted with Cleveland."

Amy admitted that she was a stranger.

"And where is your home?"

"I have none," she replied sadly.

"You are staying with friends?"

Amy shook her head. "No, I know no one in the city."

The woman grew very kind. "You poor child," she murmured; "you look as though you are in distress. Can't I help you somehow?"

Tears filled the brown eyes that were lifted pleadingly to the face of the questioner, and a dry sob was the only answer.

"Come with me, dear," said the woman, taking Amy kindly by the arm. "This is my car. Come and let me help you."

They boarded the car, and after a long ride, the two entered a finely furnished house in a part of the city far from Amy's boarding place. The girl was escorted to the woman's own room, and after giving Amy a bath and a warm supper, the benefactor sat with her young guest in front of the fire, while Amy poured out her story to the only sympathetic listener she had met.

When she had finished, the woman said, "You have not told me your name."

"You may call me Amy. I have no other name."

Again the woman spoke slowly. "You cannot find work. No one will receive you. But why should you care? You are beautiful."

Amy looked at her in wonder. The woman explained how she

had many girls in her home, who with fine dresses and jewels lived a life of ease and luxury.

At last Amy understood. With a shudder she rose to her feet.

"Madam, I thank you for your kindness, for you *have* been kind. But I cannot stay here."

She started toward the door, but the woman stopped her.

"My dear child, you cannot go out at this time of night again, and you could never find your way back to your lodging place. Stay here. You need not leave this room, and you may bolt the door on this side. Tomorrow you may go if you wish."

Amy could do nothing but stay. As she laid her tired head on the clean pillow that night, nestling in the warm blankets and watching the firelight as the flames leaped and played, she heard the sound of music and merry voices, and thought of the cold, poorly furnished bedroom, with coarse sheets and dirty pillows, at her lodging place. Her mind reviewed the scenes of the weary tramp about the streets and the unkind faces that would not give her a chance at work. What would the end be when her money was gone? she wondered.

The next morning when she awoke, for a moment she could not remember where she was. Then it all came back just as a knock sounded on the door.

"Who is it?" she called.

"Your coffee, ma'am" came the answer. She unlocked the door and admitted an old black woman with a neat tray, on which was sitting a dainty breakfast.

Later, after she was dressed, the Madam of the house came to her.

"Do you still feel you must go?" she asked.

"Yes, yes, I must. Don't tempt me."

The woman handed her a card with her name and address. "Well, go, my dear. And when you are driven to the street again because you have no money and are cold and hungry come to me if you will, and earn food and clothing, warmth and ease, by the only means open to you."

Then she went with Amy to the street and saw that she took the right car.

As Amy said goodbye, the tears filled her eyes again. How lonely and desolate the poor girl felt as she shivered in the sharp air. And how hopelessly she took up again her fight against the desperate odds.

She struggled bravely for as long as she was able. But the end came at last, just as the woman said it would. Without money, Amy was finally turned out of her boarding place. One dreadful night she spent on the street.

The next day she found her way, half frozen and weak from hunger, to the Madam's place.

CHAPTER TWENTY-SIX

FRANK GETS IN DEEPER

That Frank Goodrich had managed to keep himself free from all appearance of evil since the night he so nearly became with his hands the thief he *had* become in his heart was not because of any real change in his character.

He gambled no more, not from a matter of principle, but because he feared the results. And he accepted Whitley's sarcastic advice about religious services, not because there was any desire in his heart for a right life, but because he felt it was good policy.

Like many others, he was as bad as he dared to be. And while using the church as a cloak to hide his real nature, he was satisfied if he could keep up the appearance of respectability. In short, he was a splendid example of what that old satanic copybook proverb "Honesty is the best policy" will do for a life if it be lived up to in earnest.

He was not a little alarmed over his sister's conduct, because he feared that Whitley, in a spirit of revenge, would demand payment of the notes, which could only mean his open disgrace and ruin.

His intrepidation reached a climax two weeks after Dick's return when Frank received a curt note from Jim that read: "You will remember that I promised to surrender those notes of yours upon certain conditions. Those conditions now can never be met, and it becomes necessary for us to make other arrangements. You will meet me with a horse and buggy at Freeman Station tomorrow night, ten-thirty. Wait for me at the crossroads south of the depot. If anyone learns of our meeting, it will be all up with you."

Freeman Station was a little cluster of houses near the great hay farms twelve miles from Boyd City, and the drive was not one to be made with pleasure.

But there was no avoiding it, and about dusk Frank set out. It had been raining steadily for several days and the mud was hub deep, while in many places the road was under water. Once he had to get out and, by the flickering light of his lantern, pick his way around a dangerous washout. Several times he was on the point of giving up and turning back, but thoughts of Whitley's anger drove him on; and at last he reached the place, several minutes after the train had passed on its way across the dark prairie.

As Frank stopped at the corner, Whitley appeared by the side of the buggy and clambered in without a word. Taking the reins from Frank, he lashed the tired horse with the whip and they plunged forward into the night.

Once or twice Frank tried to open a conversation with his companion, but received such short replies that he gave up and shrank back in the corner of the seat in miserable silence.

After nearly an hour, Whitley brought the horse to a halt, jumped out of the buggy, and began to unhitch. Against the dark sky, Frank could see the shadowy outlines of a house and barn.

"Where are we?" he asked.

"At my place, nine miles south of town," Whitley answered. "Help me put up the horses."

Frank obeyed.

"No, don't take the harness off," Jim told him. "You'll want him before long." Then he led the way to the house.

Taking a key from its hiding place beneath one corner of the step, he unlocked the door and entered; and while Frank stood shivering with the cold and wet, Whitley found a lamp and made a light. The room where they stood was well carpeted and furnished, and upon the table were the remains of a meal, together with empty bottles and glasses, and lying on the chair was a woman's glove.

Frank looked around curiously. He had heard rumors of Whitley's place in the country, but this was his first visit.

"Well," said Jim shortly, "sit down while I build a fire and get something to drink. Things are not very gay here tonight, but we'll do the best we can."

When the room was warm and they had removed their coats and Jim had partaken freely from a supply of liquor on the sideboard, he stretched himself in an easy chair and spoke more pleasantly. "Well, I suppose you are ready to pay those notes, with the interest."

Frank moved uneasily. "You know I can't," he muttered. "I thought from your letter that we might make other arrangements. Amy, you know, might come back—"

"Cut the malarkey!" interrupted Whitley with an oath. "Your esteemed sister is out of this deal for good." Then, as he lit his cigar, he added, "We might fix things in another way, though, if you only had the nerve."

"How?" asked Frank.

"That printer of Udell's has some papers in his possession that I want. Get them for me and I'll turn over your notes and call it square."

Frank looked at his companion perplexed. "What do you mean?" he questioned at last.

"Just what I say. Can't you hear? Get the papers and I tear up your notes," repeated Whitley impatiently.

"But how does that tramp happen to have any papers of value to you?" asked Frank.

"That is, most emphatically, none of your business, my friend. All you have to do is get them, or—" He paused significantly.

"But will he give them to me?" Frank inquired.

Whitley looked at him a few moments in amused contempt, then said in a mocking voice, "Oh, of course he will be glad to favor us. All you need to do is put on your best Sunday-school manners and say sweetly: 'Mr. Falkner, Mr. Whitley would like those papers that you have in the long leather pocketbook tied with a shoestring.' He'll hand them over instantly. The only reason I have taken all this trouble to meet you out here tonight is because I am naturally too easily embarrassed and don't want to ask for them myself."

Frank was confused and made no reply until Whitley asked, "Where does the fellow live now?"

"I don't know," Frank answered, "but he's in old man Wicks' office every evening—has a desk there, and works on some fool church work."

Whitley nodded. "Then you will no doubt find the papers in Uncle Bobbie's safe."

"But how am I to get them?" asked Frank, still bewildered.

"I don't know, you idiot! You can't buy them. You can't bluff him. And he won't scare. There's only one other I way I know," suggested Whitley.

"You mean steal them?"

Whitley looked at him with an evil smile. "That's rather a hard word for a good Christian, isn't it? Let's just say, obtain possession of the documents without Mr. Falkner's knowledge. It sounds better."

"I'm no thief!" snapped Frank.

Jim lifted his eyebrows as he skillfully flipped the ashes from his cigar.

"Oh, I see. You did not rob the old gentleman's safe that night I saved you from committing murder. You only negotiated a trifling loan with your loving parent. You'll be telling me next that you didn't gamble, but only whiled away a leisure hour or two in a social game of cards. You know, I honestly believe, Frank Goodrich, that you are more kinds of a fool than any man I have ever had the pleasure to know. The case in a nutshell is this: I must have those papers. I can't go after them myself. You've got to get them for me."

"I won't," Frank refused sullenly. "I can't."

"You can and you will," retorted the other firmly, "or I'll turn those notes over to my lawyer for collection inside of twenty-four hours, and the little story of your life will be told to all the world. My young Christian friend, you can't afford to tell *me* that you won't."

For another hour they sat before the fire, talking and planning, and then Frank drove alone, through the mud and rain, back to the city, reaching his home just before daybreak.

CHAPTER TWENTY-SEVEN

A BAD SITUATION AND A COOL HEAD

A few nights later, as Dick sat at his work in Uncle Bobbie's office, a rubber-tired buggy drove slowly past close to the curbing. Through the big front window Dick could be seen plainly as he bent over his desk just inside an inner room, his back toward the door, which stood open.

A burly Negro leaped to the sidewalk without even stopping the vehicle. So absorbed was Dick with the task before him that he did not hear the outer door of the office open and close again. And so quickly did the huge man move that he stood within the room where Dick sat before the latter was aware of the black man's presence.

When Dick at last raised his head, he found himself looking straight into the muzzle of a big revolver.

"Don't move or ye're a goner," growled the man. Reaching out with his free hand, he shut the door between the rooms, thus cutting off the view from the street.

Dick smiled pleasantly, as though his visitor had called in the ordinary way. "What can I do for you?" he asked politely.

"Yo jest move away from dat desk fust; den we can talk,"

barked the man. "I don't 'spect you's got a gun handy, an' we don't want no foolin'."

Dick did as he was told, got up, and seated himself on the edge of a table in the center of the room. But the man did not notice that Dick had placed himself so that a heavy glass paperweight was just hidden by his right leg.

"I wants yo to unlock dat safe," said Dick's visitor.

"I can't," answered Dick. "I don't know the combination."

"Huh," grunted the man. "Yo can't gib me no such guff as dat."

"You're making a mistake," Dick argued earnestly. "I only have a desk here. I don't work for Mr. Wicks, and have no business with the safe. Besides, they don't keep money there anyway."

" 'Taint money I'm after dis trip, mistah. Hit's papers. Dey's in a big leather pocketbook, tied with a shoestring."

In an instant Dick understood. The papers were indeed in the safe, but as he said, he did not know the combination. "Papers?" he asked, trying to gain time to think.

"Yeah, papers. Dat yo keeps dere." He nodded toward the safe as he carefully seated himself in the chair, his eyes on Dick. "I wants 'em quick." The hand that held the revolver came slowly to a level with the dark face.

"I'm telling you the truth," insisted Dick. "I don't know how to open the safe."

The black man looked puzzled. Seeing his momentary advantage, Dick let his hand fall easily on his leg, close to the paperweight.

"Besides," he said carelessly, "if it's my papers you want, that's my desk behind—"

He stopped himself suddenly, as though he had said more than he intended.

Glistening white teeth showed themselves in a broad grin at what the man perceived to be Dick's mistake. Forgetting himself, he half turned in the revolving chair while the muzzle of the gun was shifted for just the fraction of a second.

It was enough.

With the swiftness of a fox, Dick's hand shot out, and the heavy weight caught the man on the right forearm. At the same moment Dick kicked with his leg, toppling the man from his seat. With a groan of pain as he hit the floor, the Negro released the gun, letting it fall from his hand. By the time the man turned to pick himself off the floor, wincing in pain, Dick was back comfortably on the edge of the table, but now holding the weapon on his would-be assailant.

"Don't shoot! Don't shoot!" shouted the frightened man.

"Tell me who sent you here?" demanded Dick.

"Mistah Goodrich," the ruffian replied.

Dick was startled, though his face registered no surprise.

"I means Mistah Frank."

Still showing no surprise in his manner, Dick asked, "How did he know that I had any papers?"

"I dunno, mistah. He only say as how he wants 'em. An' he's waitin' round de corner in de carriage."

This was a new twist to the situation. Dick was puzzled.

He thought a moment, then stepped to the phone and, still covering the black man with the revolver, rang up the operator and asked for Mr. Wicks' residence. When the answer came, he said, "Excuse me for disturbing you, Mr. Wicks, but I have a man here in the office who wants to get into your safe, and I need you badly. You had better come in the back way."

"I'll be there in a shake" was the reply. "Hold him till I get there."

Not more than five minutes passed before Dick heard a knock at the back door. Dick admitted him and then burst into a hearty laugh at the old gentleman's strange appearance. In his haste, Uncle Bobbie had simply pulled on a pair of rubber boots and donned an overcoat. With the exception of these articles, he was still in his nightshirt and stocking cap. In his hand he carried a pistol half as long as his arm, but he was as calm as Dick himself, though breathing hard. "To be sure," he puffed, "I'm—so—blamed—fat—can't—hurry—wind's no good—"

Dick explained the situation in a few words. "I wouldn't have called you in, sir, if young Goodrich were not in it. But, you see, I don't know what to do."

"To be sure," agreed Uncle Bobbie. "To be sure. Sometimes a good fellow like him gets tangled up with bad people in such a way you just got to let them alone. Tares and wheat, you know, tares and wheat. To be sure, Christianity ain't like arithmetic, and you can't save souls like you'd do problems in long division, nor count results like you'd figure interest. What do you say? Suppose you skip down to the corner and fetch him up here?"

Dick glanced at the black man.

"Never you mind him," said the old gentleman with a scowl. "He knows old Uncle Bobbie won't stand for no foolishness." He brandished his weapon in the air.

Dick slipped out of the back door and soon returned holding Frank firmly by the collar. As they entered, Uncle Bobbie said to the man under his charge, "Now's your chance, Bill. Get out before we change our minds." And the astonished Negro bolted without waiting for another word.

"Now, Frank," the old gentleman began kindly when Dick had placed his prisoner in a chair, "tell us about it."

Almost too frightened to speak above a whisper, young Goodrich told them the whole miserable story.

"Too bad, too bad," muttered Uncle Bobbie when Frank had finished. "To be sure, it ain't no more than I expected. Gambling church members ain't got no call to kick if their children play cards for money. What'll we do, Dick?"

Dick was silent, but unseen by Frank, he motioned toward the door.

Uncle Bobbie understood.

"I reckon you're right," he said slowly. "Tares and wheat—tares and wheat. But what about them notes?"

"I'll fix Whitley," replied Dick.

Frank looked at him with surprise.

"Are you sure you can do it?" asked Uncle Bobbie; " 'cause if you can't—"

"I'll write him a line tonight," Dick promised, then turned to

Frank. "You can go now," he told him, "and don't worry about Jim Whitley; he will never trouble you about collecting the notes."

Frank stammered some unintelligible reply and rose to his feet, ready to exit.

"Wait a minute, young man," Uncle Bobbie said. "I want to tell you something before you go. To be sure, I don't think you'll ever become a very bad man, but you've shown pretty clearly that you can be a mighty mean one. And I'm afraid you'll never be much credit to the church, 'cause a fellow's got to be a man before he can be much of a Christian. Pieces of men don't count much on either side; they just sort of fill in. But what you want to do is to be decent, and to quit trying so blamed hard to be respectable and well thought of. Now, run on home to your ma, and don't tell nobody where you've been tonight. Mr. Falkner will look after your friend Whitley."

CHAPTER TWENTY-EIGHT

FLIGHT TO THE BACKWOODS

The sun was nearly three hours high above the western hilltops in the Ozark mountain district of Arkansas. A solitary horseman stopped in the shadow of the timber that fringed the edge of a deep ravine.

It was evident from the man's dress that he was not a native of that region, and from the puzzled expression on his face as he looked anxiously about, it was clear as well that he had lost his way.

Standing in the stirrups, he turned and glanced back over the bridle path along which he had come, peering carefully through the trees to the right and left. Then with an impatient oath, he dropped to the saddle and sat staring straight ahead at a lone pine upon the top of a high hill a few miles away.

"There's the hill with the tree beyond Simpson's all right," he murmured to himself, "but how in thunder am I to get there? This path doesn't go any farther, that's for sure," and from the distant mountain he turned his gaze to the deep gulch that extended out beyond his feet.

Suddenly he leaned forward with another exclamation. He had caught sight of a log cabin in the bottom of the ravine, half hidden by the bushes and low trees that grew upon the steep banks. Turning his horse, he rode slowly up and down the edge of the canyon for some distance, searching for an easy place to descend, coming back at last to the spot where he had first halted.

"It's no go, Salem," he said; "we've got to slide for it."

Dismounting, he took the bridle rein in his hand and began to pick his way as best he could down the steep incline, while his four-footed companion reluctantly followed. After some twenty minutes of stumbling and swearing on the part of the man, and slipping and groaning on the part of the horse, they stood panting at the bottom. After a short rest, the man clambered into the saddle again, and fording a little mountain brook that laughed and sang and roared among the boulders, rode up to the clearing in which the cabin stood.

"Hello!" he shouted.

There was no answer, and but for the thread of smoke that curled lazily from the mud-and-stick chimney, the place seemed deserted.

"Hello," he called again.

A gaunt dog came rushing from the underbrush beyond the house, and with hair bristling in anger, howled his defiance and threats.

Again the horseman shouted, and this time the cabin door opened cautiously and a dirty-faced urchin thrust forward a tousled head.

"Where's your father?" said the horseman.

The head was withdrawn, and a moment later put forth again. "He's gone ter the corners."

"Well, can you tell me the way to Simpson's? That's where I'm headed, but I can't seem to get out of this infernal hole of a canyon."

Again the head disappeared for a few seconds, and then the door was thrown wide open and a slovenly woman, with a snuff stick in one corner of her mouth, came out, followed by four children. The youngest three clung to her skirts and stared with fearful eyes at the man on the horse, while he of the tousled head threw stones at the dog and commanded him in a shrill voice,

"Shet up, dad burn ye, Kinney, shet up!"

"Wanter go ter Simpson's at the corners, do ye?" inquired the woman. "Wal, yer right smart offen yer road."

"I know that," replied the stranger impatiently. "I've been hunting turkeys and lost my way. But can I get to the corners from here?"

"Sure ye kin. Jist foller on down the branch 'bout three mile till ye come out on the big road. Hit'll take ye straight ter the ford below ol' Ball whar the lone tree is. Simpson's is 'bout half a quarter on yon side the creek."

The man thanked her gruffly, and turning his horse, started away.

"Be ye the feller what's comin' t' Sim's ter hunt?" she called after him.

"Yes, I'm the man," he answered. And he rode into the woods.

Catching the oldest urchin by the arm, the woman gave him a vigorous cuff on the side of the head and then whispered a few words in his attentive ear. The lad started off down the opposite side of the ravine at a run, bending low and dodging here and there, unseen by the stranger.

The hunter pushed on his way down the narrow valley as fast as he could go, for he had no time to spare if he was to reach his destination before night, and he knew there was small chance of finding the way back after dark. But his course was so rough and obstructed by heavy undergrowth, fallen trees, and boulders that his progress was slow and the shadow of the mountain was over the trail while he was still a mile from the road at the end of the ravine.

As he looked anxiously ahead, hoping every moment to see the broader valley where the road lay, he caught a glimpse of two men coming toward him, one behind the other, winding in and out through the low timber. While still some distance away, they turned sharply to the left and, as it seemed to the man on the horse, rode straight into the side of the mountain and were lost to sight.

Checking his horse, he watched for them to come into view again; and while he waited, wondering at their strange disappearance, the men urged their mules up a narrow gully that was so hidden by the undergrowth and fallen timber as to escape an eye untrained to the woods and hills. After riding a short distance, they dismounted, and leaving the animals, quickly scaled the steep sides of the little cut and came out in an open space about two hundred yards above the trail along which the solitary horseman would eventually have to pass. Dropping behind the trunk of a big tree lying on the mountainside, uprooted by some gale and blackened by forest fires, they searched the valley below with the keen glance of those whose eyes are never dimmed by printed page or city lights. Dressed in the rude garb of those to whom clothes are a necessity, not a means of display, tall and lean with hard muscles, tough sinews and cruel, stony faces, they seemed a part of the wildlife about them. And yet there was at the same time a touch of the mountain grandeur in their manner and in their unconscious air of freedom and self-reliance, as there always is about everything that remains untouched by the conventionality of the weaker world of men.

" 'Bout time he showed up, ain't it, Jake?" said one as he carefully rested his rifle against the log and bit off a big piece of long green twist tobacco.

"Hit's a right smart piece ter ol' Josh's shack an' the kid done come in a whoop," returned the other, following his companion's example. "He can't make much time down that branch on hossback an' with them fine clothes of his'n, but he orten ter be fur off."

"D'ye reckon he's a blamed revenoo'r sure, Jake?"

"Dunno. Best be safe," answered Jake with an ugly scowl. "Simpson allows he's jist layin' low hisself, but ye can't tell."

"What'd Sim say his name war?" asked the other.

"Jim Whitley," returned Jake, taking a long, careful look up the valley.

"Soun' like it be a revenoo name t' me."

"Dunno," said Jake, spitting out a brown mouthful.

"An' whar from?" inquired his companion.

"Sim say St. Louie, or some place like that. Shhh—thar he come."

They half rose and crouched behind the log, pushing their cocked rifles through the leaves of a little bush. With guns ready, they covered the horseman below, whom they took for a federal agent.

"If he's a revenoo he'll sure see the path ter the still," whispered the one called Jake, "an' if he turns ter foller hit into the cut, drap him. If he goes on down the branch, all right, let him be."

Completely unaware of the rifles that wanted only the touch of an outlaw's finger to speak his death, the stranger pushed on his way past the unseen danger point toward the end of the valley where lay the road.

The lean mountaineers looked at each other. "Never seed hit," said one, showing his yellow teeth in a mirthless grin, "an' I done tol' Cap las' night, hit was as plain as the main traveled road an' orter be covered."

"Mebbe so," replied the other; "then agin he mighter ketched on an' kep' goin' t' fool us."

The other sprang up with an oath. "We'uns ain't got no call ter take chances," he growled; "best make sure." And with his rifle half raised, he looked anxiously along the trail, but the stranger had passed out of their view.

A few minutes longer they waited and watched, discussing the situation. Then returning to their mules, they rode out of the little gully and on down the branch in the direction the object of their suspicion had taken.

Just across the road from the mouth of the ravine down which the hunter had come was another little log cabin, and in the low doorway an old woman sat smoking a cob pipe.

"Howdy, Liz," greeted one of the men. "Seed anythin'?"

"Yep," returned the woman. "He done ast the way ter Simpson's. 'Low'd he'd been huntin' turkey an' lost hisself. I done tol' him he orter git someone ter tromp roun' with him er he might git hisself killed."

She laughed shrilly and the two men joined in with low guffaws.

"Reckon yer right, Liz," said one. "Jake, why don't ye hire out ter him?"

Jake slapped his leg.

"By gum!" he exclaimed, "that thar's a good ide'. I'll shore do hit. An' I'll see that he don't find nuthin' bigger'n turkey too, less'n he be too blasted inquisitive. Then I'll. . . ."

He finished with an evil grin. "You'uns tell Cap I've done gone ter hunt with Mr. Whitley iffen I don't show up."

And beating his mule's ribs vigorously with his heels, he jogged away down the road, while his companion turned and rode back up the little valley.

Enraged at Frank's failure to procure the papers held by Dick Falkner, and alarmed at the latter's letter telling him of young Goodrich's confession, Jim Whitley had come into the wild backwoods district southwest of Boyd City in order to hide and await developments.

He was more determined now than ever to gain possession of the evidence of his crime, and in his heart was a fast-growing desire to silence once and for all the man whose steady purpose and integrity was such an obstacle in his life.

But he could see no way to accomplish his purpose without great danger to himself. And with the memory of the gray eyes that had looked so calmly along the shining revolvers that night in the printing office was a wholesome respect for the determined character of the man who had coolly proposed to die with him if he did not grant his demands. He feared that should Dick find Amy and learn the truth, he would risk his own life rather than permit him to go unpunished. And so he resolved to bury himself in the mountains until chance should reveal a safe way out of the difficulty, or time should change the situation.

CHAPTER TWENTY-NINE

WHITLEY PLAYS A LOSING GAME

The afternoon following his adventure in the little valley, Whitley sat on the porch of the post office and store kept by Simpson, his host, telling his experience to a group of loafers, when the long mountaineer called Jake rode up to the blacksmith shop across the street. Leaving his mule to be shod, the native joined the circle just in time to hear the latter part of Whitley's story.

"Lookin' fer turkey, war ye, mister?" drawled Jake with a wink at the bystanders.

"Yes, have you seen any?" replied Jim.

"Sure, the brush's full of 'em if ye know whar ter hunt," Jake answered.

The company grinned and he continued.

"I seed signs this mornin' in the holler on yon side ol' Ball when I war huntin' my mule. An' thar's a big roost down by the spring back o' my place in the bottoms."

Whitley was interested.

"Will you show me where they are?" he asked.

"Might, if I could spare the time," replied Jake slowly. "But I gots my crops ter tend."

Another grin went around the small group. "Jake's shore pushed with his crops," remarked one. "Raises mo' corn'n 'ary three men in Arkansaw," remarked another, and with this they all fired a volley of tobacco juice at a tumble bug rolling his ball in the dust nearby.

Needless to say, the conversation resulted in Whitley's engaging the moonshiner for seventy-five cents a day to hunt with him, and for the next two weeks they were always together.

All day long the native led the way over the hills and through the deep ravines and valleys, taking a different course each day, but always the chase led them away from the little ravine that opened on the big road. When Whitley suggested that they try the country where he had lost his way, his guide only laughed contemptuously, "Ain't ye killin' turkey ever' time we goes out? Ye jist foller me an' I'll shore find 'em fer ye. Ain't nuthin' over in that holler. I done tromped all over thar huntin' that dad-burned ol' mule o' mine, an' didn't see nary a sign o' gobblers. Mos' times they's roun' the south side the ridge. Ye jist lemme take ye roun'."

And Whitley was forced to admit that he was having good luck and no cause to complain for lack of sport. But he was growing tired of the hills and impatient to return to the city, while his hatred of the man whom he feared grew hourly.

Seeing that his employer was fast getting tired of the hunt, Jake guessed shrewdly, from the man's preoccupied manner, that hunting was not the real object of Whitley's stay in the mountains; and the mountaineer gradually became more and more suspicious. His careless, good-natured ways and talk changed to a sullen silence and he watched Whitley constantly.

One morning, just at daybreak, as they were walking briskly along the big road on their way to a place where the guide said the game was to be found, Jake stopped suddenly. Motioning Jim to be silent, his host stood in a listening attitude.

Whitley followed his companion's example, but for a minute Jim could hear nothing but the faint rustle of the dead leaves as a gray lizard darted to his hiding place, and the shrill scream of a blue jay called his sleepy mates to breakfast. Then the faint thud, thud, thud of a galloping horse came louder and louder through the morning mist. Someone was riding rapidly toward them.

Whitley was about to speak when the other, with a fierce oath and a threatening gesture, stopped him.

"Git inter the brush thar quick an' do's I tell ye. Don't stop ter talk. Git! An' gimme yer gun."

Too astonished to do anything else, Jim obeyed, and the moonshiner, hastily thrusting the rifle under a pile of leaves by a log nearby, forced his companion before him through the underbrush to a big rock some distance from the road. The sound of the galloping horse came louder and louder.

"Stand thar behin' that rock an' if ye stir I'll kill ye," whispered Jake. He then took a position behind a tree where he could watch Jim as well as the road. He waited with rifle cocked and murder written in every line of his hard face.

Nearer and nearer came the galloping horse. Whitley was fascinated by the drama playing out before him. He moved slightly so he could peep over the rock. A low hiss from Jake fell upon his ear like the warning hiss of a serpent, and half turning, he saw the rifle pointing full at him. Whitley nodded his head, and placing his finger upon his lips to indicate that he understood, Jim turned his face toward the road again just as the horse and his rider came into view.

The animal, though going freely, was covered with dust and dripping with sweat, which showed a creamy lather on his flanks and where the bridle reins touched his neck. The rider wore a blue flannel shirt, open at the throat, corduroy trousers, tucked in long boots, and a black slouch hat, with the brim turned up in front. At his belt hung two heavy revolvers, and across the saddle he held a Winchester ready for instant use. He sat his horse easily as one accustomed to much riding, but like the animal, he showed the strain of a hard face.

Whitley was so worked up that all these details impressed themselves upon his mind in an instant, and it seemed hours from the moment the horseman came into view until he was opposite the rock, though it could have been but a few seconds.

The watcher caught one glimpse of the rider's face—square-jawed, keen-eyed, determined, alert, stained by wind and weather—before suddenly—

"Crack!" exploded the rifle behind Whitley.

Like a flash the weapon of the rider flew to his shoulder.

"Crack!" and the bark flew from the tree within an inch of Jake's face.

Whitley saw the spurs strike and the rider lean forward in his saddle to meet the spring of his horse.

"Crack!" Jake's rifle spoke again.

A mocking laugh rolled back from the road as the flying horseman passed from sight. Then, "I'll see you later" came in ringing tones, and the thud, thud, thud of the galloping horse died away in the distance.

The mountaineer delivered himself of a volley of oaths, while Whitley stood quietly looking at him, his mind filled with strange thoughts. The man who could deliberately fire from hidden ambush with intent to kill in cold blood was just the sort of man for his purpose.

"Who is he?" Jim asked at last when the other stopped swearing long enough to fill his mouth with fresh tobacco.

"A revenoo, an' I done missed him clean." He began to curse again.

"He came near getting you, though," said Jim, pointing to the mark of the horseman's bullet.

"Yep. Hit war Bill Davis. Ain't nary another man in the whole blamed outfit could a done hit." He looked almost with admiration at the fresh scar on the tree.

"But what was he doing?" asked Whitley.

Jake looked at him with that ugly, mirthless grin. "Mebbe he's huntin' turkey too."

Whitley laughed. "I guess he was riding too fast for that." But when his companion replied, his laughter instantly ceased.

"Thar's one that orter think of follerin' him right smart soon," said Jake.

"What do you mean?" asked Whitley.

"I mean you, mister," Jake replied. "The boys has had thar eye on ye fer some time. We know yer huntin's all a show, an' now

Bill Davis he's come in. I ain't right shore myself or I'd kep' mum an' he'ped the boys kill ye."

Whitley turned pale. "Do you mean that the people here think I'm a revenue agent looking for moonshiners?"

"That's 'bout hit, mister."

"In league with this Mr. Davis?"

"They'll be fer takin' ye out one o' these nights shore," the backwoodsman informed him.

For some time Whitley remained silent. He was thinking hard.

"Jake, I'll tell you something," he said at last. "The boys are mistaken. I'm not here to get anybody into trouble, but because I'm in a hold myself."

"As how?" asked Jake, moving nearer and speaking in a lower tone.

"I won't tell you how unless you'll help me," answered Whitley cunningly; "and if you will, I'll pay you more money than you can make in this business in a thousand years."

The moonshiner's eyes gleamed.

"Bill Davis is shore after us an' that means trouble ever' time," he said slowly. "Ye hear'd him say as how he'd see me agin, an' I never knowed him ter miss before."

He looked at the bullet mark on the tree again.

"Tell ye what, Mister Whitley, I'll chance 'er. But we ain't got no time ter talk now. We gotter git away from here, fer some o' the boys'll be along purty soon. We'll jes' mosey roun' fer a spell an' then go back ter the corners. I'll send the boys off on a hot chase an' fix Sim so's ye kin git erway t'night, an' then ye kin come ter my shack. Hit's on the river below that hill with the lone tree on top, jes' seven mile from the corners. Ye can't miss hit. I'll be thar an' have things fixed so's we kin light out befo' the boys git back."

They reached Simpson's in time for dinner, and Jake held a long whispered conversation with the man everyone called Sim, while Whitley sat on the porch after the meal.

As Jake passed him on his way to the mule that stood hitched in front of the blacksmith shop as usual, the mountaineer said, in the hearing of those nearby, "Hit's all right fer tomorrow, is hit, Mister Whitley? An' we'll go over t'other side o' Sandy Ridge?"

The words "all right" were accompanied by a quick wink that Whitley understood.

"Yes," he answered carelessly, "I'll be ready. I want to rest this afternoon and get a good sleep tonight. I'll be with you in the morning."

Jake rode off. All the rest of the day Whitley was the mark for many scowling glances, while many whispered words were passed between the gaunt natives as they slouched in and out of the post office.

Later, when the loafers had seemingly disappeared, Simpson came, and leaning carelessly against the doorpost within a few feet of Whitley, said in a low voice, "They's all watchin' ye from the shop yonder. Be keerful an' don't let on. Yer hoss is tied in the brush down the road apiece. Ride easy fer the first mile."

Jim rose slowly to his feet, stretched his arms above his head, and yawned noisily. "Guess I'll turn in," he said. As he passed Simpson, he put a roll of bills into his hand. The landlord stepped out on the porch and took the chair Whitley had just left, while Jake's new partner in deception slipped quietly out by the back door and crept away to his horse.

An hour later, Whitley knocked at the door of the cabin on the riverbank and was admitted by Jake.

"Did ye make hit all right?" the mountaineer asked as Jim entered.

The other nodded. "Simpson is sitting on the front porch, and all the boys think I'm in bed."

Jake chuckled.

"Cap an' the boys are way up the holler after Bill Davis, an' I'm in the brush watchin' you. Now let's git down ter the biz right sharp. Ye mentioned a tidy sum o' money, I reck'lect."

Whitley soon told enough of his story, omitting names and places, to let his companion understand the situation.

When he had finished, Jake took a long pull from a bottle and then said slowly, "An' ye want me ter put that feller what holds the papers out o' yer way?"

Whitley nodded. "It'll pay you a lot better than shooting government agents, and not half the risk."

"What'll ye give me?" asked Jake.

"You can name your own price," replied Whitley.

The outlaw's eyes glittered and he answered in a hoarse whisper, "I'll do hit. What's his name, an' whar'll I find him?"

"Richard Falkner. He lives in Boyd City—"

Slowly the man who had just agreed to commit a murder for money rose to his feet and stepped backward until half the width of the room was between them.

Whitley, alarmed at the expression on his companion's face, rose also, and for several tense moments the silence was broken only by the crackling of the burning wood in the fireplace, the shrill chirp of a cricket, and the plaintive call of a whippoorwill outside. Then with a look of superstitious awe and terror upon his thin face, the moonshiner gasped in a choking voice, "Boyd City—Richard Falkner—mister, ain't ye mistaken? Say, are ye right shore?"

Whitley replied with an oath, "What's the matter with you? You look as though you had seen a ghost."

The ignorant villain started and glanced over his shoulder to the dark corner of the cabin. "Thar might be a ha'nt here, shore 'nough," he whispered hoarsely. "Do ye know whar ye are, mister?"

Then as Whitley remained silent, he continued. "This here's the house whar Dickie Falkner war borned, an' whar his mammy died, an'—an' I'm Jake Tompkins. Me'n his daddy war pards."

Whitley stood dazed.

He looked around the room as though in a dream. Then slowly he realized his situation, and a desperate resolve crept into his heart. Carefully his hand moved beneath his coat until he felt the handle of a long knife while he began edging closer to his companion.

The other seemed not to notice and continued, as though talking to himself. "Little Dickie Falkner. Him what fed me when I war starvin', an' gimme his last nickel when he war hungry hisself, when I was away from home an' tryin' t' git back without a penny t' my name. An' ye want me ter kill him."

He drew a long shuddering breath. "Mister," he went on, "ye shore made a bad mistake this time."

"I'll fix it though!" cried Whitley, and with a vile oath he leaped forward, the knife poised above his head to strike down his companion.

But the keen eye of the man used to danger had seen his stealthy preparation, and Whitley suddenly found his wrist caught in a grasp of iron.

The city-bred villain was no match for his mountain-trained adversary and the struggle was short.

Keeping his hold upon Whitley's wrist, Jake threw his long right arm around his antagonist and drew him close in a crushing embrace. Then, while he looked straight into his victim's fear-lighted eyes, he slowly forced the uplifted hand down and back.

Whitley struggled desperately, but his left arm was pinned to his side and he was held as in a circle of steel. In vain he writhed and twisted, but he was helpless in the powerful grasp of the mountaineer.

Slowly the hand that held the knife was forced behind him. He screamed in pain. The glittering eyes that looked into his never wavered. Jake's right hand behind Jim's back touched the knife, and Whitley saw that evil grin come upon the cruel face. Slowly the city man's arm was twisted until his fingers loosened the hold of the weapon, and the handle of the knife was transferred to the grasp of the strong man who held him.

Then there were two quick, strong thrusts, a shuddering, choking cry, and the arms were loosed as the stricken man fell in a heap on the cabin floor, on the very spot where years before the dying mother had prayed for her son.

"You—have—killed—me—" Whitley gasped.

"I reckon that's 'bout hit, mister."

"Tell—Falkner—I—lied—Amy—is—innocent—and tell—"

But the sentence was never finished.

CHAPTER THIRTY

CHANGE COMES TO BOYD CITY

After several weeks of careful investigation and study of the conditions and needs of Boyd City by the committee suggested by Rev. Cameron in his address, a plan was at last arrived at, the main points of which were as follows:

That an organization be formed to construct a building which, by providing employment for men without work, would offer a ministry much like the Jerusalem Church's already-functioning house, but would be much larger in scope and would involve the entire city, both in its functioning and in its financing. In time, it would be likely that several buildings might be required in order to carry out all the facets of ministry proposed by the committee.

A recreation room—even a small gymnasium was suggested—along with a library, a reading room, classrooms, social parlors, and small medical facility for the care of the sick were all recommended as intrinsic elements of the ministry, which would have two chief aims: to minister to those in need, and to help them find work. It was said there should be a department—one for men and one for women—where the destitute could earn something to eat and a place to sleep by working in wood yards, farms, or factories that were connected to the institution. The whole organization would be under the charge of some Christian man, who would coordinate these various functions of ministry, as well as conduct classes throughout the week in Bible study and also on various topics that would be aimed at helping the men and women integrate themselves functionally into society—various skills, job training, government. These would be conducted not just by the director but by members of the community and from the different churches. The director himself, or his choice of another, would deliver an address on the teaching of Christ every Sunday afternoon in the large auditorium.

Every department of the institution was to be free to the public twenty-four hours a day. It was expected that in time the particular department that provided work for the needy, much like had already been seen to work successfully in the Jerusalem Church's pilot program, would be self-supporting. In order to raise financing initially, however, for the entire organization, it was recommended that shares in the society be sold for twenty-five dollars each, members of the community banding together for the common good in hopes of raising two to three thousand dollars to begin construction. In future years, these shareholders would pay fifteen dollars per share owned, every share entitling them to one vote in the decision-making process of the society, the money going toward the ongoing operation of the institution and to pay its director.

The purpose and plans of the society were to be fully set forth in a little pamphlet and given to every citizen in Boyd City. The people were urged to cooperate with the institution by refusing to give any man, able to work, either food, clothing, or lodging, on the ground that he could obtain the needed help by paying for it in labor at the institution. The townspeople were further asked to assist the work by contributing clothing, by employing laborers, and by using the products of the businesses the institution would develop.

The office of the superintendent of the institution was to be in direct communication with the police station, and anyone applying for help but then refusing to work when work was offered would be turned over to the authorities to be dealt with for vagrancy.

The hope was expressed that the city would cooperate by contributing liberally to the building fund and by using the workers in their street-cleaning department.

The success of the entire scheme, the committee stressed in closing, was that all parts of the city's society cooperate together— the Catholic church, various Protestant churches, the city government itself, the business community, and other social agencies. Most often, they said, civic, social, spiritual, moral, and employment needs are addressed by each church or group's setting up its *own* little program that stresses only one particular facet of the total need. Therefore, all the efforts, done independently, are ineffective. The police deal with the problem of crime. A social agency gives out food. A church leads a Bible study. The Salvation Army takes a band down to the worst part of town and plays hymns. But the problems persist because there is no united effort. The gospel of Christ, they said in closing, was a total gospel to the total man, not a piecemeal one. The churches, and the community, needed to work together in harmony if that gospel was to have a practical and dynamic impact in their city.

When the time came to hear the committee's report, the opera house was crowded as it seldom was for any political speech or theatrical performance. The young people from the various church groups occupied the front seats on the floor of the house, and back of them sat the general public. On the stage with the committee sat many leading businessmen, bankers, merchants, and city officials whose support for the project had already been obtained. There was not a single minister on the stage.

After stating the object of the meeting and reviewing the action of the previous one at Zion Church, where Cameron had spoken, the president of the joint Young People's groups emphasized that this was not a meeting merely of the young people's societies from the various churches, but rather a meeting of the entire community and that everyone present should feel a part of the proceedings, either by voice or ballot. Then he said, "Now Mr. Richard Falkner, chairman of the committee that was formed between the youth groups and the business community, will make his report and will speak for a few minutes on the subject."

As Dick rose and came slowly forward to the front of the stage and stood for a moment as though collecting his thoughts, many throughout the audience could not help thinking: *Can it be possible that this is the same man who, as a tramp, once went from door to door seeking a chance to earn a crust of bread?* And then as they looked at the calm, clear-cut, determined features, and the tall, well-built figure, neatly clothed in a business suit of brown, they burst into involuntary applause. A smile crept over Dick's face as he bowed his handsome head in grateful acknowledgment. Then he held up his hand for silence.

A hush fell over the audience, and in a moment they were listening, with intense interest, to the voice of the once tramp printer.

"Our president has already given you an account of the meeting preceding this. So now I will merely tell you the wishes of the council appointed at that time. I will try to voice their thoughts and aims as those involved have voiced them in our meetings."

He told of the discussions the committee had had, of the help they had received, and then he carefully detailed the plan, enlarging on the different aspects of it as he proceeded.

As he spoke, Dick forgot himself and forgot his audience. He saw only the figure of the Christ, and heard Him say, "Inasmuch as ye have done it unto one of the least of these my brethren, ye have done it unto me," while his hearers sat lost to their surroundings under the magic spell of his words. He demonstrated an eloquence that even his most intimate friends never dreamed he possessed.

George Udell sat in wonder. Could this splendid man now holding such a huge audience enraptured with his flashing eye and glowing face, with burning words and graceful gestures, be the poverty-stricken creature who once fell at Udell's feet fainting with hunger? *Truly,* he thought, *the possibilities of life are infinite. The power of the human soul cannot be measured, and no man guesses the real strength of his closest friend.*

As Dick finished and turned to resume his seat by the side of

Uncle Bobbie, a thunderous applause came from the people. In vain the president tried to restore order, but they would not stop.

At last Dick, trembling with emotion, came back to the front of the stage and held up his hands. "I thank you again for your kindness and the honor you show me," he said as the crowd quieted. "But may I further trespass on that kindness by reminding you that this matter will never be met by clapping hands or applauding voices. Too long in the past have we applauded when our hearts were touched, and allowed the sentiment to die away with the echo of our enthusiasm. Too often we offer the pastor a shake of the hand and a kind word about his sermon, while we walk out the church door never to think of his words again, much less attempt to live them. Too often we are moved by a beautiful song, but never think that to make the song a true reality, we must live and behave as the lyrics suggest. Shall it be so this time? Once again I ask you, men and women, in the name of Jesus Christ who died on Calvary, what will you do for the least of them, His brethren?"

A long pause came, during which Dick resumed his seat. Then Banker Lindsley rose. Instantly the people became quiet and all turned toward Boyd City's leading financier.

"The committee has requested me to ask all those who wish to become charter members of an association as suggested in the report of the council to meet here on the stage immediately following this meeting."

He stood to one side; then the president came forward again and dismissed the assembly with a few words. In the minutes that followed, however, it seemed there were more people pushing their way forward toward the stage than were trying to exit at the rear of the huge hall.

As the group gathered, Mr. Lindsley looked around. "Where's Falkner?" he asked. No one knew. They searched the hall, but Dick could not be found. At length the company remaining was called to order, and the agreement was finally reached to meet in the Commercial Club the next Wednesday night to begin formulating a constitution and bylaws, and to begin electing officers and thus begin the business at hand.

Half an hour later some of the people on their way home from the meeting noticed a tall figure, dressed in a business suit of brown, standing in the shadow of the catalpa trees on the avenue, looking upward at a church spire, built in the form of a giant hand, and at the darkened stained-glass window, in which was faintly visible the figure of Christ holding a lamb in His arms. Later, they might have seen the same figure walking slowly past a beautiful residence a few blocks farther up the street, and when opposite a corner window, pausing a moment to stand while his lips moved as though whispering a prayer for one whose memory filled the place with mingled pleasure and pain.

About one o'clock on the following Wednesday, Uncle Bobbie Wicks dropped into the printing office.

"Good afternoon, Mr. Wicks," said Dick, looking up from his work. "You want to see a proof of those letterheads, I suppose. Jack, take a proof of that job of Uncle Bobbie's."

Uncle Bobbie took a chair and a few moments later Dick's young helper brought them the proofsheet. He looked over the work a moment, then lifted his head and remarked, "The new association meets tonight, doesn't it?"

Dick nodded, and the old gentleman continued nonchalantly as he arose to go, "Stop by for me when you go, will you? We'll walk over together."

"But I'm not going," said Dick.

Uncle Bobbie dropped back in his seat with a jar. "Not going!" he exclaimed. "Why, what's the matter with you?" He sat staring at the young man.

"Nothing's the matter," replied Dick with a smile. "I cannot become a member of the association when it is organized, and so I have no right to attend the meeting tonight. I would like to join after a time, but I cannot now."

"Why not?" said Wicks.

"Because I haven't the money," Dick replied.

Uncle Bobbie settled back in his chair with a sigh of relief. "Oh, is that all? I thought maybe you'd changed your mind about something you said."

"No, nothing like that," Dick answered quietly, but he did not explain how he had spent everything he had saved in his search for the wealthy hardware merchant's daughter. Perhaps Uncle Bobbie needed no explanation.

"Well, let me tell you, you're going anyhow, and you're going to have voting power too," announced Uncle Bobbie. "Be a pretty kettle of fish if after that speech of yours you weren't in the company. Be like tryin' to make cheese without any milk."

"But I haven't the money and that's all there is to it. I will join in as soon as I am able."

"Well," returned Uncle Bobbie, "you can borrow it."

"From whom?"

"From me if no one else," retorted Wicks. "Who do you think?"

"But I can give you no security."

"Security my foot! What would I do with security from one of my friends! Isn't your Christianity security enough?" asked Uncle Bobbie with a gruff smile.

Dick laughed. "Is that the way men do business in Boyd City?"

"I doubt it," returned Uncle Bobbie. "But it's the way I do business when I'm doing the Master's business. And that settles it."

When Dick and Uncle Bobbie reached the Commercial Club that evening, they found it filled with a large company of interested townspeople and businessmen; and when the opportunity was given, over two hundred enrolled as members of the Association, as it was called, thus raising some five thousand dollars with which to construct the new facility. It appeared there would be sufficient money remaining to maintain and fund it for a year, even after all construction costs were paid.

Mr. Lindsley, the banker, was elected president, with Mr. Wallace, a merchant, vice-president. Then with great enthusiasm, a unanimous ballot of the Association was cast for Mr. Richard Falkner as secretary, while to Dick's delight, Uncle Bobbie was given the place of treasurer.

The papers of the city in the days following gave a full and enthusiastic account of the new movement. And when the citizens saw that the Association was really a fact, that it was really going to happen, with men in charge who were well qualified to fill their positions, then even greater confidence in the plan began to emerge in the community, which resulted in greater numbers soon joining in as members.

A prospectus setting forth the object of the Association, together with its plans and constitution, was drawn up, printed, and then sent out to all members and made available to the entire city. The newspapers continued to speak well of the plan; and finally, through the influence of the strong businessmen who were involved, the city itself appropriated an additional three thousand dollars to the building fund, and one thousand a year, for five years.

With such backing as it now had, the Association began preparation for active work. A fine building site was purchased, with plenty of room for expansion; and drawings were begun for the main building, which would house the kitchen, meeting rooms, a large hall, the hospital, a modest recreation room, several parlors, and the housing facilities for the staff. Once that was completed, additional smaller facilities would be built to provide sleeping accommodations and some work stations for the beginning of certain small, self-sustaining businesses.

Prior to construction, however, it was thought that it might be beneficial for Dick to travel about to study various plans and institutions that were operating similar works in several of the large cities. There was nothing quite like their own association, they all agreed; yet several YMCA's were carrying out related operations, a few churches had joined hands in certain areas to minister effectively to their communities, and there were also several private and government-backed agencies that bore examination. Perhaps, it was thought, through a study of the strengths and weaknesses of all these organizations, some useful ideas could be gleaned that would help them toward their own goals.

To this end, Dick asked Udell for a month's leave of absence, and made preparations to take the train north and east.

"Well, goodbye, old man," said Udell when Dick stepped into

the office on his way to the depot. "I can tell that one of these days I'm going to lose a mighty good printer."

"I'll be gone only a month, George," laughed Dick.

"A month, this time," replied George. "But next time, it might well be for keeps."

"I won't leave you again, George. Not without a good reason."

"Just what I'm afraid of."

"But you know," said Dick as he grasped his employer's hand with hope shining in his eyes, "why I am glad for this chance to go east again."

"Yes, I know, my friend," Udell answered. "If Clara was somewhere out there in the world without a friend, I reckon I'd go too."

"Thank you," replied Dick solemnly. "I'm glad you understand."

"God bless you, Dick. I hope you find her."

So Dick went. And his travels took him to many places. Whenever he reached a town, he would first go to the YMCA to secure a room. Then he would embark on a two- or three-day investigation of that city's ministries which he felt he might profitably learn from. There was a great deal to see simply in observing how each Y conducted its affairs. Wherever there was a mission in operation in the lower parts of town, he visited it, taking mental notes. He attended more profitless church services and walked by more tightly locked church houses than he cared to remember. But whenever he did encounter a church or a club or an organization that was attempting to reach out to the downtrodden in any manner whatsoever, he heartily joined in with them for a day or two—both to help them briefly in their work and to see from the inside what sort of impact they were having in their own communities.

Wherever he went, when he explained the purpose of his mission, he was welcomed warmly into the ranks of his fellow ministers. And thus his month passed as he worked his way, first to St. Louis, then to Chicago, and slowly eastward.

CHAPTER THIRTY-ONE

UNEXPECTED REUNION

After those terrible weeks, which had drifted hopelessly into months of despair trying in vain to find work and some way to preserve her dwindling means, Amy's resources had at length dried up and she knew she was penniless. And after one terrible night on the streets of Cleveland, she had finally admitted defeat and returned to Madam's house, where she was kindly received.

Under the woman's skillful treatment, Amy rapidly regained her strength and beauty. Never doubting that Whitley had made it impossible for her ever to return to Boyd City, she felt she was dead to the kind world she had once known, and looked upon the life she was entering as her only refuge from the cruel world she had now learned to know.

Several of the girls proved to be very kind and sympathetic companions. Little by little Amy grew accustomed to her surroundings and in a measure learned to look upon the life they led from their point of view. And when the time came, after being there about two weeks, for her to join the company in the parlor, she accepted her lot as inevitable and with hopeless resignation.

When she had carefully dressed herself in a silken evening gown provided by Madam, she made her way alone down to the wine rooms.

The scene that met her eyes was beautiful and fascinating. The room was large and brilliantly lighted. The furniture, accoutrements, and pictures on the walls were of the finest, with rare bits of statuary half hidden in banks of choicest flowers. Upon the floor were carpets and rugs, in which the foot sank as in beds of moss, and luxurious chairs and couches invited the visitor to ease and indolence. From behind silken curtains came soft strains of music, and deft waiters glided here and there, bearing trays of expensive wines and liquors.

Seated at the card tables, drinking, laughing, and playing, were the wealthy patrons of the place, and mingling with them were the girls of Madam's house—all of exceptional grace and beauty, dressed in glittering evening attire. But hardly one of them eclipsed the radiant creature who stood with flushed cheeks, shining eyes, and terrified heart, hesitating on the threshold.

Madam, moving here and there among her guests, saw Amy as she stood in the doorway and went to her at once. Leading the girl to a little alcove at one end of the room, she presented her to a middle-aged man who was seated by himself and who seemed to be waiting for someone. Amy did not know that he was waiting for her. As the three stood there chatting, a servant came quietly to Madam's side and whispered something in her jeweled ear.

"Certainly," she answered; "tell them to come in."

Then turning, she stepped to a table, rapped with her fan to attract attention, and cried out over the din, "The Salvation Army people want to come in and hold a brief prayer meeting here for us. What do you say?"

There was a babble of voices, shrieks of feminine laughter, and an oath or two from the men. Some shouted, "Let them come!" Others protested, until Madam stopped the clamor by saying sharply, "Of course they shall come in. You know it is never my custom to refuse these people. I respect and admire them. They believe in their own teaching and live what they preach, and I want it understood that they shall not be insulted in this house. Jerry—"

A huge ex-prizefighter stepped into the room from a side door.

"You all know Jerry, Gentlemen," continued Madam with a

smile, "and if you are not acquainted with him, you can easily obtain an introduction by making some slighting remark, or offering an insult to these Salvation soldiers."

As the little band of men and women filed slowly in and took their position in the center of the room, Madam gave a signal and everyone rose and gathered about the Salvationists—all except the girl in the alcove, who turned her back to the group and stood partly screened by the lace draperies of the archway.

The visitors opened their service with a song, chosen with good taste and rendered with much feeling—not loud as they might have done it on the street, but soft, low, and pleading. Many eyes glistened and many lips trembled when the song came to a close, and as the singers dropped to their knees, not a few heads involuntarily bowed.

One after another the little band prayed, pleading with God to be kind and merciful to the erring, asking the Father, in the name of Jesus, to pity and forgive. Truly it was a picture of great contrasts—of brightest lights and deepest shadows—almost as when the Son of God prayed for His enemies, and wept because they were His enemies.

Three of the six had offered their prayers and then the fourth began: "Our Father and our God . . ."

At the first word, uttered in a clear, manly but subdued tone, the girl behind the curtain started violently, and as the prayer continued slowly, in that voice so full of powerful truth and vigor, she raised her head and the rich blood colored her neck and cheek. Little by little the hard look in her eyes gave way to one of mingled wonder, doubt, and awe. Then the blood fled back to the trembling heart again, leaving her face as white as the marble figure near which she stood. And then, as though compelled by a power superior to her own will, she turned slowly and stepped from the hiding place into full view. As if stricken dumb, she stood until the prayer was finished. The captain gave the signal and the little company rose to their feet.

"Oh, God!" cried the man who had prayed last as he saw the girl and sprang forward. But he was not quick enough, for before he could cross the room, she sank to the floor with a moan of unutterable anguish.

When Dick had arrived in Cleveland two days before, he had taken a room at the YMCA and then checked in with the local Salvation Army, of which he had heard a good report, to see what sort of ministries it was involved in. After explaining his mission to the captain, Dick was invited to participate in several street services with them. This was now his second day as a temporary enlistee in the small band.

All of a sudden, without prelude or warning, his secondary mission had in an unexpected moment been fulfilled as he found himself dropping on one knee beside Amy and reaching out to support the senseless girl in his arms.

All was confusion immediately. Men and women crowded about their companion, while the Salvationists looked at one another in pity, surprise, and wonder.

Then Madam spoke: "Girls, be quiet. Gentlemen, make way. Amy has only fainted. Bring her in here."

The stalwart prizefighter touched Dick on the shoulder, and the latter, with the lovely form still in his arms, followed, as in a dream, the man and Madam to her own private apartment.

A doctor came, in answer to a hurried call, and after no little effort the color slowly returned to the cheeks, and the long, dark lashes began to tremble.

The physician turned to Dick. "Leave us now. She must not see you at first."

Dick looked at Madam. "May I have a few words privately with you?"

The woman nodded, and with the army captain, they retired to another room, leaving Amy in the charge of the doctor and one of the Salvation lasses.

Then Dick told Madam and the captain the whole story of Amy's life and home, how she had gone away because of her father's mistake, how Whitley had deceived her, and how they had searched for her in vain. Then as he told of the mother's broken health and of the sorrowing friends, though he made no mention of himself, they could not but read as he spoke of others, something of his own personal trouble on account of Amy's straits.

Tears gathered in Madam's eyes, and when the tale was finished, she said, "Somehow I have always felt that Amy would never remain with us."

And then she told of the poor girl's bitter experience alone in the great city, and how as a last resort, she had accepted her present situation. "She is more refined and gentle than the others," continued Madam, "and in my heart, I have always hoped that she would leave here. But what could she do? She had no friends, no money, no place to go, no job, no home. And in this wretched business we can scarcely afford to have feelings. Oh, this life is a very hell on earth, and bad as I am, I would never lay a straw in any girl's way who wanted to get out of it. I am very glad you came in time. You know, Captain, that I have never opposed your work. Without protest I have seen you take several girls from my place. I sometimes could not help actually envying them a little, but of course, such a religious life would never suit me."

They discussed the situation for some time. Finally Madam said again, "Mr.— I don't even know your name."

Dick opened his mouth to answer.

"Never mind," the woman continued. "I don't want to. You wear that uniform and that's enough for me. But what I want to say is this: just let Amy remain here for a day or two. One of the Salvation girls will stay with her, and can do more for her right now than you. Then when she is strong enough, you may come and take her if she will go. And I am sure she will. She will be as safe here as in her father's home."

The captain nodded. "Madam has given her word," he said. "I can vouch for it. You come with me and arrange for the future, while your friend regains her strength again. Our Sarah will remain with her and keep us posted."

Dick agreed. And after hearing from the doctor that Amy was resting easier, they bade Madam good night and reentered the room where again the music played, jewels sparkled, wine flowed, and the careless laugh and jest were heard.

With a shudder of horror, Dick thought to himself, *How could Amy ever come to such a place!* And never, though he lived to be an old man, could Dick look back upon that night and the days following without turning pale. How he lived through it, he never knew. Perhaps it was because he had suffered so much in his own up-and-down career that he was enabled to bear that which otherwise would have been impossible. And the consciousness of the great change in his own life led him to hope for Amy when others would have given up in despair.

While Dick and his friends planned for Amy's future, Sarah, the Salvation girl, remained by the girl's bedside, caring for her as a sister. Not one hint of reproach or censure fell from her lips—only words of lovingkindness or hope and courage. At first the poor girl refused to listen, sobbing convulsively that her life was ruined and begged that they leave her alone in her disgrace and sin.

But Sarah herself could say, "I know, sister. I have been through it all, and if Jesus could save me, He can save you too."

So at last, love and hope conquered, and as soon as she was strong enough, she left the place and went with Sarah to her humble home. There Dick called to see her.

"Mr. Falkner," Amy said sadly, after the pain and embarrassment of the first meeting had somewhat passed off, "I do not understand. What makes you do these things?"

"What things?"

"Trying to help people . . . helping *me*."

"Didn't I tell you once," Dick answered, "that nothing could make me change, that nothing you could do would make me less your friend? For a while you made it impossible for me to help you, but the desire, the wish, was there just the same. And besides," he added gently, "you know I'm a Christian now."

Amy hung her head.

"Yes," she replied slowly, "you are a Christian. These people from the Salvation Army are Christians too, but I—I—am—oh,

Mr. Falkner, won't you help me now? Indeed, I need you to be my friend."

"You know, of course, that I will do anything," Dick promised.

"Tell me what I should do. I cannot go back home like this. I do believe in Jesus, and that He sent you to me. I'm so tired of this world, for I know the awfulness of it now. And these good people have taught me that one can live close to Christ even in the most unfavorable circumstances."

Dick told her of his plan, how his new friend, the captain, had arranged for her to live on a farm in northern Missouri with the family of the captain's brother, and that they only wanted her consent to begin the journey there at once. Would she go?

"But how can I?" asked Amy. "I have no money, and have never been taught to work."

"Miss Goodrich," answered Dick, "can you trust me in this?"

Amy was silent.

"You must let me help you," Dick continued. "Thank God I can do it now. Prove to me that you are still my friend by letting me make this investment for Christ. Will you?"

She agreed.

The next day they bade goodbye to the sturdy soldiers of the cross who had been so true to them, and started on their westward journey.

Dick saw Amy safe in her new home, and then with a promise that she would write to him regularly, and with an agreement that he would send letters and papers to her, addressed to the people with whom she lived, he left her, for he was satisfied that she was in kind hands and that a new life was about to open before her.

But when Dick was once more aboard the train, alone with his thoughts, without anxiety for Amy's immediate welfare upon his mind, a new struggle began.

He loved Amy dearly, had loved her almost from the moment she came into George Udell's printing office three years before, loved her in spite of the difference in their social position—when he was only a tramp and she was the favored daughter of wealth, when he was an unbeliever and she was a worker in the church—loved her when he saw her losing her hold on the higher life and drifting with the current, loved her when she left home, and, as he thought, honor behind.

And he was forced to confess, in his own heart, that he loved her still in spite of the fact that their positions were reversed. Now he was a respected man, trusted by the community, while she, in the eyes of the world, was a wayward girl with no friend but himself.

What of the future?

Dick's dream had always been that he would win such a position in the world as would enable him, with confidence, to ask her to share his life. But there was always the feeling that he never could be worthy. And with the dark picture of his own past before him, he knew he had no right to think of her as his wife.

But now the question was not with his position, but rather with hers. Could he think of taking her for a wife now? On the one hand, his love pleaded in the affirmative. Yet the change in her life argued against it. Would not people think he was taking advantage of her lowly condition, and thus think worse of both of them? Would such be fair to Amy?

Yet as his own past life came before him like a horrid vision, just as it had done that morning when he learned of his father's death, it spoke to his sense of justice. That she had sunk low should no more alter his view of her than his own past life altered Christ's view of him as a man worthy to be saved. He saw his childhood home, smelled the odor of the fragrant pines upon the hills, and heard the murmur of the river running past the cabin. Again he heard his drunken father cursing in his sleep, and caught the whisper of his mother's dying prayer. And again he saw himself as a young boy creeping stealthily out of the cabin into the glory of the morning, with a lean hound his only companion.

Slowly and painfully he traced his way along the road of memory, recalling every place where he had advanced, every place where he had fallen, going step by step from the innocence of boyhood to the dreadful knowledge of the man of the world. He had fought, had fallen, had conquered, and had risen again, always advancing toward the light, but always bearing on his garment the smell of the fire, and upon his hands the stain of the pitch.

And now because he was safe at last and could look back upon those things, should he look differently upon another? Would not Amy also conquer, and when she had conquered, would not Christ as freely welcome her back into the fold as He had welcomed him? Christianity held out as many glorious hopes for her as for him. Her past might be past as well as his. Why should he not shut the door upon it forever, and live only in the present and the future?

Then his mind fell to picturing what that future, with Amy by his side, might be. They were equals now, before God and their own consciences. Why should he care what the world might think or say?

And so, the fight went on in the battleground of his heart until the whistle blew a long blast for the station, and looking from the window of the car, he saw the smelter smoke and dust of Boyd City.

CHAPTER THIRTY-TWO

STUNNING NEWS

John Barton and his wife Anna, with whom Amy was now making her home, came to love their new daughter in a very short time.

Both of them fully sympathized with the girl in her sad position, though one would never dream that the quiet, reserved John knew as much of life as he did of his pigs and cattle, or that his jolly-faced motherly companion had ever been beyond the quiet fields that surrounded her simple dwelling. In fact, years before, they had been rescued from the world in which Amy had so nearly perished, and by the same kind hand that had been stretched out to her—the Salvation Army. And now, well on in middle life, happy and prosperous, they showed scarcely a trace of the trouble that had driven them to labor on a farm.

As hired help they had gained their experience, and by ceaseless industry and careful economy, the couple had at last come to own the place where they now lived. With no child of her own, Mrs. Barton took a mother's place in Amy's life from the first moment, and was very patient with the girl who had never been taught to do the simplest household task.

Amy returned the loving kindness in full measure, and determined to be a help to those who so much helped her. Thus she advanced rapidly in the knowledge of her duties about the home and farm.

Dressed in the plain working garb of a farm girl, with arms bare and face flushed by the heat of the kitchen, one would scarcely have recognized in her the beautiful young woman who once moved with Boyd City's society leaders, or the brilliant novice who stood hesitating at the entrance to a life of sin in Madam's wine parlor. And certainly, one would never have classed the bright eyes, plump cheeks, and well-rounded figure with the frightened, starving, haggard girl who had roamed the streets of Cleveland a few short months before.

But great as was the change in Amy's outward appearance, the change within was even greater. She was no longer the thoughtless, proud, pleasure-loving belle that her parents had trained, nor was she the hard, reckless, hopeless creature that the world had made. She was a *woman* now, with a true woman's interest and purpose in life. The shallow brilliance of the society girl had given place to thoughtful earnestness, and the dreary sadness of the outcast had changed to bright hopefulness.

One warm day in June, Mrs. Barton laid the last neatly ironed garment on the big pile of clothes nearby and noisily pushed her irons to the back of the stove.

"Thank goodness, that's the last of it for this week!" she cried.

Throwing out the dishwater, Amy mimicked the voice of her friend, "And thank goodness that's the last of that!" She hung the empty pan in its place.

Mrs. Barton wiped the perspiration from her steaming face. "Come on, let's get out of this inferno for a while and do our patching in the shade. I'm going to melt if I stay here a minute longer."

Soon the two were seated in their low chairs on the cool porch, with a big basket of mending between them.

"Why, there's our man back from town already!" exclaimed Mrs. Barton a few minutes later as her husband drove into the barnyard. Then with a mischievous twinkle in her blue eyes, she called, "Hurry up, John. Amy wants her letter."

John smiled in his quiet way as he came up to the porch and handed the girl an envelope with the Boyd City postmark. Then the old people both laughed at Amy's embarrassment when, rising, Mrs. Barton said in her teasing voice, "Come on, hubby, I'll fix your dinner. We've kept it warm. Can't you see the lass wants to be left alone with her treasure from her man?"

When Mrs. Barton returned a while later to the porch and her mending, she hardly noticed that Amy's hands were idle and her work was lying untouched in her lap as she sat looking wistfully far away across the sunlit meadows and pastures. But after a long talk with her husband concerning his business in town, Mrs. Barton's jolly face wore an expression of seriousness that was unusual.

Both women took up their tasks in silence and plied their needles with energy, while their thoughts were far away; but one thought of a great city in the faraway east, the other, of a bustling mining town in the nearer west.

At last Mrs. Barton spoke with a little sigh, not knowing how to ease into what she knew she must eventually tell. "Amy, dear," she said, "I suppose you will be leaving us one of these days before long."

The girl answered with a smile. "Are you so tired of me that you are going to send me out into the world again?"

"No, no, dear. You have a home with John and me as long as you live. Surely you know that, don't you, Amy dear?" There was a wistful note in the kind voice. The older woman dropped the stocking she was darning, leaned forward, and placed her hand on the arm of Amy's chair.

A rush of tears was her answer as the girl caught the toil-stained hand and carried it passionately to her lips. "Of course I know, Mother. I was only funnin'."

"But I'm awfully in earnest," replied the other.

There seemed to be a hidden meaning in her words and Amy looked at her anxiously. "I do not understand why you think I should leave you," she said seriously.

"Because—because—I—this life must be so degrading to you. You could live so differently at home," Mrs. Barton finally answered.

Amy looked at her steadily. "That cannot be your reason, Mother," she returned gently. "You know that a woman degrades herself when she does nothing useful, and that I count my present place and work far above my old life at home. Why, just think," she added with a quiet smile, "John said last night that he couldn't tell my biscuits from yours. And wasn't dinner all right today? And isn't this a beautiful patch?" She held up her work for inspection.

The other shook her head while she smiled in answer. "I know, dear girl, you do beautifully. But that's not it. There are your father and mother and brother. You know you can't stay away from them forever."

Amy's face grew troubled, while her hand nervously sought the letter hidden in her bosom.

"You do not understand, Mother," she replied slowly. "My people do not want me to come home. My father said I should not, until—until—" She hesitated.

"But surely your father has forgotten his anger by this time," Mrs. Barton reasoned, "and when he sees you he will be glad to forgive and take you back."

The brown eyes looked at the woman in startled surprise. "When he sees me?" Amy repeated.

But the other continued hurriedly. "And there are the letters, you know."

Amy's face grew red. "Why the letters?" she murmured.

"Because he loves you, dear, don't you see?"

"He has never told me so," Amy replied.

"Not in words perhaps," agreed Mrs. Barton.

Amy was silent.

"He will come for you one of these days," her companion continued, "and then you will go with him."

The girl sadly shook her head. Turning her face, she looked away across the fields again, where silent, patient John sturdily followed his team as he plowed the rich ground.

The shadow of the big sycamore was stretching across the barn lot almost to the gate where the cows stood watching for the boy to come and let them in. A troop of droning bees were paying their last visit for the day to the peach tree that flung its wealth of passionate blossoms almost within reach of the porch. And over the blue distant woods the last of the feathery banks of mist hung lazily, as though tangled in the budding branches, reluctant to say good night.

Suddenly leaving her chair, Amy threw herself on the floor and burst into tears as she buried her face in the lap of the older woman, whose own eyes were wet as she softly smoothed the brown hair of the girl she had taken to her mother's heart.

"You do love him, don't you, dear?" she asked.

"Because I love him so, I must never see him again," answered Amy between her sobs. "He—he—is so strong and good and true—he could not care for one who would only bring reproach upon his name."

"I know, dear girl, and that is why you must go home. Take your own place in the world again, and then the way will be clear between you and him."

Amy lifted her head. "Oh, if only I could!" she cried. "But you do not know—my going home would only widen the distance between us. My father—"

She paused again. Her quivering lips could not form the words.

"Amy, I am sure you are mistaken. You must be. When you meet your father, it will all come right, I know."

Again there seemed to be a hidden meaning in her words. Amy repeated her words: "*When* I meet my father?" she said slowly.

Mrs. Barton grew flustered.

"Yes—I—we—you know John has been trying to sell the place for a long time. We want to go back to Cleveland, you know—"

She hesitated, struggling to find the right words for the awkward news.

"—and today—he learned—that a buyer was coming to see it—from Boyd City—"

Amy's face grew white as she rose, trembling, to her feet.

"My father!" she gasped, "—coming here?"

The motherly woman took the frightened girl in her arms.

"There, there, dear, don't be afraid," she soothed. "All will be for the best, I am sure. John and I will stand by you and you shall go with us to Cleveland if you wish. But I am sure your father will be glad to take you home with him. And you ought to go. You know you ought, not for your family's sake alone, but for his, you know."

And so they talked as the shadows grew, until in the twilight John came from the field with his tired team. Then they went into the house to prepare the light evening meal.

CHAPTER THIRTY-THREE

FORGIVING BUT UNFORGIVEN

Adam Goodrich had by no means forgiven his beautiful daughter for the blow dealt his pride, though one could not easily detect from his manner that there was anything but supreme self-satisfaction in the life of this worthy leader in the Jerusalem Church.

Mrs. Goodrich's health was broken, but she still remained the same society-loving, fashion-worshiping woman, who by her influence and teaching had made the way of her child so hard. It never occurred to the mother that Amy's conduct was the logical and legitimate, indeed, almost the inevitable, outcome of her training and example. She looked upon everything that had happened as stemming from weaknesses in the girl.

Frank, true son of his father, never mentioned his sister but with a curl of his lip, and lived his life as though she had never existed. The family still attended the church once each week, still contributed the same amount to the cause, Mr. Goodrich still cast his vote as deacon according to what he termed his conscience but which was in reality his own warped sense of convention, and still found fault with Cameron for his low tastes and his new methods of so-called "ministry." They all continued to laugh at the new Association as a dream of fools and misguided enthusiasts. Adam had long wanted to add a good farm to his possessions, and after some correspondence with the agent who had advertised the Barton property, he boarded the train one bright day to pay a visit of inspection to his contemplated purchase. Reaching the little city of Zanesville in the evening, he spent the night at a hotel. In the morning he called upon the agent, and the two were soon whirling along the road behind a pair of wiry little ponies.

The drive of eight or ten miles passed very pleasantly between the real estate man and his prospective customer, in such conversation as gentlemen whose lives are spent in the bustle of the money world indulge in between moments of activity.

At last they neared the farm, and bringing the ponies to a walk, the agent began pointing out the most desirable features of the property: the big barn, the fine timber in the distance, the rich soil of a field nearby, the magnificent crop of corn, the stream of water where cattle stood knee-deep lazily fighting the flies, and the fine young orchard just across the road from the house.

"Yes, the building is old," the agent agreed as they drove up in front of the big gate, "—but it is good yet, and with just a little expense, could be converted into a model of modern convenience and beauty."

As they drove into the yard and got out to unhitch the ponies, Mrs. Barton came to the door. "Just come right in, Mr. Richards. John is over in the north field; I'll go for him."

"Oh no, Mrs. Barton, I'll go," replied the realtor. "This is Mr. Goodrich. He would like to have a look around the farm. Mr. Goodrich, just wait here in the shade and I'll go after Mr. Barton."

"I believe, if you don't mind, I'll have a walk through the orchard until you return," replied Adam.

"Certainly, certainly," said both the agent and the farmer's wife, and the woman added nervously, "Just make yourself at home, Mr. Goodrich. You'll find the girl out there somewhere. Dinner will be ready in about an hour."

Leisurely crossing the road, Adam paused at the orchard gate to watch some fine young shoats that were running about with their mother. From the pigs, his gaze wandered about the farm buildings, the fields, and the garden. Turning at last to enter the orchard, he saw a young woman, clad in the homely everyday dress of a country girl, her face hidden beneath a large sunbonnet of blue gingham. She was gathering apple blossoms.

Something in her manner or figure struck him as being familiar, and with his hand on the gate he paused again. As he stood watching her, who was unconscious of his presence, she sprang lightly from the ground in an effort to reach a tempting spray of blossoms; and at her quick movement the sunbonnet dropped from her head, while a wealth of brown hair fell in a rippling mass to her waist. Then as she half turned, he saw her face distinctly, and with a start of surprise and astonishment, he recognized her as his daughter.

Under the first impulse of a father's love at seeing his child again, Adam stepped forward. But with the gate half open, he checked himself and then drew back. In another instant the old haughty pride, that dominant key in his character, hardened his heart again. And when he at last pushed open the gate once more, whatever was left of his love was fairly hidden.

When Amy first caught sight of her father advancing slowly toward her beneath the blossom-laden trees, she forgot everything and started quickly toward him, her face lighted with eager welcome, ready to throw herself into his arms and there pour out her whole tearful story and beg his love and forgiveness.

But when she saw his face, she dared not, and stood with downcast eyes, trembling and afraid.

"So this is where you hide yourself while your family faces your shame at home," began Adam coldly. "Tell me who brought you here and who pays these people to keep you."

The girl lifted her head proudly. But what a different kind of pride it was than that which beat in the heart of her father! Amy's was the pride of womanhood. "No one pays them, sir. I am supporting myself."

The man looked at her in amazement. "Do you mean that your position here is that of a common servant?"

"There are worse positions," she replied, not without a trace of sadness in her voice. "The people here are very kind to me. They treat me like a daughter, and I love them."

"But what of your family? You are a disgrace to us all! What can I tell them when I go back and say that I have seen you?"

"Tell them I am well, and as happy as I deserve to be." She pressed her hand to her bosom where a letter was hidden.

"But what will people say when they know that my daughter is working on a farm for a living?" asked the angry father.

"They need never know unless you tell them, if the truth is so painful to you," said Amy.

Then the proud Adam Goodrich lost all control of himself. That this girl, who had always yielded to his every wish without so much as daring to have a thought of her own, should so calmly, but firmly, face him in this manner and speak to him thus enraged him beyond measure. He could not understand. He knew nothing of her life since that night he had refused to listen to her explanation, and now in his anger he taunted her with being unduly familiar with Dick Falkner; and then, because her face flushed, he thought he had hit on the truth and grew almost abusive in his language.

But Amy only answered, "Sir, you are mistaken now, just as you were when you drove me from home. Mr. Falkner had nothing to do with my leaving Boyd City."

"You are my daughter still," stormed Adam, "and I will force you to leave this low position and come home to us. You cannot deceive me with your clever lies about supporting yourself. What do you know about servant's work? That cursed tramp printer is at the bottom of all this, and I'll make him suffer for it as long as I live. I will force you to come home."

Amy's face grew pale, but she replied quietly, "Oh no, Father, you will not do that, because that would make public my position, you know. I have no fear of your proclaiming from the housetops that your daughter is a hired girl on a farm. I know you well enough. You would never do such a thing for fear of your own reputation.

"But, Father," she said in a softer voice as Adam stood speechless with rage, "Father—forgive me for this, for I know that I am right. Let me stay here and prove that I am not useless to the world, and then perhaps I will return to you. In the meantime, keep my secret and no one shall know that your claim on society has been lessened because your daughter is learning to do a woman's work."

Just a shade of sarcasm crept into her voice, but her father did not notice it, for he saw the agent and the farmer coming. "Very well," he returned hurriedly; "you have chosen your path and must walk in it. But you cannot expect me to acknowledge a servant as my daughter."

Turning his back, he went to meet the men, while Amy slipped off to the house with her blossoms.

Mrs. Barton needed no word to tell her of the result of the interview from which she had expected so much; so with a kiss and a loving word, she permitted the girl to go upstairs, where she remained until Mr. Goodrich had left the place.

After completing the purchase of the farm, Adam wrote his daughter from the office of the agent in Zanesville: "The place where you are living now belongs to me, and the Bartons must give possession at once. If you will promise never to speak to that man Falkner again, you may come home and be received into your old place, but on no other terms will I acknowledge you as my daughter. Refuse and you will be thrown on the charity of the world, for you cannot remain where you are, and you will never see a penny of Goodrich money."

Amy took the letter to her friends, together with her reply. By every argument of love they tried to induce her to go with them back to Cleveland, but she refused them amid many tears. And when she would not be persuaded, they were compelled to leave her. With many expressions of love, they said goodbye and departed for their old home in the eastern city.

Before going, they arranged with friends in a neighboring town to give her a place in their already crowded home until she could find means of support. There was some talk in the town where they lived concerning a need for a teacher in the fall, and it was hoped Amy might apply and be found suitable.

CHAPTER THIRTY-FOUR

THE ASSOCIATION TAKES SHAPE

Upon Dick's return from his Cleveland trip, he had thrown himself into his work with feverish energy. Yet in his heart, the struggle over his love for Amy and his thoughts of the future continued.

As the weeks of the summer went by and Amy's letters came, telling of her life on the farm, and how she was learning to be of use in the world, he had read between the lines to see her changing views of life, and her deepening maturity, and he found his love for her growing still stronger.

But then suddenly a letter came, bidding him goodbye, and telling him that she was going away again, and that for her sake he must not try to find her, that she was deeply grateful for all he had done, but it was best that he forget he had ever known her.

Dick was hurt and dismayed. Bitterly he chastised himself for being so hesitant to declare his love. Was it now too late forever? Many doubts, one of which was the fear that perhaps she had given up in her fight against the devil, eventually sent him into the black depths of despair.

"I never saw such a man," said George Udell to Clara Wilson one evening as they caught a glimpse of him bending over a desk in Uncle Bobbie's office; "he works like a fiend."

"Like an angel, you ought to say," replied Clara. "Didn't I tell you he was no common tramp?"

"Yes, dear, of course," agreed George.

"Where do you suppose Amy Goodrich is now? Do you know, I have fancied at times that Mr. Falkner learned something on his last trip that he has not told us?"

"What makes you think that?" asked George.

"Somehow he seems so different since he returned," answered Clara.

George shook his head. "I thought so too, for a while," he replied. "But I talked with him just the other day, and I'm afraid he's all but given up hope on her. He works to hide the hurt. But I'll tell you one thing, if anything could make a Christian of me, it would be Dick's life. There's something more than human in the way he stands up against all he's had to face. And the change in him, in the way he treats people, and his outlook on life, well, it makes me wonder if there's not something to it after all."

In the middle of August Dick received a letter, handwritten and barely legible, from a post office in Texas:

> Dere Dikkie: I take my pen in hand to let u no that Ime wel an hoape u are the same. Jim Whitly is ded. He don tried to nife me an i fixed him. he wanted to hire me to kil u fer some papers an we was in you ol caben kross the river from the still. He said ter tel u that he lied to u an that Amy is inosent. I dont no what he means but thot u ort ter no. I skipped—burn this. Yor daddys pard.
>
> Jake Tompkins

Throughout the remaining summer months and into the fall, construction continued on the Association building, and by mid-October it was sufficiently completed to begin being used, though the finish work would continue on for some time.

One morning the pastor of the Jerusalem Church sat in his study looking over the morning mail. There was the usual number of magazines, papers, and sample copies of religious periodicals, with catalogues and circulars from publishing houses; an appeal to help a poor church in Nebraska whose place of worship had been struck by lightning; a letter from a sister in Missouri, asking for advice about a divorce case; one from a tinware man in Arkansas, who inquired about the town with a view of locating there; and finally one with a Boyd City postmark, bearing the familiar mark of the Association, which informed him, over the signature of Richard Falkner, Secretary, that it had been unanimously voted upon to ask him if he would be willing to occupy a leadership position in the new work.

Cameron carried the letter, with a grin on his face, to the kitchen.

"Well," said his wife, "didn't I tell you that one preacher would have a hand in whatever work of this kind was started here? Of course you'll accept?"

"I don't know," Cameron answered. "We must think and pray about it. You know how I'd love to, yet there is something wonderful about such a thing moving forward *without* the clergy, from the people, as it were, the laity, the grass roots."

"You'll do the right thing," she answered. "Of that much I *am* certain."

The next day Cameron called for a consultation with Elder Wicks. Uncle Bobbie said, "To be sure, it's mighty hard for me to advise you in a thing like this. As a member of the church I might say turn down the offer in order to give more time to matters of the Jerusalem Church. But as a member of the Association, I would say—accept the offer. I don't know what to do."

The old gentleman thoughtfully stroked his face for a few moments, then suddenly grasped the arms of his chair and nearly shouted, "As a Christian, I say accept!"

And so Cameron became the manager of the new work. And his first recommendation to the directors was that they send their secretary away for a vacation. His employer Udell was consulted and heartily agreed, for Dick, poor fellow, needed it, though at first he flatly refused to go.

But Dr. Jordan imparted to him the cheerful information that he would die if he didn't, and Uncle Bobbie finished matters by declaring that he had no more right to kill himself by overwork than any other way.

" . . . and besides," added the old gentleman, "you ain't paid me that hundred dollars yet. To be sure, the note ain't due for some time, but a fellow has got to look after his own interest, you know."

The first address delivered by Cameron in the auditorium of the Association building during the last week of October was from the text, "Ye shall know the truth, and the truth shall make you free." The room was crowded, and the young minister had never declared the teaching of his Master with greater freedom, earnestness, and vigor.

To the astonishment of the people, when Cameron offered an invitation at the close of the service, who should come forward to declare his belief in Christ as the Son of God but George Udell.

CHAPTER THIRTY-FIVE

TWO CONVERGING STREAMS

In southwestern Missouri, in the White Oak district, there are many beautiful glens and sheltered valleys where a sturdy people have tamed the wildness of nature and made it obedient to their will.

The fields lie fertile and fruitful on either bank of murmuring streams, clear to the foot of the hills where the timber grows. Always a road winds down the valley, generally skirting the forest, and the farmhouses are nearly all built of logs, though more modern and finished dwellings are fast taking the place of these primitive homes. Every few miles, one may see little schoolhouses, most often made of good lumber and painted white, with heavy shutters and a high platform in front. For the Ozark settler takes great pride in his schoolhouse, which is also a church and a political rallying point, and a meeting place for the backwoods "literary" clubs. For though he may live in a rude log hovel himself, the settler of this region must have his hall of education made of boards and carefully painted.

To this romantic region Dick Falkner went to spend his vacation during the early days of November, the loveliest season of the year in that section of the country.

Mr. Cushman, who was a successful farmer living in the White

Oak district, and an old friend of Uncle Bobbie's, gladly welcomed the young man, of whom his old partner Wicks had written so highly. When Dick left the train at Armourdale, a little village in the lead and zinc fields, he was greeted at once by his host, a bluff, pleasant-faced elderly gentleman whom he liked at first sight, and who, in turn, was completely captivated by his guest before they had been together half an hour.

Oak Springs Farm, which was to be Dick's home for the next couple weeks, took in the whole of a beautiful little glen and many acres of timberland on either side. Crane creek had its source, or rather one of its sources, within a hundred feet of the house, where a big spring bubbled from beneath the roots of a giant oak, and the water went chattering and laughing away to the south and east.

Three-quarters of a mile from Oak Springs, just over the ridge in another hollow, another stream gushed bright and clear from beneath another ancient oak and went rushing away to join its fellow brook a mile distant, where the little glens broadened into a large valley, through which the creek hurried onward to the great river, miles away in the heart of the wilderness.

It was all very beautiful and restful to Dick, wearied and worn by the rush and whirl of the city and stifled with the dust and smoke from factory and furnace. The low hills, clothed with foliage, richly stained by October's brush, and the little valley lying warm in the sunlight were a welcome change to the dead monotony of the prairie, where the sky shut down close to the dull grown earth, with no support of leafy pillars. And the mother quail, with her full-grown family scurrying to cover in the corner of the fence, the squirrel scolding his mate in the treetops or leaping over the rustling leaves, and all the rest of the forest life were full of interest when compared to the life of busy men or chattering sparrows in the bustling mining town.

Though Mr. Cushman and his wife had raised a large family of boys and girls, only one, a daughter, remained with them on the farm. The others had, one by one, taken their flight from the home nest to build home nests of their own in different parts of the great world wilderness.

Kate was a hearty, robust, rosy-cheeked country lass of eighteen, the youngest of the flock, her father's chum, with all his
frank, open ways, and her mother's companion, with all her loving
thoughtfulness. Kate possessed the charming freshness, innocence,
and purity of one who had never come in touch with those who,
taught by the world she had never known, would have shammed
her virtues even as they tried to imitate the color of her cheek.
Along with the freshness of her smile, however, Kate displayed a
worrisome naivete, an indication that while she may have been
innocent as a dove, she had not been taught the wisdom of the
serpent. Sadly, such an ill-fitting combination is often alluring to
those well-acquainted with the harsh realities of the world. Not
concerned with protecting that innocence, but only using it, the
result of their involvement with such as Kate is often deception.

After meeting the mother and daughter and enjoying such a
supper as one scarcely finds except on a prosperous farm, Dick
sank to rest that night with a long sigh of relief. Strangely enough,
the last picture on his mind before he fell asleep was of a little
schoolhouse that he had seen just at sunset, scarcely a quarter mile
up the valley. He found himself drowsily wondering who taught
the children there, while a great owl, perched in an old apple tree
behind the chicken house, echoed his sleepy thoughts with its
"Whoo! Whoo!"

On the following afternoon, with a whoop and hallo and whistle, the noisy troop of boys and girls came tumbling out of the
doorway of the White Oak school, their lunch pails and baskets
on their arms, homeward bound from the irksome duties of the
day.

The young teacher, after standing a few moments in the doorway, watching her charges as they galloped down the road and
out of sight in the woods across the valley, turned wearily back.
Seating herself at a rude desk in the rear of the room, she began
her task of looking over the copybooks left by the rollicking
youngsters. Had she remained on the porch a moment longer she
would have seen a tall, well-dressed gentleman coming leisurely
up the hill.

Dick had been roaming all the afternoon over the fields and through the brown woods. He now came slowly up the road, crossed the yard, and stood hesitating at the threshold of the building. The teacher, bending low at her desk, did not see him for a moment through the open door. But when she raised her head, she looked straight into his eyes.

Dick would have been dull indeed had he failed to interpret that look. And Amy would have been more than dull had she failed to see the love that shone in his glance of astonishment and pleasure.

For an instant neither spoke.

Then Dick said simply, "It seems I have found you again."

She gave a soft, pretty laugh.

"I hope you will forgive me, Miss Goodrich," Dick went on. "I assure you this meeting is entirely by accident. I only stopped for a drink of water."

"Please, help yourself, Mr. Falkner," offered the girl, finding her voice at last. There was, however, still a slight choke in it. "There it is." She pointed to a wooden pail and tin dipper near the door.

"But . . . I had—no idea," Dick faltered. "That is, I am spending my vacation here in the Ozarks, or rather, I came here to rest." He paused awkwardly. "I—I did not dream of your being here, or of course I should not have come, after receiving your last letter. Forgive me, and I will go away again."

He turned to leave, but then paused. He walked back toward where she sat at the desk.

"There's just one thing, though, that I must say before I go," said Dick. "Are you in need of any help? If so, let me be of use to you. I am still your friend."

The brown head was raised and two glistening eyes, proudly pleading, looked at Dick.

Through a mist in his own eyes he saw two hands outstretched and heard a voice say, "I do need your help. Don't go. That is— I mean—leave me here now and come again tomorrow, and I will tell you everything. Only trust me this once."

Dick took the outstretched hands in his and stood for a moment with bowed head. Then he whispered softly, "Of course I will stay. Shall I come at this same hour tomorrow?"

Amy nodded, and he turned and left the building.

Had Dick looked back as he strode swiftly toward the woods, he would have seen a girlish form in the door watching him, and had he listened as he climbed the fence, he might have heard a sweet voice say falteringly, "Oh, Dick, I love you."

All throughout the morning of the next day, Dick wandered aimlessly about the farm, but somehow he never got beyond sight of the roof of the little white schoolhouse in the distance. He spent an hour watching the colts that frolicked in the upper pasture, beyond which lay the children's playground. Then going through the field, he climbed through the screen of leaves and branches. Once Amy came to the door, but only for a moment, when she called the shouting youngsters from their short recess. Then recrossing the valley half a mile above, he walked slowly home to dinner along the road leading past the building. How he envied the boys and girls whose droning voices reached his ears through the open windows.

While Dick was chatting with his kind host after dinner as they sat on the porch facing the great oak, the latter talked about the spring and the history of the place, how it used to be a favorite camping ground for the Indians in winter. He pointed out the field below the barn, where they had found arrowheads by the hundreds. Then he told of the other spring, just over the ridge, and how the two streams came together and flowed on, larger and larger, to the river. And then with a farmer's fondness for a harmless jest, he suggested that Dick might find it worth his while to visit the other spring, "For," he said, "the schoolmarm lives there, and she's a right pretty girl. Sensible too, I reckon, though she ain't been here only since September."

When the farmer had gone to his work, Dick walked down to the spring house, sat down on the twisted roots of the old oak, and looked into the crystal water.

So Amy lives by a spring just like this, he thought, *and often sits*

*beneath that other oak, perhaps, looking into the water just as I am
doing now.*

A blue-jay perched on a bough above screamed in mocking
laughter at the dreamer down on the ground. An old drake, leading
his family in a waddling row to the open stream below the house,
solemnly quacked his protest against such a willful waste of time.
And a spotted calf thrust its head through the barnyard fence to
gaze at him in mild reproach.

In his revery, Dick compared the little stream of water to his
life, running fretted and troubled, from the very edge of its birth-
place. He followed it with his eye down through the pasture lot
until it was lost in the distance. Then, looking into the blue vista
of the hills, he followed on, in his mind, where the stream grew
deeper and broader.

Suddenly he sprang to his feet and walked hastily away along
the bank of the creek. In a little while he stood at the point of land
where the two valleys became one, and the two streams were
united; and with a long breath of relief, he found that the course
of the large stream, as far as he could see, was smooth and un-
troubled, while the valley through which it flowed was broad and
beautiful.

At the appointed time, Dick went to the schoolhouse, met
Amy, and walked with her through the woods toward the farm
where she lived, while she told him of her life since they last met,
of her father's visit and his threats, and of her fear that he would
force her to go home, of how the farm had been sold, and how
through her friends she had obtained her present position in the
school. She told of her pride and her desire to wipe out her disgrace
alone, as she had brought it upon herself. Above all, she longed
to be of use in the world, and to once again be clean and pleasing
to God.

As she talked, Dick's face grew bright.

"It is so good to hear you talk so," he said. "This is good news
indeed. I'm so glad for your sake." Then with a smile, he added,
"I see you do not need my help, now that you can be of so much
help to others."

"But won't you help me plan for the future?" asked Amy, trying to hide the slight tremble in her voice. "Won't you tell me what is best to do? I have thought and thought, but can get no further than I am now."

"Let us say nothing about that for a while," replied Dick. "We can talk that over later."

And so it came about that the farmer's advice, spoken in jest, was received in earnest, and for two happy weeks the two lived, unrestrained by false pride or foolish prejudice, walking home together through the woods or wandering beside the little brooks, talking of the beauties they saw on every hand, or silently listening to the voices of nature. But at last the time came when they had to part, and Dick tried to give his best answer to her question about what she should do.

"I think you should go home," he advised.

"But you must know what that means," answered Amy. "I'll have to do no church work and become a useless social butterfly again. And besides, the conditions my father insists upon—" She blushed and hesitated.

"Yes," said Dick, "I know what your going home means for me. But you need not be a useless butterfly again, as you say. Write your father and tell him of your desire, that you cannot contend to be a useless woman of society. I am sure he will ask you to come home. When your present term of school finishes, you can take your old place in the world again. You will find ways to be of use to others, and I am certain your father will gradually learn to give you more liberty."

"And the past?" asked Amy with a blush.

"Is past," said Dick emphatically. "No one in Boyd City knows your story, nor need they ever know."

"But one man there can tell them," answered the girl, looking away.

"No, there's not even one," replied Dick quietly. And then as gently as he could he told her of Whitley's death. But of his own relations with him and the real cause of the fight in the cabin, he said nothing.

It was hard for Dick to advise Amy to go home. In their present life they were equals, with no stigmas about what they were or had been. If she went back to Boyd City, all would be changed. But he felt, for her own sake, that she had to be reinstated with her family and friends before anything else could follow.

And so it was settled. No word of love was spoken between them. Dick would not permit himself to speak them because he did not want Amy to be influenced by her present surroundings. On Amy's part, she felt her work could be complete only when she had returned to her old position and had proven herself by her life there.

Thus they parted, with only a silent clasping of hands, as they stood by the brook that chattered on its way to join the other, though there was a world of love in both the gray eyes and the brown—a love nonetheless strong because unspoken.

Upon Dick's return to the city, he took up his work again with so light a heart that his many friends declared that he had entirely recovered his health, and their congratulations were numerous and hearty.

During the holidays there was some gossip among the towns-people when it was announced in the *Whistler* that Miss Goodrich would soon return to her home. The article stated that she had been living with some friends in the east, finishing her education, and the public, feeling morally certain that Adam himself had written the article, accepted the polite lie with a nod and a wink.

Mrs. Goodrich, though her mother-heart was glad at the re-turn of her child, received the girl with many tearful reproaches. And while Amy was hungering for a parent's loving sympathy and encouragement, she could not open her heart to the woman who mourned only because of the blow dealt her family pride and social ambition.

Adam was formal, cold, and uncompromising, while Frank paid no more attention to his sister than if she were a hired servant in the house. Only the girl's firm determination, awakened womanhood, patience, and Christian fortitude enabled her to ac-cept her lot.

In spite of the daily reproaches, stern coldness, and studied contempt, she went steadily forward in her purpose to regain the place she had lost; and somehow, as the weeks went by, everyone noticed a change in her. Amy's father dared not check her in her work, for something in the clear eyes that looked at him so sadly, yet at the same time so fearlessly, made him hesitate.

It was as though she had spoken, "I have been through the fire and have come out pure gold. It is not for you to question me."

And though she attended to her social duties, her influence was always for the good, and no one dared to speak slightingly of spiritual things in her presence, while the poor people at the mission learned to love the beautiful young woman who visited their homes and talked to them of a better life, and never failed to greet them with a kindly word when she met them on the street.

Of course Dick could not call at her home. He knew well that it would only provoke a storm. Nor did Amy ask him to. They met only at church or at the mission, and nothing but the commonest greetings passed between them. But they each felt that the other understood, and so were happy, content to wait until God, in His own way, should unite the streams of their lives.

CHAPTER THIRTY-SIX

THE STRONG AND THE PROUD

It was about nine o'clock in the evening. Dick was in his office at the Association building, writing some letters pertaining to the work.

Suddenly the door burst open, and to his great astonishment, Amy entered hurriedly, out of breath, and very excited.

"I'm sorry for interrupting you," she began as soon as she could speak, "but I must tell you." But then before she was able to say more, she sank down into a chair and began to cry bitterly.

Dick's face was serious. He stepped to the window, drew the curtain, then turned the key in the lock of the door.

"What is it?" he asked. "Please be calm. You know you have nothing to fear from me."

Amy brushed away her tears. Looking up into his face, she said, "I'm not afraid of you. But—but—our secret is out."

Dick nodded that he understood, and she continued. "You know that Frank has been at Armourdale the last few weeks, looking after papa's interests in the mines there, and—and he came home this afternoon."

"Yes, I know," replied Dick calmly.

"I was in the living room and he and Father were in the library.

I did not mean to listen, but the door was open and I heard them say your name," Amy told him.

"Yes," replied Dick again.

Amy continued. "Frank met Mr. Cushman and spent several days at the farm where they are prospecting, and—of course learned that we were together there. Father believes the awfullest things and threatens to kill you—and—and I slipped away because I—I thought you ought to know."

The poor girl finished with a sob and buried her face in her hands.

Dick thought rapidly for a few moments. He remembered that he had never told Amy how, at the time of her flight, her father had accused him of taking her away, and he saw how that belief would be strengthened by her brother's story. Then as his heart bitterly rebelled at the thought of such a misunderstanding, and of the danger to Amy, he made up his mind without hesitation.

"Miss Goodrich," he said, "can you let me talk to you plainly?"

She nodded and grew quiet.

"I have known all along that these things would come out sooner or later. I have foreseen that the whole story must be told, and have prayed that the time might be put off until your life could put to rest the thought that the past was not passed forever, and now I thank God that my prayers have been answered. No harm can come to you now, for your Christian witness is no vain trifle, but a living power that will help you to bear the reproach that must come. Had this happened before you were strong, it would have driven you back again. But now you can bear it. But, Miss Good—Amy . . . I—I don't want you to have to bear this alone. Won't you let me help you? You know that I love you. I have told you so a thousand times, though no word has been spoken. And I know that you return my love. I have seen it in your eyes, and I have waited and waited until the time should come for me to speak. That time is here now. Amy, dearest, tell me that you love me and will be my wife. Give me the right to protect you. Let us go to your father together and tell him all. He won't dare refuse us then."

The beautiful girl trembled with emotion.

"You must not. Oh, you must not!" she protested. "Don't—don't tempt me."

She buried her face in her hands again. "You—you cannot take for your wife one who has made such mistakes as I have made."

"Amy dear, listen," urged Dick. "You and I are Christians. We have both made mistakes. But Christ has forgiven and accepted both of us. God has only one love for each. There is only one promise, one help, one heaven for us both. Amy dear, don't you see that we are equal both in our sin and in our acceptance by God? Because of my past, I could never reproach you for yours. Won't you forget it all with me?"

The girl lifted her face and looked into his eyes long and searchingly, as though reading his very soul.

Had there been anything but love in Dick Falkner's heart, he would have argued in vain. But with unflinching gaze he returned the look, then pleaded, "Amy, listen. On the soul that has been pardoned in the name of Jesus Christ, there is no stain. Won't you put your past beneath your feet as I have put mine, and come to me upon the common ground of Christ's love and forgiveness? Come, because we love each other, and for the good we can do."

Amy's lips trembled. Holding out her hands she replied, "Oh, Dick, I do love you. Help me to be strong and true and worthy of your love. I—I—have no one in all the world but you."

He stooped down and gently kissed her, then she stood and he held her tightly to himself.

"I must take you home now," he said after a moment.

"No," she answered hurriedly. "The folks will think that I am calling on some of the neighbors, even if they miss me at all. I often run out that way in the evening. It is not late, and I'm not afraid."

"Listen to me, dearest," he implored. "You must not see your father alone until I have told him everything. I will go up to the house with you now and we will settle this matter once and for—"

A loud knock at the door interrupted him.

Amy trembled in alarm. "Don't be frightened," urged Dick. "No harm can come to you from this moment on. Thank God you have given me the right to speak for you."

The knock was repeated.

"Step in here," he said, leading her to a chair in the next room, "and be a brave girl. It must just be some fellow on business. He'll be gone in a moment."

Leaving her with the door partly closed, he stepped across the room just as the knock came the third time.

Dick threw open the door. Without waiting for an invitation to enter, Adam Goodrich strode inside with a look upon his face that could not be mistaken. Dick was astonished beyond measure to see him, though not a muscle of his face quivered as he spoke. "Good evening, sir. What can I do for you?"

"You can do a good deal," replied Adam with venom in his tone. "But first lock that door. We want no visitors here tonight."

Without a word, Dick turned the key again.

"Now, sir, I want to know first: Is it true that you were with my daughter in the Ozark Mountains this summer? Don't try to lie to me this time. I'll have the truth or I'll kill you," Adam vowed with deadly calm.

"I have never lied to you, sir," answered Dick, "never so much as a word. And I have no desire to do so now. It is perfectly true that I did meet your daughter last summer while on my vacation."

"I knew I was right!" raved Goodrich. "I knew you led her away from home. Why did you ever come to this city? Why did I ever have to lay eyes on you! Here," he said, as he frantically tore a blank check from his checkbook, "fill this out for any amount you choose and go away again. I tell you, if you don't, I'm not sure what I might do! I could kill you, if I dared. You have ruined me forever—you—"

"Stop, sir!" cried Dick.

When Adam looked into his face, he saw again that nameless something which compelled him to obey.

"You have said quite enough," continued Dick calmly, "and you are going to listen to me now. But first, I want to beg your pardon and apologize for the language I used when you called upon me before—"

He heard a slight rustle in the next room and continued hurriedly on.

"—when you accused me of taking your daughter from her home. I as good as called you a liar. I beg your pardon now. I was excited. I know that you were only mistaken. You would not have listened to me then, nor believed me, had I told you what I knew. But the time has come when you *shall* listen and be forced to know that I speak the truth."

Goodrich sat as though fascinated, angered beyond the point of being able to speak. Once he attempted to answer, but a quick "Silence, sir! You *shall* hear me" kept him still.

Dick proceeded to detail the whole story, omitting nothing from the evening when he had rescued Amy from her drunken escort, to the day when he had said goodbye in the Ozark Mountains. When he had finished, Adam sat silent for a moment.

Can it be possible, thought Dick, *that I have misjudged this man and that he is grateful for the help I have given Amy?*

But no. Dick had not misjudged him.

There was not a thought of gratitude in Adam Goodrich's heart. Thankfulness for his daughter's salvation from a life of sin had no part in his feelings, only blind rage that his pride should be so humbled.

Leaping to his feet, he shouted, "Proof, you miserable scoundrel! The proof, or I'll have your life for this!"

Dick remained perfectly calm.

"You shall have the proof," he promised quietly. Turning, he stepped to the next room, coming back an instant later with his arm around Amy's waist.

Adam sprang forward.

"You . . . you here at this hour!" he cried, beside himself with wrath. "Go home at once! You . . . take your hands off her, you ruffian!" he raged at Dick.

Dick stood without moving a muscle, and Goodrich started toward him.

"Stop," Dick warned, still without moving. Again the older man was forced to obey a will stronger than his own.

"Father," Amy began, "I am going to marry Mr. Falkner. I—"

"Why, you ungrateful—!"

"Please!" interrupted Dick in a strong voice; "—please, Mr. Goodrich, be still! Do not force me to use more unpleasant means to compel you to show your loving daughter the respect she deserves."

"I heard you and Frank talking in the library," Amy went on, "and when you said that you would kill him, I came to warn him, and—and—his story is every word true. Jim Whitley was a bad man and would have done me harm. Oh, Papa, don't you see what a friend Mr. Falkner has been to me? You forced me into the society that might have ruined me, but he has helped me to a better life. I love him and I will be his wife. Won't you forgive us for the past, Papa, and let us live our lives together?"

Never in his life had it been Dick's lot to see a face express so much, or so many conflicting emotions—love, hate, pride, passion, remorse, gratitude—all following each other in quick succession. But finally pride and anger triumphed and the answer came, not in the man's words but the expression of his face. There Dick found the clue to his own course.

"You are no longer a daughter of mine," Goodrich announced. "I disown you. If you marry that man who came to this town as a common tramp, I will never recognize you again. You have disgraced me. You have dragged my honor in the dust."

He turned toward the door.

But again Dick's voice, clear and cold, forced him to stop.

"Sir," he said, "before God I tell you that you, and not your daughter, are to blame. By your teaching, you crippled her character and made it too weak to withstand temptation, and then by your brutal unbelief and your insensitive pride, which is a mockery to the God in whose church you sit every Sunday, you drove her from home."

"Are you quite through?" Adam asked with a haughty sneer.

"Not quite," answered Dick. "You value most of all in this world pride and your family position. Can't you see that by the course you are taking, you yourself proclaim your disgrace and forfeit your place in society? We three alone know the story I have just related to you. But if you persist in this selfish and prideful course, the whole world will know it."

He paused. Adam's face slowly changed. For while his nature could not forgive, pity, or feel gratitude, such reasoning as this forced its way upon his mind—a mind ever ready to cheat the opinions of men.

"What would you suggest?" he asked coldly.

"Simply this," answered Dick. "You and Amy go home together. No one shall ever know of this incident. Live your life as usual, except that you shall permit me to call at the house occasionally. Gradually the people will become accustomed to my visits, and when the time comes, marriage will not be thought so strange. I know it does not lie in my power to compel you to love and forgive as Christ would have you. Such can only come from a heart more open than you have shown yours to be. But remember, this woman is to be my wife. And you shall answer to me if you make her life difficult."

"Very well," answered Adam after a moment's pause. "I see I have little choice but to submit. I will do anything rather than have this awful disgrace made public. But understand me, while you may come to the house occasionally, and while you force me to consent to this marriage by the story of my daughter's disgrace, I do not accept you as my son, or receive the girl as my daughter. For my honor's sake, I will appear to do both, but I shall not forget."

Then turning to Amy, he commanded, "Now, come home."

"Good night, dearest," whispered Dick. "Be brave."

And as he opened the door, he smiled at her father, wishing him also a pleasant good night.

CHAPTER THIRTY-SEVEN

A STORY ALL TOO COMMON

Another spring and summer came to Boyd City, and then drifted toward autumn.

Amy continued to grow. Dick began to call on her at the house, and by slow degrees their engagement became known and accepted by the citizenry of Boyd City. Not once, in the course of a year, did Adam Goodrich speak so much as a word to his future son-in-law. Dick, however, always greeted both Mr. and Mrs. Goodrich with the cheeriest of smiles, and there were faint indications, by the time a year had passed, that he might be making inroads in his attempt to win over Amy's mother. He rarely ever saw Frank.

The following spring Dick Falkner and Amy Goodrich were married by Rev. Cameron in the Jerusalem Church. By this time, Dick was held in such high esteem by the town that to fail to attend would have done irreparable harm to Adam Goodrich's reputation. He therefore not only attended the joyous ceremony, but also walked the bride down the aisle and dutifully answered the minister's question, "Who giveth this woman to be married to this man?" But after taking his seat at his wife's side, he remained stoically somber throughout the remainder of the proceedings. Finding suddenly some urgent business that required his attention, the father of the bride managed to escape the humiliation of the happy reception which was to be held at the auditorium of the Association building.

By this time the Association was engaged in a thriving range of ministries to the poor of the vicinity. The reading room at the church had been discontinued and incorporated into the Association work; and the institution for helping the unemployed had expanded from merely a supplier of kindling wood into a center for several such businesses, and had also become part of the larger work of the Association.

One evening seven months after the wedding, the supervisor of the original home for the unemployed was sitting with his wife before a cheery fire in their little parlor. The cold November rain outside came beating against the windowpanes in heavy gusts, and the wind sighed and moaned about the corners of the building and down the chimney.

Suddenly they heard a knock at the door.

The old man rose and went into the next room, which was used as a kind of reception hall. He could hear the rapping sound more clearly now. He crossed the room and opened the door. In the light that streamed out he saw a woman.

"Come in!" he cried, reaching out his hand and taking her by the arm. "Come in out of the rain. Why, you're soaked through!"

"Oh, thank you, sir," said the bedraggled woman. "They told me this was a place where people in trouble could come. I'm so hungry and tired . . . and cold."

Indeed, she looked it. Her dress, though of good material and nicely made, was dirty with mud and rain. Beneath the sailor hat, from which the water ran in sparkling drops, her hair hung wet and disheveled. She was shivering uncontrollably and had clearly been out in the freezing rain much too long. The moment the man's wife laid eyes upon the suffering soul, she feared the worst, not only for the girl herself, but also for the child she was obviously carrying. The girl's eyes were wild with pleading, her cheeks sunken and ashy pale, while the delicately turned nostrils and finely curved, trembling lips were blue and cold. Beyond all doubt she had once been beautiful.

Mr. Gray, old in experience, noted all this and more as he said, "We are not allowed to keep women here, but it's a little different in your case."

"Of course you will stay with us," declared his wife. "I know, I know," she added as the girl looked at her in a questioning manner. "Anyone can see your condition. But bless your heart, our Master befriended a poor woman, and why should not we?"

Mrs. Gray led the girl into the other room and removed her hat and loosened her clothing.

Then going to the door, she whispered to her husband, "I think you had better go for Dr. Jordan. He'll be needed here."

When Mr. Gray returned with the doctor, the patient, dry and clean, was wrapped in the soft blankets of Mother Gray's own bed, with an old nightdress on, and with a hot water bottle at her tired feet.

But warmth and kindness had come too late. The long, weary tramp about the countryside and then the city, in the cold and rain, the friendless shutting of doors in her face, the consciousness that she was a mark for all eyes, and the horror of what was to come, with the cold and hunger and exposure, had done its work. When the morning sun, which had chased away the storm clouds, peeped in at the little chamber window, Dr. Jordan straightened up with a long breath and said, "She will suffer no more pain now, until the end."

"And when will that be, Doctor?" asked Mother Gray.

"In a few hours, I think. I cannot tell exactly," replied the doctor.

"And there is no hope?"

"Absolutely none," answered the physician.

"Ah, well, perhaps it is better so," murmured the old lady. "This world is not the place for such as she. Christ may forgive, but men won't. The man alone goes free. Will she come to, do you think, before she goes?"

"It is probable that she will rally for a little while, and you may find out her name perhaps. There was no mark on her clothing, you say?" asked Dr. Jordan.

"Not the sign of a mark, and she would tell me nothing. And see, there is no wedding ring," Mrs. Gray replied.

They were silent for some time, and then, "She is awakening," announced the doctor.

The blue eyes opened slowly and looked wonderingly about the room. "Where am I?" she asked feebly, trying to raise her head.

"There, there, dear. Lie still now and rest. You have been sick, you know. We are your friends and this is the doctor."

"Mother—I—who are you?"

"Your mother shall come when you tell us where to send for her."

The poor creature looked for a full minute into the kind old face above her, and then slowly the look of wonder in her eyes gave place to one of firmness, pain, and sorrow, and the lips closed tightly, as though in fear that her secret would come out.

"Oh, honey, don't look like that!" cried Mrs. Gray. "Tell us who you are. Have you no mother? Let us send for her at once that she may come to you."

The lips parted in a sweet, sad smile. "I'm going to die then? You would not look so if I were not. Oh, I am so glad." And in another moment she was sleeping like a child.

"Poor girl," muttered Dr. Jordan, wiping his eyes. Then turning to Mrs. Gray, he said, "I fear you will have to take her mother's place. I must go now, but I will look in again during the day. Don't have any false hopes. There is nothing to be done except to make the end easy."

For an hour the stranger slept with a smile on her lips, and then opened her eyes again. But there was no pain, no fear in them, only a shadow of trouble as she asked in a whisper, "Where is it?"

With one hand Mrs. Gray smoothed back the hair from the forehead of her patient, and with the other pointed upward. The troubled shadow passed from the eyes of the young mother, and she slept again. Later in the day, the doctor called, and once more the girl awoke.

"I thank you, Doctor," she murmured in a weak voice, but shook her head when he offered her medicine.

"But, dear child, it is only to relieve you from pain."

She answered, "If I must go, let me go as I am. Oh, this world is so cold and harsh. God knows that I do not fear to die. Christ, who welcomed little children, now has my baby, and He knows that in my heart I am innocent."

"But won't you tell us of your friends?" asked Mother Gray.

"No," she whispered. "I have no friends but you and God."

And no argument could prevail upon her to change her mind. Her only answer was a shake of the head.

That evening, just after dusk, she whispered to her kind nurse, "Won't you please tell me your name?"

"They call me Mother Gray."

"May I call you that too?" said the stricken girl.

"Yes, honey, of course you may," answered the woman. "Of course you may."

"And why do you cry, Mother?" she asked, watching the tears roll down the wrinkled cheeks. "Are you not glad that God is going to take me? Oh, I forgot, you are afraid for me."

"Is there nothing I can do for you, dear?" asked Mrs. Gray through her tears. "Would you like to see a minister? Our Brother Cameron is such a good—"

"No, no minister, please. I am tired, and he can do me no good now. I would rather die alone with you."

She turned her head away and dropped into sleep again.

Later, after Rev. Cameron had come and gone without seeing her, she opened her eyes again. Mrs. Gray was still sitting by her bedside with a sad smile on her face.

Just then a low knock came at the door and a sweet voice called gently, "May I come in, Mother Gray?"

It was Amy, who had come at Cameron's request.

The sufferer half rose in her bed. "Who is it?" she gasped. "I— I—know that voice."

"There, there, dearie," returned the nurse gently. "It's only our friend Amy Falkner."

"Yes, come in," Mrs. Gray called behind her, and Amy softly pushed the door open and entered.

"I thought perhaps I could help you, Mother Gray," she said as she removed her hat and arranged a beautiful bunch of flowers on a little stand in the center of the room. Then turning to the sufferer, she was about to speak again when she paused and her face grew white.

The wide eyes of the dying girl stared back at her in doubting wonder, while the trembling lips tried to whisper her name.

The next instant Amy threw herself on her knees, her arms about the wasted form upon the bed. "Oh, Kate . . . Kate!" she cried. "How did this happen? How did you come to be here?"

It was Kate Cushman, from Oak Springs Farm.

Mother Gray quickly recovered from her surprise, and with the instinct of a true nurse, she calmed Amy and soothed the patient.

Amy controlled herself with an effort, rose from her knees, and sat down on the edge of the bed, still holding Kate's hand.

"We must send for your father and mother at once," urged Amy after a moment; "they can—"

"No, no, you must not—they do not know—in mercy, please don't tell them—it would kill them. Please promise them you will never tell them how I died," pleaded Kate.

Mother Gray bowed her head, while the tears streamed down her wrinkled cheeks. "Yes, yes, dearie, we'll promise. It's better that they do not know until it's all over, and they need never know all."

Then whispering to Amy, she added, "The poor child can't last but a little longer."

Reassured, the sufferer sank back again with a long sigh, and closed her eyes wearily. But a moment later she opened them once more to look at Amy.

"I'm so glad you're here," she said feebly. "But I can't bear to have you think that I am all bad."

And then in whispered, halting words, with many a break and pause, she told her story—a story all too common. And Amy, listening with horror-stricken face, guessed that which Mother Gray could not know and which the sufferer tried to conceal, the name of her betrayer.

"And so we were married in secret, or I thought we were," she concluded. "I know now that it was only a farce. He came to visit me twice after the sham ceremony, and I never saw him again until last night. Oh, God, forgive him . . . I did love him!"

The poor wronged creature burst into a fit of passionate sobbing that could not be controlled. In vain Mother Gray tried to soothe her. But it was of no use. Exhausted, she sank into a stupor, from which she roused only once near morning, and then she whispered simply, "Goodbye, Mother . . . goodbye Miss—Amy. Don't let Father know."

And just as the day dawned in all its glory, her soul—pure and unstained as that of her babe—took its flight, and the smile of innocent girlhood was upon her lips.

On her way home, Amy went by the house of her parents. She met her brother just coming out the door.

"You look like you've been making a night of it," he said with a contemptuous sneer. "Been consoling some wanderer, I suppose."

The young woman made no reply, but stood with her eyes fixed on his face.

"Well, get out of my way," he snapped roughly; "can't you see I'm on my way out? Why don't you go back to that fool husband of yours!"

At last Amy spoke. "I have been at the institution all night. Kate Cushman found her way there in the midst of the storm. She and the baby are both dead. Go and behold your work."

Frank started as though she had struck him, and then as she stepped aside, he fairly ran down the walk as though in fear of his life.

CHAPTER THIRTY-EIGHT

CAMERON'S BETRAYAL AND SACRIFICE

Neither Frank nor Amy, though for very different reasons, ever brought news of Kate Cushman's involvements to the ears of their father. But from the very day of her death, Frank's life seemed to begin to unravel. He was more often seen out late at night, a time or two drunk, and talk began to circulate about his reckless lifestyle. No longer did he even attempt to keep up the pretense of a religious honorability, to his father's intense but unspoken shame.

Six months later, in the little country village of Anderson, where the southern branch of the Memphis joins the main rail line, a group of excited citizens were standing in front of the doctor's office.

"You're right sure it's smallpox, are you, Doc?" asked one.

"There's no doubt about it," answered the physician.

"Who is he?" said another of the group.

"He won't tell his name, but Jack Lane says it's Frank Goodrich," replied the doctor. "He came in the day before yesterday on the Memphis from Boyd City, where they've just reported a case or two."

An angry murmur arose from the little group of men at the thought of someone coming to infect their town.

"What are you going to do, Doc?"

"I've sent to Pleasantville," the doctor answered. "There's a black fellow there who has had the disease and survived it. He'll be in as soon as he can get here. We have to find some place out of town for the man to stay, and then old Jake will take care of him."

"Thar's a cabin on my west forty that's in purty good shape," offered a man by the name of Jim Boles. "It's way back from the road, a good bit over a mile, I reckon—in heavy timber too."

"I know the place," said another. "We run a fox past thar last winter and found him denned in that ledge o' rocks 'bout half a quarter on yon side."

"That's it," interjected another. "It's sure out of the way all right."

"Well," the doctor told them, "three or four of you go over there and fix up the cabin as comfortable as possible and I'll have Jake take him out as soon as he comes."

The cabin, which was built by some early settler, had long ago been abandoned, and was partly fallen into decay. Tall weeds grew up through the ruins where the pole stable had stood, the roof and one side of the smokehouse had fallen in, and the chinking had crumbled from between the logs of the house, while the yard was overgrown with brush and a tangle of last season's dead grass and leaves, now wet and sodden with the late heavy rain. Deep timber hid the place from view, and a hundred yards in front of the hovel a spring bubbled from beneath a ledge of rock, sending a tiny stream trickling away through the forest.

Jim Boles and his helpers had just finished patching up the cabin roof and floor, after first building a huge fire in the long unused fireplace, when they heard the rattle of a wagon. Peering between the trees, they caught a glimpse of a scrawny old horse, harnessed with bits of strap and string, to a rickety wagon that seemed about to fall to pieces at every turn of the wheel. Upon the board used for a seat, sat an old Negro, urging his steed through the patches of light and shadow with many a jerk of the rope lines, accompanied by an occasional whack from the long slender pole he held in his hand. Behind him lay a long object wrapped in blankets and comforters.

"Hullo!" shouted the black man, catching sight of the cabin and the men.

"Am dis here de horspital fer de smallpox diseases? Dey dun tol' me fer ter foller de road, but all de's here roads look erlike ter me in dis here place. Nevah seed sich er lonesome ol' hole in all my born days. Reckon dar's any ha'nts in dat der ol' shack?"

"No. This cabin is all right!" shouted one of the men. "But you stay where you arc till we get away."

Immediately they began gathering up their tools and clothes.

"All right, sah, all right," grinned the Negro. "You'uns jes' clear out ob de way fer de amblance am er comin'. We dun got de right ob way dis trip, shore."

And so Frank Goodrich was before long established in the old log house, with an old black man he did not know to nurse him. A place was fixed where the doctor and others could leave such things as were needed, and Jake could go and get them.

Three days passed, and then by bribes and threats and prayers, Frank persuaded the Negro to walk to Pleasantville in the night and post a letter to Rev. Cameron, begging the minister to come to him, telling him only that he was in trouble and warning him to keep his journey secret, but saying nothing of the dread disease.

What fiend prompted young Goodrich to take such a course cannot be imagined. But let us, in charity, try to think that he was driven to it by the fright and horrors of his condition rather than by any desire to betray the minister and do him harm. Though whatever his intent, the effect was the same.

Mrs. Cameron was away in the East visiting her parents, and when the minister received the letter, he made hurried preparations. He told Dick that he might be gone several days, then left the city that very evening. At a little way-station named in the letter, he found the black man with his poor old horse and rickety wagon waiting.

"Is yo de parson?" Jake asked.

"Yes, I am a minister," Cameron answered, wondering greatly what sort of trouble Frank could be in. As he climbed up to the board seat, he questioned his guide rather sharply, but the only answer he could get was, "Mistah Goodrich dun tol' me ter hol' ma tongue er he'd ha'nt me, an' I'm shore gwine do hit. Dis here chile don't want no ghostes chasin' ob him roun'. No, sah. I'se dun fetch yo t' Mistah Goodrich an' he kin tell yo what he's er mind ter."

None of this added to Cameron's peace of mind, and the moments seemed hours as the poor old horse stumbled on through the darkness of the night. At last they entered the timber, and how the man ever guided his crippled steed past the trees and fallen logs and rocks was a mystery to Cameron. But at last they saw the lights of the cabin.

"Dar's de place, sah. Dis here's de horspital. We dun got here at las'."

The driver brought the horse to a standstill near the tumbled-down smokehouse.

"Go right in, sah. Nobody dar but Mistah Goodrich. I put away dis ol' hoss." And he began fumbling at the ropes and strings that made the harness.

Cameron, nearly overcome by this time with curiosity, stepped to the door of the cabin and pushed it open. By the dim light of a dirty kerosene lantern, he could see nothing at first; but a moaning voice from the far end of the room drew his attention in the right direction. "Is that you, Brother Cameron?"

The minister stepped forward and to the side of the cot. "Frank, what are you doing here? What is the matter?"

"I'm sick," answered the young man in a feeble voice. "I wanted to see you. I'm awful glad you came."

"But why are you in this miserable place? I don't understand," said Cameron.

"Smallpox," muttered the sick man.

The minister involuntarily started back.

"Folks in town are afraid," Frank went on; "that old black man takes care of me. He has had it."

Thoughts of his wife went fleeting through Cameron's spinning brain. Without realizing he was doing so, he took a step or two backward.

"Oh, Brother Cameron, don't leave me here alone!" cried Frank. "I can't die like this."

For one brief moment Cameron trembled. He saw his danger and the trap into which he had fallen. He thought of his important work and of his wife, and took another step toward the door. Then he stopped.

"Oh, I can't die alone," moaned Frank again.

Suddenly the scripture from Matthew came to the young minister's mind, the scripture he had quoted so many times from his pulpit. The words of his Master rang loud in his brain: "I was sick and you cared for me . . ."

Another moment he hesitated, then realized he was being called to follow in his Master's footsteps of servanthood. With a prayer to his God for help and courage, the minister made up his mind.

"Why, of course I'll not leave you, Frank," he said with a cheerful smile, taking a seat. "Surely you know that."

And so, several days later his friends in the city received letters from this man of God saying that he would be detained a few days. All the while he remained by the side of the wretched sufferer in the old cabin in the lonely woods.

The disease was not slow in its work, and before many hours had passed, it was clear to Cameron that the end was approaching. Frank also realized that death was not far distant, and his horrible fear was pitiful.

"Brother Cameron," he whispered hoarsely, as he held his pastor's hand, while the old black man crouched by the fireside smoking his cob pipe, "I must tell you, I've lived an awful life— people think that I'm a Christian—but I've lived a lie—"

Then with a look that made Cameron shudder, and in a voice strong with terror, he screamed, "Oh, God! I shall go to hell. I shall go to hell! Can't you save me, Brother Cameron? I always said you were a good fellow. Why do you let me die here like a dog? Don't you know I want to live? Here, you cursed nigger, go fetch a doctor! I'll haunt you when I'm dead if you don't."

The black man trembled in fright, dropped his pipe, and half rose as though to leave the room, but sank back again with his eyes fixed on Cameron, who was bending forward, his hand on the forehead of the dying man.

"God knows all, Frank," said the minister.

"Yes," muttered the other. "God knows all—all—all." Then in a scream of anguish again, he cried, "He has been watching me all the time! He has seen me everywhere I've gone. He is here now! Look! Don't you see His eyes! He's watching—watching—Oh, I have fooled men, but I couldn't fool God. Oh, Christ, I want to live. Save me—save me—"

And he prayed and pleaded for Jesus to help him. Then he turned to Cameron. "I must get out of here. Don't you hear them coming? Let me go!" he cried as the minister held him back on the bed. "Let me go! Don't you know that I can't look God in the face? I tell you, I'm afraid!"

For a moment he struggled feebly and then sank back exhausted. But soon he began to talk again, and the minister heard with horror the dark secrets of his life.

Suddenly he ceased muttering, and, with wide-open eyes, stared into the darkness. "Look there, Brother Cameron!" he cried, hoarse with emotion. "Amy! Don't you see her? She disgraced the family, you know—ran away with that low-down printer. But look! Who is that with her? Oh, God, it's Kate—Kate—Yes, Kate. I'll marry you. It can't be wrong, you know, for you to love me. Only we must not marry now, for Father would—Look Cameron—"

His voice rose in a scream of fear.

"—she's got smallpox! Drive her out, you nigger. Take her away to that cabin in the woods where you kept me. Shh—Don't tell anyone, Cameron, but she wants me to go with her. She's come to get me. And—yes—yes—Kate, I'm coming—"

And he sank back on the bed again.

Jake was without much success trying to mumble a prayer, while the minister sat with bowed head. The lantern cast flickering shadows in the corner of the room, and the firelight danced and fell. A water bug crawled over the floor, a spider dropped from the rude rafters, and from outside came the sound of the wind among the bare branches of the trees and of the old horse feeding on the dead grass and moldy leaves about the cabin.

Suddenly the man spoke once more. "No, sir, I will never disgrace you. I am as proud of our family as you are yourself. I am—home—day . . ."

The sentence trailed off into a few unintelligible words in which only "Mother" and "Amy" could be distinguished. And then, with a last look about the cabin, from eyes in which anguish and awful fear were pictured, he took in one last deep breath, and was gone.

The next day Jake dug a grave not far from the house, and at evening, when the sun was casting the last long shadows through the trees, the black man and the minister lowered the body of the rich man's son, with the help of the rope lines from the old harness, to its last resting place. A few minutes later, Jake came to the front of the house. "Ready to go, sah?" he asked.

"Go where?" said Cameron.

"Why, go home, ob course," replied Jake. "I reckoned yo'd be mighty glad ter get erway from dis here place."

"I'm not going anywhere," the minister answered. "You may unhitch the horse again."

The old man did as he was told, then scratching his woolly head, said to himself, "By golly, I neber thought ob dat. I guess I'll hab ter take care ob him next."

In the days that followed, Cameron wrote long letters to his wife, preparing her, with many loving words, for what was, in all probability, sure to come before she could even reach home again. He also prepared an article for the *Whistler*, telling of Frank's death, but omitting all that would tend to injure the young man's character. Only to Adam Goodrich did he write the full and dreadful truth.

Other letters containing requests in regard to his business affairs, he addressed to Dick Falkner and Uncle Bobbie Wicks, and one to the president of the Association, in which he made several recommendations in regard to the work. All of these he placed in the hands of the faithful black servant to be mailed after his death, if such should be the end.

When symptoms of the dread disease appeared, he calmly and coolly began his fight for life. But in spite of his efforts, the strength gradually ebbed from his body.

One night, just before the break of day, he called to the man who was by now his dear friend and whispered as he came to his bedside, "It's almost over, Uncle Jake. My Master bids me come up higher." Then giving his friend a smile, he went on. "You have been very kind to me, and the good Father will not forget you. But I feel a change coming . . . and soon."

And so, talking calmly of the Master's goodness and love, he fell asleep, and the old Negro sat with a look of awe and reverence on his dusky face. And then old Jake did a thing he had never before done in his life. He slipped to his knees and began to pray.

"O Lawd!" he cried in a mournful voice full of emotion, "take care ob dis here man, yo serbent from da city. Take care ob him an' effen yo kin, Lawd, bring him to da light ob yo day. An' take care ob me too, Lawd, 'cause I'se dun da bes' by him as I cud. An' keep the ha'nts from me in dis here place, Lawd . . ."

Thus prayed the superstitious old black man, with tears streaming down his dark rugged cheeks, until the glorious sunlight filled the cabin and the chorus of birds greeted the coming of the day. And though such was not in reality the case, old Jake felt that for the first time in his life he had truly looked death in the face. And he found it not to be so horrifying a thing as he had long feared.

At length he rose from the floor, feeling refreshed but not understanding why, went outside, immediately hitched up his wagon, and went to the village to mail the letters that had been entrusted to him. He would return in the afternoon to do what needed to be done.

———

Much that passed in the weeks following cannot be written here. Mrs. Cameron's grief and anguish were too keen, too sacred, to be recounted in unsympathetic print. But sustained by that power that had ennobled the life of her husband, and kept by the promises of faith that had strengthened him, she went on doing her part in the Master's work, waiting in loving patience the day that would unite them again.

CHAPTER THIRTY-NINE

STRANDS AND THREADS

Two weeks after Cameron's letters reached Boyd City, the president of the Association called on Dick and Amy, and spent an hour with them talking of the work.

"Mr. Falkner," he said at length, "in Rev. Cameron's letter to me, he strongly recommended that you be called to take his place as full-time director of the Association. With your consent, I would like to announce that recommendation at our next meeting."

With serious expression Dick nodded, thinking of his departed friend.

"You understand," he replied slowly, "we'll have to think and pray about this. Can you give us a week to think the matter over?"

"I understand," returned the president. "A week will be fine."

Several days later Dick and Amy invited Elder Wicks to their home for dinner. They laid out the situation to him, and the offer that had been made, and asked for his counsel. When he had heard everything, Uncle Bobbie merely grasped his young friend by the hand and said simply, "Behold, I have set before you an open door."

The following week, at the next meeting of the Association committee, the president made the recommendation that Richard

Falkner be called as director. The motion was unanimously approved, and Dick accepted their offer the next morning.

"I told you the day would come sooner or later when I'd be losing a mighty good printer," said George Udell when Dick informed him of his intention to leave Udell's Print Shop. "But I'm pleased and proud of you, Dick," he added, giving his hand a hearty shake.

"And I'm grateful to you for giving me a start," returned Dick. "None of this would have been possible without you."

"Heathen that I was, eh!" laughed George.

"I doubt you were quite the heathen some of the church people made of you. All that's now passed, in any case," said Dick. "And you know you can call me anytime to fill in if things get too hectic. Like that first day I walked in here."

"I'll never forget it," mused Udell. "The first day either Amy or I laid eyes on you. We've all changed a mite since then!"

"And the Lord be thanked for that!" laughed Dick.

The same day, late in the afternoon, George Udell was bending over some work he had to finish before going home. He did not hear the door open when Clara Wilson walked in. She stood close by for some time before he finally looked up.

"I—I—thought I'd stop and ask if you'd like to come over to the house this evening," said Clara.

"Hum-m-m, anything important?" asked George, leaning against the press.

He shut off the power and stepped across the room just as the phone rang. "Hello . . . Yes, this is Udell's. . . . I'm sorry, I'm just closing up—it's past six. . . . No, I'm sorry, I can't do it. I have an important engagement tonight. . . . All right—goodbye."

"Oh, if you have an engagement I will go," Clara said, moving toward the door.

"You needn't be in a hurry," returned George with one of his peculiar smiles. "My engagement has been put off so many times it won't hurt to delay it a few minutes longer. And besides," he added, "the other party has done all the putting off so far, and I rather enjoy the novelty."

The young lady blushed.

That evening, sitting on the front porch of the Wilson home, at long last George Udell's proposal was accepted. When they later went inside to tell the news to Clara's mother, the lady exclaimed, "Law sakes! I do hope you'll be happy. Goodness knows you ought to be; you've waited long enough!"

When Dick began his work at the Association, a pall still hung over the town on account of Cameron's absence. On his third day, sitting at his old friend's desk, attempting the heart-breaking task of cleaning out the director's office and returning photographs and personal belongings to the pastor's wife, Dick began to long for the activity of Udell's Print Shop and the hum of machinery and the clanking of the large presses.

Suddenly a lanky young lad of thirteen, who swept up about the place, burst into the office without so much as a knock of warning.

"Mr. Falkner—Mr. Falkner!" he cried. "Come . . . come quick!"

Almost before the words had left the boy's lips, he had turned and was gone again. Dick jumped out of his chair and followed him down the hall.

Running outside after the boy, Dick saw a crowd gathering in the distance. The mass of townspeople was shouting, hands waving in the air, and others streaming out of homes and buildings to join them. Steadily the growing assembly was moving toward the Association building.

At the head of the throng, to all appearances oblivious to the hubbub his presence was creating, upon a thin board seat, behind a tired old horse that was pulling an ancient rickety wagon with reins made from worn-out leather and string, sat an old Negro whose woolly black hair was speckled with gray.

At first Dick stood watching the procession with a bewildered expression on his face. Then, hardly daring to believe the shouts that were now reaching his ears, his heart began to pound in tremulous anticipation, and he burst into a run toward the scene.

He approached the wagon, running faster and faster, a huge

smile of exceeding joy breaking out over his countenance.

The shouts were unmistakable now! Could it possibly be true? he asked himself as he ran. Yet the tears making tracks down his burning cheeks convinced him that it *must* be true!

Dick reached the wagon. Instinctively the happy followers separated to make way for him to pass through. The driver stopped his horse.

"Is yo Mistah Falkner—?" he began.

But Dick heard no more, nor stopped to attempt an answer. He was too busy climbing aboard, still weeping, to take the outstretched hand of Jake's lone passenger, seated in back, wrapped in blankets, but smiling broadly.

"I—I don't understand," he stammered in disbelief. "We thought . . . the letters—"

Cameron laughed. It was a feeble laugh, it is true, but full of returning life.

"I'm sorry, my friend," said the minister. "But it seems Jake here is none too used to praying for the sick. The moment he laid his hands on me and prayed, though I was asleep, I began to recover. He thought I was dead, went to mail my letters, and came back to find me not only still alive, but sleeping better than I had for days. I began to eat again, and as you can see, he has nursed me almost back to health."

"Jake . . . Jake! How can we thank you!" cried Dick, turning toward the front where the faithful black man sat patiently. "This—this—is wonderful! Oh, but—" and Dick turned back toward Cameron, "they've gone and made me director of the Association!"

Cameron laughed. "I can't think of better news to come home to!" he said. "I've been going to ask the committee to ask you to join me as a co-director for some time."

Dick was too dumfounded to reply.

"Now, Dick, please," added the minister. "Won't you please run home to my wife. I want her to hear the news from you, and I know you can get to her before Jake's horse will be a quarter of the way."

Without another word, Dick was off the wagon and sprinting down the street as fast as his legs would carry him. Halfway down the block he leaped into the air, gave a whooping "Ya-hooo!" of jubilation, then continued toward the parsonage.

So now Rev. Cameron and Dick Falkner work side by side at the Association.

Dick is a fine and mature-looking man in his early thirties, with all trace gone of the youthfulness that accompanied him when he first arrived in Boyd City. Amy, in her late twenties, is more beautiful than ever in the simple dress and hairstyles that she feels more become her as Mrs. Richard Falkner than the expensive adornments to which she had been accustomed earlier in her life. The society pages in the *Whistler* rarely mention her now. But to a good many of the working men and women of Boyd City who have gained their start in life through the Association, she is considered an angel whose smile helped them through difficult times.

Charlie Bowen is in an eastern college preparing himself for the ministry. His expenses are paid by Mr. Wicks.

"To be sure," said Uncle Bobbie, "we reckon a feller might as well invest in young men as anything else; and the church needs preachers who know a little about the business of this world as well as the world that's comin'. To be sure, college only puts the trimmin's on, but if you've got a Christian man that's all *man* to begin with, they sure do put him in shape, and I reckon the best ain't none too good for God. I'll miss the boy in my office and don't know how I'll get along without him, though I reckon if we look after Christ's interests He won't let us go broke. And after all is said and done, it's mighty comforting for such old, uneducated blokes as me to know that it ain't the trimmin's the good Father looks at. You can't tell a preacher by the long words in his sermon no more'n you can tell what kind of life's inside a church by the length of its steeple."

In spite of his anxiety, Uncle Bobbie's office continued to do a fine amount of work in Boyd City, and he continued to be a friend to all.

The Goodrich Hardware Store also thrived. The worthy proprietor continued to faithfully attend the Jerusalem Church, and upon occasion could be seen condescending to a scarcely perceptible nod toward the young co-director of the Association in Boyd City when they chanced to meet on the street. Though the truth that Rev. Cameron had in essence laid down his life for Frank Goodrich utterly escaped the father, the mere fact that the minister had been with Adam's son at the moment of Frank's death seemed to somehow soften Goodrich's heart toward the young minister he had long despised. Occasionally he shared some light word when they shook hands on Sunday morning, and once or twice the good minister was even asked to Sunday dinner.

Though for some years he never favored his daughter or her husband with a like invitation to his home, Adam Goodrich's pride had been dealt what might be hoped was a mortal blow by the news that came to his eyes about his son from Cameron's deathbed hand. And soon a new form of pride began faintly to blossom inside him, and that in the person of the new granddaughter brought him by the young Mr. and Mrs. Falkner.

Uncle Bobbie was heard to remark, "To be sure, youngsters can bring out the best in a man. Perhaps we'll see the father's heart in that poor man come to life yet."

EPILOGUE

Five years later, two men traveling on the train were discussing the business outlook of the area as they approached Boyd City.

"This town is a wonder to me," said one, pointing out the window.

"Why?" asked his companion, who was making his first trip through that part of the country. "Isn't it a good business town?"

"Good business town!" exclaimed the other. "It sure is. There's not a more thriving place in this section. Of course, it all depends on what business you're in. It's the character of the place that's so amazing! You go in there with the wrong kind of goods, and you won't do a dime's business in a year."

"How so? What's the character of the place got to do with it?"

"Five, maybe six years ago there wasn't a tougher city in the West. Every other door on Broadway opened into a joint, and now—"

"Oh, now I remember," interrupted the other; "struck by a church revival or something, wasn't it? And built some sort of Salvation Army Rescuing Home or Mission of some kind?"

"I'm not sure about the church revival," returned the other slowly. "And I don't think the Salvation Army was behind it.

Started by the businessmen from what I gather; though I think the churches are all behind it now."

"So do you know what happened exactly?"

"I had a friend there. He's moved now. But he said to me that the whole town was struck by what he called common sense, good-business Christianity. As for the rescue home, I don't know what they call the establishment. It does all sorts of things—finds jobs for those out of work, feeds the hungry, gives a night's lodging to the homeless, but also does things like providing entertainment and teaching. I think there's several thriving businesses it runs, even holds concerts in its auditorium. It's quite an operation; I've never seen anything like it. And no run-down mission sort of place either. Why, it takes up a whole city block, and one of the finest, most attractive blocks in the business portion of the city. Nearly every man you meet owns a share or two in it."

And indeed, the two travelers might well wonder at the change a few years had brought to this city in the great coal fields of the southern Middle West.

In place of bars and saloons that once lined the east side of Broadway and the principal streets leading to it, there are now substantial buildings and respectable business firms. The gambling dens and brothels have been forced to close their doors for lack of business. Cheap entertainers and hucksters list the city as "no good" and pass it by, while the best of musicians and lecturers are always sure of crowded houses.

Most of the churches of all denominations are filled to capacity, and several have been forced to enlarge. The Ministerial Association still meets and still often misses the mark of where the Spirit of God is moving. But fortunately that Spirit has hundreds of loyal followers and intent listeners in the city who manage to keep the churches moving in the directions of His choosing in spite of bureaucratic inertia.

The city streets and public buildings, even the lawns and fences, by their clean and well-kept appearance, show an honest pride and a purpose beyond mere existence. But a stranger might notice, first of all, the absence of loafers on street corners, and the bright, interested expressions and manners of the young men he chanced to meet.

Does all this seem strange to you, dear reader, as to our friend, the traveling man on the train?

Believe me, there is no mystery about it. It is just the change that comes to the individual—or the family, or the church, or the city—that applies, *really* applies, Christ's teaching to his daily life.

High purpose, noble activity, hard work, virtue, honesty, cleanliness, putting the welfare of others above your own, generosity, gracious words, gentle deeds of kindness. God has but one law for the corporation and the individual, for the child and the adult, for the family and the nation. The teaching that will transform the life of a man or woman will just as readily change the life of a city or a country . . . if only it be applied—*lived*—in the small moments of every day between each man and woman and the business and personal affairs in which they are involved.

The reading room and first plan for helping unemployed men make kindling wood had both accomplished their purpose. Now the Association was able to carry on those works with hundredfold fruit, in addition to providing a place where boys and girls, men and women, could hear good music, uplifting talk and helpful entertainment, and where good citizenship, health, morals, and spiritual principles were all taught in the name of Jesus.

The offerings of the Association were free in every department, but rules for wholesomeness and order were strictly enforced, and if either was ignored, visitors were asked to leave or were removed. The Association, by its joint ownership on the part of the citizenry, remained self-supporting and even profitable; and from a business standpoint, for the good it brought the city, all would agree that it paid marvelous dividends.

As Uncle Bobbie Wicks tells his customers from other towns, "Folks come to Boyd City 'cause they ain't afraid to have their boys and girls walk down the street alone."

And after all, that is maybe one of the best recommendations a city can have.

Perhaps the happiest couple in that contented, prosperous city, as well as the best-loved of all her citizens, is the young co-manager of the Association, Mr. Richard Falkner, and his beautiful wife Amy.

One day, about a year after his return to Boyd City, Rev. Cameron took Dick aside.

"You know, Dick, when I was out there—alone—thinking I was dying," the minister said with serious expression, "I had the chance to think about a good many things. I thought about my preaching, about everything I'd ever said from the pulpit. And I wondered if my life matched my words. I thought, too, about this work we are trying to do here. And I could not help but think that this is a more lasting, more eternal work of Christ than is my preaching every Sunday morning. You know, Dick, a part of me *did* die out there.

"When you're that close to death, your priorities get clear in a hurry. I thought about my wife . . . about you . . . and about what kind of people we're put on this earth to become. And I've discovered since then that the part of me that used to worry about earthly things—that part of me *is* dead. Because I've faced death, and I know now what *really* matters. And I pray to God I never forget."

A short while after this, Cameron took a week off and went away, alone, to erect a monument, he said, to a past life as a reminder of what comprises *true* life. Only one man in the city knew his destination.

And now, once a year, Dick and Amy pay a visit to a lonely spot near the little village of Anderson.

There, where the oaks and hickories cast their flickering shadows on the fallen leaves and bushes, and the striped ground squirrel has his home in the rocks, where the redbird whistles to his mate, and at night the sly fox creeps forth to roam at will, where nature, with vine of the wild grape, has built a fantastic arbor and the atmosphere is sweet with woodland flowers and blossoms. Not far from the ruins of an old cabin, they will kneel before a rough mound of earth, marked with a simple headstone, beside which stands another stone, the two monuments honoring the death of the one's brother and the testimony of the other's mentor.

One bears no inscription except the name and date.

The other, as a reminder of an earlier empty grave, and of the Man's words who had briefly occupied it, reads: "Inasmuch as ye have done it unto one of the least of these my brethren, ye have done it unto me."

AFTERWORD

Most people don't bother with introductions in books, and even fewer read past the end of the story. They want to get right to the main course and finish it.

I often skip introductions and other material myself, saving them to read *after* I've finished a book and am more interested in the author and the book's background.

So if a reader doesn't read this, I won't be offended. But for those of you who are interested in knowing about this book, its author, why it was written, why it was necessary to "edit" it, who I am, and what business is it of mine to "change" what was once a bestseller, then to you I offer these comments. I hope some of you enjoy this story more deeply by knowing a few of the circumstances surrounding its history. Perhaps the rest of you, after reaching the conclusion of the narrative, will have found your way here through curiosity, retracing your steps to the introduction also.

I am a man who loves books—all kinds of books! Whenever I walk into a house my eyes immediately scan the room for a bookshelf. If I find one, I cannot help being drawn toward it to begin perusing its contents.

I love to leaf through a nicely bound volume, to caress a fine binding in my hands, to browse through libraries. I even enjoy the musty smell of an old used bookstore as much as the aroma of a handsome leather-bound Bible. I like to examine different kinds of paper, different type styles, different binding techniques, developments in cover embossing and interior engravings, and changes in paper through the years. And as part of this, I am always looking for some unusual or antique bookcase, having more than a dozen different little book collections I am working on.

And of course . . . I love to read. That's what started it all!

My love of books led to the opening of my first bookstore nineteen years ago (I have been selling books ever since) and started me on the road to writing (which I have been doing almost as long), and more recently has led into the related fields of both editing and publishing. So I continue to be involved with books at every stage—from blank page to finished title on a bookstore's shelves, and especially sitting down in front of the fireplace to read. I love every aspect of the process!

I also love *old* things—old tables, old barns, old safes, old fences, old landscapes, old castles, old bureaus, old toy trains, old Bibles, and old movies. Give me a choice between a functional oldie and the same thing shiny new and I'll usually take the old. There's something about the old work that feels more full of life than its fresh counterpart just off the assembly line. Who can compare today's radio fare with Haydn, Mozart, or Handel, or the so-called "talents" of today's sit-com or game-show stars with Fred Astaire? In fact, I'd rather walk through an ancient English garden where feet have trod before me for centuries than a newly landscaped sterile park. Likewise, I'd much rather spend time in a book that is well thumb worn—even a little dirty, whose binding is flexible from use—than a stiff, new volume fresh from the bookstore.

Thus, over the years I've become absorbed in books by authors of yesteryear, authors whose stories hearken back to nostalgic eras—times which, if not easier, somehow seem less complex, even with their hardships, than these present frenzied years of the twentieth century. There is nothing intrinsically better about vintage age. Yet the flood of "newness" that contemporary society presses upon us tends to drown out the sometimes quieter voices from the past. And it is my conviction that these ancient voices, though perhaps expressing themselves in different, occasionally in quaint and old-fashioned ways, nevertheless contain much truth for us today.

Old books make me excited. And when I get excited about something, my first thought is, "With whom can I share this?"

Therefore, my love of good stories and treasured authors always seems to carry the desire to share my favorite books with friends. Unfortunately, many of my favorite authors are dead and their books, some which were bestsellers in their own day, are out of print and unavailable except in used bookstores and through rare and antique book dealers.

Hence, coupled with my interest in the antique object and in my reading and writing historical fiction, is an ever-present itch to bring to light old books and authors that are favorites of mine but which have for one reason or another been lost to the reading public. Along with this has come the desire to get their books back into print by re-editing, updating, and generally doing what is necessary to make a hundred-year-old book suitable for today's market. Oftentimes, though the stories and characters and spiritual themes of a book are still compelling, I as a writer am aware that the language has changed so the style of some of these older titles is not compatible with today's literary climate.

Out of this, about twelve years ago, emerged a process of rewriting some of my favorite old books, hoping thereby to be able to share them with you, my reading friends of the late twentieth century. At first I began by hauling my typewriter to the counter of my bookstore, where I would sit and type a few lines between waiting on customers. This lasted only for four or five titles. By then it was apparent that enough people were in favor of what I was doing to enable me to write full time. I restructured my business, giving me more time to devote to writing and editing, and now, in addition to writing my own books, I have edited twenty-two by the three authors of the late nineteenth and early twentieth centuries whom I would consider my favorite novelists: George MacDonald, Ralph Connor, and Harold Bell Wright.

All three men were spell-binding storytellers, able to draw characters out of real life. All were godly men of virtue whose spiritual perspectives form the basis for all their writing. All three were ministers who turned to writing fiction *after* beginning their careers in the pulpit. The lives of all three overlapped. Two were Scots. All three wrote from firsthand experience, weaving plots together with spiritual threads and sub-themes, giving each of their books wide appeal on several distinct levels. And all three became prolific best-selling novelists, writing over one hundred books with estimated sales between fifteen and twenty million. And yet, in our generation, of those one hundred books, only a scant five or ten have remained in print and readily available up to a decade ago. Thus began my attempt to revive interest in them. I hope you have enjoyed this second revived work from the pen of Harold Wright Bell. His classic work, *Shepherd of the Hills*, has also been edited and is also available from Bethany House Publishers.

—Michael Phillips